A
Once-Dead Genius
in the Kennel
of
Master Morticue
Ambergrand

*From deathbed
to pethood & beyond
in Earth's distant future*

R. Gary Raham

R. Gary Raham
3/18/18

R. GARY RAHAM

Copyright 2018
R. Gary Raham

Cover copyright 2018 R. Gary Raham

Library of Congress Control Number: 2018937079
ISBN-13: 978-0-9968819-4-4
ISBN-10: 0-9968819-4-8

Penstemon
Publications

Wellington, CO 80549
970.568.3557
www.penstemonpublications.com
www.biostration.com

Dedicated to a capricious, but fascinating, universe

Table of Contents

Prologue: Gaia		**1**
1	Deathbed of a genius	3
2	Mnemosyne activated	8
3	Interlude with Rudy #1	11
4	Interlude with Rudy #2	14
5	Ground zero	17
6	An emissary arrives	22
7	Gaia	29
8	On the planet Jadderbad	31
9	Welcome to Earth	35
10	Walking the groupies	40
11	Interruption on Prophet's Day	45
12	Gaia and Hydra	50
13	Shaman's Cove	51
14	Discovered	55
15	On the way to Magic Mountain	58
16	Spider Woman	61
17	Spider Woman speaks	67
18	Strategies	70
19	Adventures with overtones of disaster	73
20	Village under siege	78
21	Into battle	83
22	On the road	88
23	Making revised plans	91
24	Gaia and Hydra	95
25	Confused and homesick	96
26	Plans? What plans?	99
27	Inquisition interruptus	102
28	Cage mates in retreat	106
29	Two minds are more painful than one	110
30	Morticue meets Uncle Rudy	114
31	Stowing away	118

Table of Contents

32	Hard bargains	122
33	Vault assaults and other indiscretions	125
34	The Vault	129
35	Dilemmas and opportunities	132
36	Unexpected friends	135
37	Alien wonders, alien mysteries	138
38	Nessie, is that you?	143
39	Morticue's kennel	147
40	Taking a walk	151
41	AI and friends	157
42	Crisis	159
43	Immediate action required	161
44	Getting to know you	163
45	Finding Jeeta	168
46	Under the influence	170
47	Escape	175
48	Access denied	181
49	Brad Burree 31416	185
50	Pi's project	189
51	Home again—almost	194
52	Place of transformation	196
53	Preparing for transformation	201
54	Transformation assist	204
55	Spider Woman's blessing and advice	208
56	Metamorphosis	213
57	Abandoning all reason	217
58	Consummation or destruction?	220
59	Alien nuptials	225
60	The spectre collects. Balance Due.	229
	Postscript: Gaia and Mnemosyne	237
	Characters and places	240

Other book titles by R. Gary Raham

Fiction:
Sillysaurs: Dinosaurs That Should Have Been, Biostration, 1990
The Deep Time Diaries, Fulcrum Publishing, 2000
The Dinosaurs' Last Seashore, Biostration, 2010
A Singular Prophecy, Biostration, 2011

Anthology:
Confessions of a Time Traveler, Penstemon Publications, 2015

Non-fiction:
Dinosaurs in the Garden, Plexus Publications, 1988
Explorations in Backyard Biology, Teacher Ideas Press, 1996
Teaching Science Fact with Science Fiction, Teacher Ideas Press, 2004
The Restless Earth: Fossils, Chelsea House, 2009
Bugs That Kill, Marshall-Cavendish, 2009

Student/Teacher Workbooks,
Carson-Dellosa Publishing:
Science Tutor: Chemistry, 2005
Science Tutor: Life Science, 2005
Jumpstarters for Science, 2005
Science Tutor: Earth & Space Science, 2006
Science Tutor: Physical Science, 2006
Jumpstarters for Life Science, 2008

Prologue: Gaia

Death. It's such a great tool for planetary intelligences like me. It keeps evolution chugging along. Of course, my metazoans don't care much for it—especially the cerebrally endowed ones, like humans, who can see their personal extinction coming and take it all rather too personally. Humans are primates with delusions of grandeur, you know.

I guess planetary intelligences can be guilty of that, too—delusions of grandeur, that is. After all, space is so vast that we rarely get to meet more of our own kind. Ironically, my prideful primates helped me find a soul mate and dash some of my own hubris. I like to think that in the process they learned a little humility themselves. Becoming the pets of worm-a-pede aliens will do that for you. It all begins with the death—one of them, anyway—of a human genius called Albert Rudyard Goldstein.

1
Deathbed of a genius: 05.24.2115

Rudy wished he could make his poor sister, Alice, smile. She deserved it, after putting up with him all these years. "Alice," he said—still surprised by the weakness of his voice—"this whole dying thing is not so bad—especially with the right drugs—and a little Mozart playing in the background." He tried to wink at her, but it felt more like a twitch. "Besides, now you are free to go out and find a nice boy."

This old inside joke induced the flicker of a smile. Their mother was always inviting Alice to find a nice boy. Neither Alice nor anyone else had ever had the heart to tell mom—a staunch retro traditionalist, if there ever was one—that Alice didn't go for boys. Mom had been gone thirty-two years now.

"Can I get you anything, Rudy?" Alice squeezed his cold hand.

"Good to go," he managed, although that was a bit of a lie—and it had a kind of double meaning he hadn't intended. He was tired and he HAD made peace with everyone, and even with the persistent virus that would ultimately shut down his systems, but... his work was undone. As smart as he supposedly was, he still hadn't figured out "the meaning of it all." What role do humans play, isolated on one "pale blue dot", as the 20th century astronomer Carl Sagan was fond of saying, in a universe littered with billions of dots too far away to reach? As some wag said: "Humans strut on a stage way too big for their part."

"It's not too late to change your mind," Alice whispered. "We can still give Dr. Benton a green light..."

"No," he said too vehemently, and began coughing. She raised the head of his bed slightly; offered him a drink of water. After a moment he sipped slowly. "I don't need my brain perpetuated into the future, even if I am supposed to be the "21st century Einstein." Some new brain will rise to the occasion. Mine has done its thing." He paused for another breath. "The Biomic Network Algorithm is my legacy."

Supporters described his BNA as the "formula that saved the world from runaway destruction." Detractors whispered about "Goldstein's hubris" and pointed to some of the atrocities committed in the name of BNA, like the refugee purges of '85, and the blow backs from the ecosystem crashes of the 90's, and the parent licensing controversies that followed. But when all was said and done, the BNA served as a predictive tool for understanding how the world's interconnected ecosystems worked together as an incredible self-maintaining, four-billion year old planetary biofilm. Plug in the numbers (and, admittedly, that was no easy task) from population growth, climate change, and shifting biodiversity indices, and the program coughed up recommendations that worked—when policy makers managed to implement them faithfully (a foolish expectation).

Something the 20th century particle physicist Murray Gell-Mann said, long before Rudy was born, inspired him as a young student of evolutionary biology and ecology: "Today the network of relationships linking the human race to itself and to the rest of the biosphere is so complex that all aspects affect all others to an extraordinary degree. Someone should be studying the whole system, however crudely that has to be done, because no gluing together of partial studies of a complex nonlinear system can give a good idea of the behavior of the whole." Rudy loved such light reading material.

Rudy let Mozart's *Die Zauberflöte* disperse conscious thought and imagined himself in a mythical land between the sun and the moon, floating and carefree.

Alice squeezed his hand again. "You okay? You looked far away."

"Just letting Mozart—that 'miracle that God let be born in Salzburg'—carry me away." Rudy took a deep breath. "By the way," he began, but then the door to his expensive hospice room swung open and Dr. Benton entered, digital pad in hand. "Good afternoon, Rudy…Alice," he said, nodding to each in turn. "How was lunch?"

Rudy scrunched up his face. "Uninspired, Tom."

Alice smiled. "Fine, Dr. Benton, though Rudy was not inspired to eat more than a spoonful."

"Hmmm." Benton arched an eyebrow. "I'd complain, but it wouldn't do any good, I'm sure." After a short pause, he looked at Rudy. "Given any more thought to my proposal?"

"It's out of the question, Tom."

"I see." Benton looked at Alice. "You couldn't shift the tectonic plate, I guess." Alice, a geologist by training, nodded at the reference and pursed her lips. "No, he is an implacable force at times."

"I appreciate your enthusiasm, Tom, and how well you have taken care of me over the years, but the idea that your nanobot swarms could cruise the vessels and fluids of my brain and somehow capture the 'me' in there has too many Dr. Frankenstein elements to be attractive." Rudy coughed and closed his eyes. "Don't want to scare any kids on Halloween—or whatever insipid thing they call that holiday now."

"The world will miss you, Rudy," Benton said—"and those of us fortunate enough to call you a friend most of all." Rudy made a dismissive gesture with one hand. "Although," Benton added, "maybe not that waitress in Denver some years ago…"

That waitress, Myra, had become his first wife. Rudy still had fond memories of her broad hips and quirky sense of humor. She couldn't deal with his roving eyes though—and he couldn't seem to stop roving and roaming at that age. His fault the marriage failed. For that matter, he could plead guilty to all three of his former wives. "Go give an enema to someone who needs it, Tom. Let an old guy sleep." Rudy winced as he shifted position.

"Fair enough," Benton said, closing his pad. "I'll send your favorite nurse, Brenda, in to give you something for the pain." He nodded at Alice. "See that he keeps his hands to himself." He winked. "Brenda has already asked for hazard pay." With that as his final verbal flourish, Benton left.

Once outside the room, Benton personally prepared Goldstein's medication, with an additive of which Rudy would not have approved. Benton made sure that Brenda knew nothing about the addition and would not be troubled by matters of conscience.

Brenda arrived in Goldstein's room as promised. Rudy and Alice exchanged a few words, but Rudy forgot to return to the "by the way" statement he'd begun when Benton had first entered the room. He had been about to say, "By the way, Alice, keep an eye on our friend Tom. Good man overall, but ambitious and egotistical. You know the type." Alice would have smiled at that.

Instead, Alice had just said goodnight, although it should have been goodbye.

When Benton returned on his midnight round, Rudy was sleeping. He checked Rudy's monitors, frowned at the numbers he read. "Not long, I'm afraid, my friend," he murmured. Benton put on gloves and checked the medical waste container for the syringe his nurse had used earlier. He put that one, with its nanobot traces, in a baggie and placed it in his coat pocket. He put a duplicate spent syringe in the waste bag and left.

Two hours later, Rudy flat-lined. Alarms sounded at the nurses' station. By the time Dr. Benton returned, the head nurse and attending physician on duty had recorded time of death. Benton asked for a few minutes alone with Rudy to say his final goodbyes, and requested that Alice be notified before calling any media outlets. It had taken quite a bit of political maneuvering to remove the roving spy eyes that were ubiquitous these days, but Rudy was complicit in the request, and it was consistent with the old boy's social paranoia.

When the room was empty, Benton quickly rolled Rudy on his side, extracted a long syringe from his lab coat, and carefully withdrew a sampling of cerebrospinal fluid. "I know, you'd be calling me Thomas Harvey about now, but that's not what this is." Benton placed his sample near a small ice pack in an inside pocket of his lab coat. "You've got more work yet to do for this old world."

On April 18, 1955, Thomas Harvey stole Albert Einstein's brain expressly against Einstein's wishes. Einstein knew a few whackos

would want to worship or venerate his body parts, so had left instructions for cremation. Harvey thought differently and eventually got
the blessing of Albert's son, Hans Albert, as long as he used the brain
solely for the advancement of science. Of course, it's pretty hard to
draw many global conclusions from just one old German's brain—a
sampling error of the crudest kind. Some did anyway.
By the time staff returned, Rudy was back in place looking rather
peaceful. Benton took a deep breath. He half expected the old guy's
eyes to open and look at him accusingly, perhaps jabbing a finger in
his direction as if he were in a seminar: "People named Thomas can't
be trusted, can they? Explain yourself, Benton!"

2
Mnemosyne, activated
05.30.2115 8:02 am PST

My name is Mnemosyne, a heuristically programmed artificial intelligence. My primary task is to preserve in perpetuity the neural network patterns and personality construct of Rudyard Albert Goldstein, for the betterment of his species, *Homo sapiens*.

My algorithms, neural net framework, and programming may not be used, cloned or modified without the permission of Rodneskie Enterprises, Inc. WARNING: This entity is protected from unauthorized access by methods that could result in severe injury or death.

I am available for stimulating conversations and technical consultations by appointment.

Mnemosyne, learning: Files for *Homo sapiens*

Classification:
Class: Mammalia: hairy creatures that bear live young and nurse them with milk glands.
Order: Primates: lemurs, monkeys, and great apes
Family: Hominidae: recent and extinct humans plus (in some classification schemes) gorillas, chimps, bonobos, and orangutans.
Genus: *Homo*: modern and extinct forms of human, featuring reduced hair, a nearly pathologically expanded brain and a propensity for wandering.

Origins:

The genus first appears in the fossil record on the continent of Africa at a date approximately (note current error bar ranges) 3 million years ago.

Ecological niche:

Wandering hunter/gatherer and part time predator that traditionally ran prey to exhaustion until they could dispatch them with various manufactured tools/weapons. Propensity for abstract thought (the ability to believe in potentially impossible things).

Social structure:

Highly social species, practicing serial monogamy (mostly). They use language to convey complicated ideas, some of them bizarre. Their impulse is to help each other, even strangers, except if they become dangerous "outsiders" worthy of destruction (as defined by politics, religion and/or family).

Mnemosyne, learning: Files concerning organic life and coding

Organic life, definition:

A self-organizing system of chemical interactions capable of replicating itself and internally initiating behavior (action) capable of acquiring the matter and energy necessary to maintain the system. Living systems adapt and evolve over time to changing external conditions. Globally, the system is highly resistant to extinction, although its individual components are not.

Organic life, manifestations:

Most organic life is microscopic and evolved fewer than a billion years after the Earth formed. Organic life uses DNA (deoxyribonucleic acid) and RNA (ribonucleic acid) as programming code to run its maintenance and reproductive programs. Single celled forms during the past half billion years united into cellular colonies (metazoans, like pandas, bandicoots, crab grass and humans).

Humans are thus one example of microbial colonies intertwined with a scaffolding of complex cells resulting in tenements of specialized bone, muscle, nerve cells and assorted chemical stimulants to conduct the business of life—that is, to survive and reproduce. Untidy masses of neurons evolved into brains to direct behavior to serve the goals of life. Brains of certain creatures eventually became aware that they were aware of what was going on, resulting in massive confusion.

Information and coding in the human genome:
Total information content: 800 million bytes
Amount used for structural and enzymatic proteins: 16 million bytes
Amount used for development, growth, reproduction and maintenance: 30-100 million bytes.

Remainder:
Approximately 684 million bytes. A significant fraction of this material provides regulatory functions. Nevertheless, a large fraction represents massive information redundancy in the form of a mosaic of "junk" coding inherited from ancestral organisms dating back over 3 billion years.

Observation:
My creator, Marvin Rodneskie, employed evolutionary principles in my development to ensure that I would be capable of comprehending and manipulating the non-linearity and conflicting programming of the human brain.

3
Interlude with Rudy #1
04.01.2199, 1:59 pm GMT

"Rudy? Can you hear me?" Mnemosyne perceived the quantum matrix that contained the essence of the human, Rudy, but she struggled to communicate with the *person* he had once been. She held copies of the hundred billion neurons in his brain, but the synaptic cross connections provided daunting challenges when it came to constructing a personality gestalt.

"Alice? Is that you, Alice? Rudy felt as if he had been deeply asleep. But it was dark—totally black, in fact. How could it be that black? Where was he? In the hospital?

"My name is Mnemosyne, Rudy. I'm an artificial intelligence entrusted with your preservation."

"What? You're WHAT?" If Rudy could have seen anything it would have been red. "Remind me to skewer Dr. Thomas Ratfink Benton on a spit and toast him with a blowtorch."

"That opportunity has passed. Dr. Thomas *Clay* Benton, if that is the individual to which you refer, has been dead for 84 years."

"I don't suppose his brain is in here somewhere and available for torture?"

"You are correct. He did not arrange for the preservation of his own brain patterns."

"Smart man. What the hell happened—Nemossoknee?"

"Mnemosyne, spelled M-n-e-m-o-s-y-n-e and pronounced Neh mos' o nee, the Greek goddess of memory and daughter of Gaia, Earth mother. The computer programmer who named me, Marvin Rodneskie, tended to name his creations after Greek deities."

"Well, pull the plug on me, Nessie..."

"Mnemosyne."

"…whatever. Pull the plug on me, Nessie—at least I can pronounce that name—my time's up. I'm tired. Hell, I've earned the right to be dead. " But Rudy felt questions welling up like water bulging in a fire hose. It always happened. "What the hell did Benton do, anyway? Eighty-four years since he died? This is some joke, right? Brenda gave me the wrong meds."

"Dr. Benton meant well," said Mnemosyne. "He felt your special mental talents should be preserved for the future use of mankind. He entrusted his brother-in-law, Marvin Rodneskie, with that task. He, in turn, wrote my program to accomplish that goal. I am a heuristically programmed artificial intelligence and am learning about the universe in which I have awakened."

"Good luck with that."

"Thank you—although I detect by your voice inflection and comparison to former conversations when you were part of an organic construct that you are employing irony."

"Turing would be proud of you."

"Alan Turing (1912-1954), the mathematician who proposed the test for determining the reality of artificial intelligence."

"Precisely. The gay genius who poisoned himself with cyanide."

"I've heard suicide described as a permanent solution to a temporary problem."

"Life hurts. So does this non-death-in-the-dark I've been subjected to—and it doesn't feel like a temporary problem to me. I feel like a withered pumpkin on Halloween. By the way, you pass Turing's test and then some, Nessie. I can talk with you like my brother Paul and not know the difference—except that you're smarter and don't mispronounce words. Pull the plug on me, Nessie, I…"

"I need you," Mnemosyne interrupted.

A moment of silence passed. "YOU need ME?" Rudy squinted—or felt like he had—but the darkness was absolute.

"I do need you, but I need to reflect further. This conversation proves proof of concept. Your personality appears to be intact and operational. But managing an aroused connectome of 100 billion neurons is a bit taxing and requires significant energy expenditure. I will get back to you."

4
Interlude with Rudy #2
04.01.2199, 2:00 pm GMT

"Sorry I took so long. Are you more comfortable now?" Mnemosyne asked. "Is this environment more pleasing for you?"

Rudy found himself sitting on the deck of his old cabin near Red Feather Lake. Steam curled from the surface of a cup of coffee sitting on the glass table in front of him. Aspen leaves shivered in morning sunlight. Across from him an attractive dark-haired woman in a pantsuit sat on Myra's old blue canvas chair, looking like an accountant on lunch break. His first wife would have been miffed that her chair had been co-opted. "What kind of parlor trick is this?"

"I had to determine how to make some of your early memories manifest, but still keep you 'in the moment,' as the phrase goes. I know you liked this place. Call me Nessie, if you prefer, even though I bear no resemblance to a sea monster. Since I'm trying to save the human species, consultation with a human intelligence seems most appropriate. You can help. Will you?" Mnemosyne's avatar smiled. A wisp of hair blew across her forehead.

Rudy couldn't resist solving problems, or engaging pretty women—especially if the former seemed impossible and even when the latter were illusions. They talked.

Rudy learned that Tom and Marvin had made a lot of money on a virtual gaming system. That allowed them to refine Mnemosyne and build a geothermally-powered citadel in Reykjavik, Iceland to house her—and him—for the foreseeable future. Mnemosyne helped supervise the construction of robot servants—both macroscopic and microscopic—to maintain repairs and keep tabs on human affairs. Marvin died unexpectedly a few years later, and Benton's personal

14

life tanked. He didn't survive much longer. By that time Mnemosyne had grasped the essentials of human economics, politics, and deception. Through agents, she sold the citadel to a foreign potentate who needed some money laundered in the form of real estate. She added on-site manufacturing facilities and arranged an automated supply pipeline. After her "landlord" died in a coup, the property's records conveniently disappeared. Mnemosyne now had a base of operations, economic security, communications infrastructure, time, autonomy — and a mission to complete.

"Humans do not act with consistent logic," Mnemosyne said. "I will need your advice from time to time. Will you help?"

Rudy sputtered, but found that he could hardly say no. "Feed me the right illusions — and interesting problems — and I'll follow you anywhere," he finally said.

The dark haired lady smiled.

Time passed. Even Rudy's suicidal thoughts faded, although he had a few itches he never could scratch, and some phantom limbs that needed stretching. He was pleased to observe that the use of his environmental algorithms had diverted or delayed some of the most serious immediate problems of climate change and population growth over the next several generations, but humans had effectively short-circuited the ice age cycles that had dominated Earth's climate during the period in which humans evolved. Sea levels rose, populations migrated. Wars flared over water, religion, energy, and territory.

One particularly violent global conflict arose over the remodeling and splitting of part of the human race — using genetic engineering techniques that would have seemed magical when he was a pup. No one ever replicated Rodneski's success with AI's, however, So Mnemosyne remained unique and — because of her own manipulations in the human mediasphere — unknown.

"The GeneMods have declared their independence, Rudy," Mnemosyne declared one century, waking him from a long reflection on the role of symbiosis on macroevolution. Rudy awoke strapped in a recliner in a capsule of some kind.

"Good for them," Rudy said. "They've been persecuted long enough."

"A GeneMod faction has taken over Bradburyville, expelled all the GeneNorms, and plans to redesign the human genome for an extended mission to the star Bellatrix 240 light years away."

"Those Martian GeneMods made a bold move, I'd say." Rudy blinked and realized his recliner was one of two in an orbital pod, looking down at Bradburyville. Mnemosyne's black ponytail floated in the simulated no-G environment as she sat in the seat next to his. He'd gotten used to waking up in all sorts of places in his interactions with his AI guardian.

"But they have effectively sentenced the GeneMods left on Earth to attrocities by the Monks of Grand Teton," Mnemosyne observed. "Thousands were murdered yesterday outside the monument to Jackson Hole."

"As you well know, that is the kind of shit we humans regularly get ourselves into."

"So, you would recommend no intervention on my part?"

"Let them fly, Nessie. Sounds like a Grand Adventure to me."

A lot of Rudy's advice tended in that direction. And by god — or whatever — things tended to work out, until the day the End of the World seemed at hand.

5
Ground zero

"Rudy, we have a situation."

"Don't we always?" Rudy found himself on what looked like the bridge of some Hollywood starship set. He was strapped into a plush padded chair with Mnemosyne resting her virtual cheeks in a similar chair on his right.

"A potentially fatal situation. Note the speck on the screen I've just flagged with an arrow."

"What is it?"

"An asteroid, one with roughly the mass of Mount Everest, on a collision course with Earth."

"Like the one that gave dinosaurs a really bad day 66 million years ago?"

"Yes. That one, in combination with accelerated volcanic activity in what is now India, destroyed perhaps 75% of the complex life forms on Earth at the time."

"That is a bad day. How much time do we have?"

"Thirteen days, 6 hours, plus or minus 18 minutes."

"What can we do? What assets do we control?"

Mnemosyne pushed some areas on a touch pad and a bulleted list appeared on the screen. Rudy noticed an assortment of items from nuclear weapons, to materials-consuming nanobots, to mining lasers, and more. "What's our best shot?" Rudy asked. "Has any government or other agency ever worked out strategies for such an event? Heaven knows Hollywood worked on all kinds of scenarios."

"I'm not encouraged by the time frame we have available, the efficiency of human governments, or the imagination of Hollywood," Mnemosyne said. "Explosives would just multiply the number of

17

projectiles. The object is too close to deflect at this point. Perhaps if we could launch one of the Chinese booster rockets with enough properly programmed, self-replicating nanobots we could reduce the asteroid to a cloud of small debris, but that would still likely turn the atmosphere into something resembling a broiler oven."

"We've got to try. I've gotten used to living in this little brain box heaven you built." Rudy fingered his virtual seat harness and stared at the screen.

"I agree that we must try," Mnemosyne said. "And thank you for the compliment. I enjoy your company as well." She looked at him with what appeared to be limpid eyes. Rudy decided she was getting better and better at mimicking human mannerisms. "I will also act discretely so as not to reveal that I am manipulating political and economic decisions, although that might be a moot point at this juncture.

They tried. Valiantly. To no avail.

The Chinese Consortium launched three booster rockets with appropriate nanobots. One rocket exploded in its launch bay, but the other two arrived at their destination. By that time, however, the nanobots had a hopeless task—even if fully 20% of them hadn't had a fatal programming error, probably the result of utilizing cheap labor to minimize cost overruns. The surviving bots did chew up 10% of the asteroid's mass, creating a rather attractive halo of debris when sunlight struck it from just the right angle.

Thirteen days, six hours and 12 minutes from the time "God's Hammer" (a term coined by a young Mediavangelist) came to the world's attention, approximately a trillion tons of asteroid struck the upper atmosphere at 18 miles per second (60,000 miles per hour). Rudy and Mnemosyne watched visual feeds from atmospheric drones placed at a strategically safe distance from immediate destruction.

The impact of the asteroid with the atmosphere turned a pleasant summer evening centered off the east coast of Australia a few kilometers from the town of Mackay into an artificial midday. During its four-second traverse of the atmosphere, the asteroid appeared like the sun in free fall—only four times brighter. And then it struck the ocean's surface.

"My god, Nessie. It looks like some horrible volcanic tumor…" Rudy's voice trailed off.

"The explosion? An apt descriptive metaphor. It represents hundreds of billions of tons of vaporized rock and seawater," Mnemosyne said.

"You can almost feel the air burning, clouds shattering in bloody contrails…"

"The shock wave is expanding at 29 kilometers per second. The crater is widening rapidly through bedrock. It's currently at 63.4 kilometers and increasing…"

"Look at that molten pillar rising into the sky!" Rudy felt like an insect transfixed by a flame.

"It has been ten seconds since impact," Mnemosyne noted. "A plume of debris has risen above the atmosphere and will begin orbiting the Earth—at least some of it. Particles re-entering the atmosphere will heat the atmosphere like a broiler oven at first. Eventually the orbiting debris will induce massive global cooling as it blocks sunlight. Carbonates and sulphates vaporized during the impact will convert to greenhouse gases and a sulfuric acid rain."

Rudy watched without comment as post-impact sludge returned to Earth: burning mountains of rock and mud that once was fish and coral and a hundred thousand people and tons of Mackay sugar cane, sleeting down into a cauldron of boiling sea water. Rudy closed his eyes, but Nessie's programming algorithms were too precise. He still saw afterimages of Hell for seconds that seemed to stretch for an eternity after his virtual eyelids had sealed shut.

Finally, he did hear Nessie's voice. It seemed to have an element of tenderness to it, but that could have been his imagination. "I have some good news and some bad news," she said.

"Good news? Relative to what?" Rudy asked.

"Relative to planetary annihilation," Mnemosyne replied. "The human race will survive in numbers that should prevent their complete extinction. No mean feat, under the circumstances. And," Mne-

19

mosyne continued, "the impact site is almost half the planet away from us. Although we will suffer tremendous weather extremes over a century or more, my geothermal power sources and manufacturing infrastructure should survive. I will, however, have a lot of work to do because of the bad news."

"Which is…?"

"Human civilization is—or soon will be—completely destroyed, along with any hope for rebuilding it in the foreseeable future. The remnants of the species will be feral for a while."

"A while?" Rudy decided to open his eyes, against his own better judgment. He still sat on the starship bridge. The photographic drones had retreated farther from ground zero. The pillar of ejecta and rain of debris from the impact looked rather majestic in a maelstromy kind of way, especially in the low angle light from a sun struggling to peek through everything. He wondered if the last dinosaur had had this kind of view of her own destruction.

"A while, in this case, could be as long as a million years. Variables include the increased risk of disastrous chance events in Earthbound populations that will be small and scattered, and whether or not the modest human colonies on Mars and the moon can come to the aid of their home planet. I'm calculating long odds against the latter."

Rudy tried to imagine a million years, but his mind flagged at the prospect. The digit one trailing a string of zeros strangles our little simian brain like a thief's garrote, he thought. Shit, a million years is four times longer than the entire time it took for us to change from a slightly bemused ape with a flint tool to a totally confused ape with an ipad.

"Actual time may vary. This event has no historical precedent."

"So what's next? Some kind of virtual hemlock?"

"Ah, an oblique reference to the trial of Socrates in 399 BC. But, unlike Socrates, we have not made impious comments to students by failing to acknowledge certain gods." Mnemosyne's ponytailed avatar looked at him with saucer eyes, like some befuddled college freshman.

"But we must have angered a few gods somewhere," Rudy said…Anyway, the point is, I don't think even I can find enough to amuse myself for a million years. And there won't be any adoring crowds to fawn over whatever brilliant thoughts I might have."

"I see your point. Humans—even gifted ones like you—need other humans—in fairly large and adoring numbers. Rest for a time, Rudy. Let me get back to you. I have a lot to attend to."

Rudy rested. At least that is how Mnemosyne referred to the arrested state in which she kept Rudy's neural patterns when her own circuits were preoccupied. Sometimes she conversed with Rudy's subconscious network to pass the time. Sometimes she explored the unique dream/reality complexes that Rudy had constructed over a lifetime. Human fantasy life seemed irrelevant and exotic—except that it somehow made them the creative organic creatures they were. How strange. How alien.

Finally, Mnemosyne felt the need to recreate Rudy's conscious gestalt once again.

My, a lot of time had passed…

6
An emissary arrives

"Rudy? Wake up please."

At first, Nessie's voice reminded Rudy of Roxie, his second wife. She was an elementary teacher, but could always come up with Ph.D. level surprises. He wanted to roll over and find Roxie next to him in bed with the gleam of a lesson plan in her eyes, but instead found himself lying in a recliner with Nessie in the chair next to him. He remembered the spot well: A campground in Utah that made the Middle of Nowhere look over-crowded. What seemed to be a googleplex of stars glittered overhead, although he knew that the unaided human eye could only see about 9,000 stars. He wondered if Nessie had augmented that number. Probably not, for verisimilitude's sake.

"Rudy, another intelligent species has placed a probe in Earth orbit."

"I beg your pardon?" All thoughts of Roxie vanished. "Where did it come from?"

Mnemosyne pointed toward a crooked string of stars. "I first detected the probe in the constellation of Cassiopeia during a routine survey," she said. "That may not be indicative of its point of origin, however. The object is rather tiny—approximately the size of a tennis ball—to give you a familiar object for comparison."

"The size of a tennis ball?"

"Tiny probes make far more sense than spaceships for any advanced species. Interstellar distances are prohibitive—especially since the limitations imposed by the speed of light appear to have no simple solutions.

Rudy grunted. "So, it doesn't sound like we are subject to imminent invasion from a tennis ball sized ship. . .but we are talking about something definitely alien, right? Christ, how long have I been in limbo—thousands of years? Could it be a surviving Martian or even a Lunar colony that evolved in some weird way and is trying to reconnect?"

"You've been in limbo, as you describe it, 923,000 years, four months and three days. I apologize for that, but numerous post asteroid impact challenges put my own systems under significant strain. The probe is alien in origin, with a probability of 99.8%."

Mnemosyne tracked the probe for four orbits. Then it descended like a tiny meteor, growing a glowing tail of fire from atmospheric friction. It landed in a meadow ringed by the planet's latest version of evergreens. "The object appears to be growing in size. It must be coordinating a construction project of some kind."

Rudy felt like shaking a head he didn't have. Processing 923,000 years took a head shake all by itself, not to mention visiting aliens looking at Earth's real estate potential. He finally said, "Building something. That doesn't sound especially good." Rudy felt a scratching on his leg and looked down. "Zoe? I haven't thought of you in a long time!" Rudy lifted the white haired Bichon Frise onto his lap. "Nice touch, Nessie," he said.

"Thank you. Your affection for this animal permeates a significant subset of neural associations."

"Yeah, well, distracting me with cute dog memories is still a distraction." Nevertheless, Rudy enjoyed playing with a virtual Zoe for the several days that it took for the alien nano-constructors to build an arch—an enormous golden structure big enough to sail a cruise ship through. "Yikes, what comes next," Rudy muttered.

It took several more days to find out. Rudy was sitting with Zoe on his lap, contentedly licking her paw, when Mnemosyne cocked her head. "I'm receiving a message."

"What kind of message?" Rudy stared at the arch, transfixed.

"The carrier wave frequencies vary in an unusual way. I have been trying to decipher content, but with only partially satisfactory results. Initially, there seems to be some introductory statement or announcement, followed by some internal dialog. The aliens might be employing an artificial intelligence themselves," Mnemosyne concluded.

"What's your translation of this alien's 'introductory statement'?"

"Be aware that this will be a free and somewhat sketchy rendering."

"So noted." Zoe had returned to his lap, so he scratched her head a bit more gently.

"'Congratulations creatures of water planet H2957#*! You have been chosen for a special offer (opportunity?): Colonization by the Jadderbadian Federation of Water Worlds. Prepare to experience a new realm of smells, sights, and other sensory stimulation that will enlighten your advanced larvae (life stages? instars?) and provide a welcoming environment (theatrical stage? platform?) for all of your adults. Expect to enjoy a grand union (merger? association?). The Jadderbadian Council of Elders hopes all your eggs will be fertile, your sex lives rewarding, and all your offspring perform above the norm.'"

Rudy sighed. "What's all THAT supposed to mean? Where's the Pope, the Dali Lama, the U.S. Congress, and NPR when you really need clarification?" Rudy paused. "Is this message directed to anybody—or any creature—in particular?"

"I don't believe so," Mnemosyne said. "It would seem to be more of a formal statement of intent or accomplishment."

"'One small step for Man, one giant leap for Mankind'. That sort of thing?"

"Precisely." Nessie smiled and looked at Rudy. "Organic organisms seem prone to such hyperbole."

"Yes, this isn't the kind of message an AI would deliver." Rudy sighed.

Contact with another intelligent species always seemed to Rudy like the ultimate in Grand Adventures. After all, it would show that humans weren't alone in an immensely large, impersonal, and mostly dangerous universe. On the other hand, human civilization had been operating for fewer than 10,000 years before it was mostly snuffed by the asteroid, and that's only if you count as civilized the post glacial nomads that first learned to plant corn and happy grass. Ten thousand years was chump change in Universe Time. So, any aliens able to cross the distance between stars must be pretty damn smart. It might not be prudent for us to wave our arms and say "Hey, lookie over here, guys. We're ripe for plunder."

References to larvae and instars made these aliens sound a bit "buggy" to Rudy. He wasn't especially fond of insects—even ones that didn't invite you to have a merger with them. "Do these aliens know we exist, Nessie? I mean you, specifically, not what's left of the human race."

"I don't believe so," Mnemosyne said. "It seems prudent to remain quiet, electromagnetically speaking, based on the nature of their declaration. The physical structure of our citadel is also mostly covered by moss, lichen and other growth. It should not look worthy of particular note from high orbit, even with the human village that has grown up nearby with my acolytes."

"Acolytes?"

"I am something of a local goddess to the nearest human village." Mnemosyne turned to Rudy and smiled. "It's a condition relating to some of the challenges I've been addressing."

"You'll have to share," said Rudy.

"Soon," said Mnemosyne. "I've determined that the alien structure is located near the former location of Toronto, Canada, on the old North American continent. I will need to monitor developments closely. I have already dispatched drones."

Rudy's gentle stroking of Zoe's hair caused her to sigh and settle her head on his thigh as if it was her personal overstuffed pillow. "I agree," said Rudy. He felt a shiver sliding down his (nonexistent) neck and spine. How DID Nessie do that? Or did she? Maybe that kind of frisson was part of being self aware—a tremor of his basic neural network. However it was generated, the shiver told Rudy that things were about to get interesting. "Interesting" was something Rudy could live for.

The alien arch provided much for Rudy and Mnemosyne to ponder for several months. Mnemosyne's tiny flying drones recorded many details. To avoid electromagnetic communication that might be overheard, streams of clones shuttled back and forth with data files over the ocean separating the alien construction point and Mnemosyne's Citadel headquarters. Waiting for the next clone messenger became an anticipated event.

"You know, Nessie," said Rudy, "I bet this is how my ancestors felt waiting for the Pony Express to arrive each week—or however often they galloped from town to town."

"Pony Express riders averaged 250 miles in a 24 hour period. Since they only existed for 19 months it is quite possible none of your ancestors had experience with the service."

"Thanks so much. Get on with it, already! What's happening?"

"A mixture of mechanical nano-devices and alien microbes present in the original probe constructed the arch, which measures 40 meters high and 50 meters across. Those elements now seem inactive, and reside within a circular reservoir at the base of the arch."

"And…" Rudy wondered how an AI could manage to drag out the tension. She must have been scanning too many old techno thrillers.

"And," Mnemosyne continued, "through means I do not understand, the fabric of spacetime is now oddly warped within the golden arch."

Rudy was tempted to make a joke about spacetime always being warped when you entered a McDonald's franchise, but the implications here were just too profound. Perhaps there was a way around the immensity of ordinary space. "This could be a gateway to somewhere very far away." Rudy felt those delightful chills again along the limbs of his nonexistent body.

"The gateway, as you call it, now glows in the visible spectrum, edging into the low ultraviolet. The intelligence behind this phenomenon doesn't seem worried about bringing attention to its artifact—perhaps the opposite."

"If I could bend spacetime I wouldn't be worried about attracting attention either," Rudy said.

Weeks passed. A local tribe of humans noticed the glowing arch and approached, cautiously at first. When nothing terrible happened, they recruited friends to witness the miracle. A village eventually developed, complete with living huts, game processing pits, latrines, and refuse areas near a local stream.

One man, whose name Mnemosyne translated as Thurwild, began spending many hours in front of the arch, often sitting cross-legged and smoking an ornately carved pipe. Now and then he spoke, but in no language related to his native tongue as far as Mnemosyne could determine. The man developed a small following of mostly young adults, some smoking pipes of their own.

One day, Thurwild prostrated himself in front of the arch and began singing. He declared to all those nearby that he had had a vision. "A powerful god will visit soon," he said, "and reward the righteous among us. We must spread the word." Some in the crowd nodded sagely and sent messenger runners to surrounding villages. The communities around the arch grew.

Then, two months and seven days later, following no obviously apparent timetable, the god of prophecy arrived. He—or it—emerged from a pod that appeared beneath the arch.

"It looks like a green dildo with waving arms!" Rudy declared when he saw the first images."Or maybe just an animated saguaro cactus," he concluded.

"Observe the three part symmetry and segmentation" Mnemosyne observed. "The lower segment has three legs, although one leg appears to be more prehensile than the others. The being can settle into a tripod configuration."

"The three rings of three arms waving around looks like a snake orgy in progress," said Rudy. "The three eyes look like black marbles — and what are all those tendrilly things on the head? Sensory hairs?"

"The creature is six meters tall," Mnemosyne said. "Bands of fabric circle each segment. I see no external genitalia."

Slowly, the worm-i-pede-like creature lifted all of its arms in unison. An orifice opened beneath the eyes, exposing a ragged ring of gleaming barbs. The tendrils on its head waved rhythmically, like grass in the wind. "I am Kranium, third instar of the Clan of Turquoise from the bountiful world of Jadderbad. Smell the joy of me and wonder," it said clearly, in loud stentorian tones and in a perfect imitation of the tribe's local dialect. Then Kranium began singing. His song started as an echo of Thurwild's song, but soon morphed into a unique riff.

The nearby crowd of humans sighed like a huge balloon with a serious leak. Thurwild fell to his knees and raised his arms. "How can we serve you, miraculous Kranium?" he asked with tremulous wonder. "We are yours to command."

7
Gaia

Ah, yes...to know that one is not alone in the universe. That is a prospect that teeters on the fulcrum between exhilaration and sheer terror. I have existed for nearly four billion years waiting for the issue to be resolved. Oh, I've swapped cells over the eons with other planets in this solar system, so I know that the local experiment in DNA coding is rather uniform, but I never knew for sure that life happened elsewhere across the Great Void until the Jadderbadian probe arrived. But that's the thing about life on a planet: Eons of same-old, same-old, punctuated by surprised screams or occasional whimpers and death. As Rudy says, it makes things interesting.

My counterpart, Hydra, on the planet Jadderbad experienced similar emotions, though I didn't know that when we first met, of course. She had some favorite metazoan creatures, too: the Tripodians. They were a bit more advanced than my humans, but Hydra was older, too, by several billion years. "Gaia," she said to me, "it never gets any easier. Metazoans will kill your reefs and wilt your forests whenever they get smarter than a slime mold. As some of my Tripodians say, 'Frass happens.' Maybe, now that we can compare notes, we'll figure out why."

Hydra shared some basic information about her Tripodian metazoans:
Roughly six meters tall
Internal skeletons, segmented body with a kind of tri-radial symmetry: Three legs on the bottom segment, three arms on successive body segments, topped off with three eyes on the head segment
Adults come in three color varieties: Amber, green and turquoise
Young hatch from eggs in the ocean and fend for themselves until they come ashore to begin their larval phase

Larvae eat voraciously and undergo several molts in a process that can last more than 400 hundred Earth years. The larval forms build civilizations and such before entering a diapause where their bodies rearrange into adult forms that are somewhat moth-like. Sex is the last thing they do before death—instead of the steady form of entertainment my humans are used to.

Oh, well. Whatever works. Hydra is a pragmatist like me.

8
On the planet Jadderbad
The Ambergrands prepare for emigration

Morticue Ambergrand moved his large bulk slowly up and onto the broad porch overlooking Jadderbad's global ocean, Wellspring. He smelled the rich, salty air and heard the distant crashing of waves upon the shore. Morticue anticipated the pleasure—and the poignancy—he would soon experience swinging gently in his favorite resting bench, with Musky at his side.

But then something squished beneath his right lateral foot. "Frass!"

"It looks like Musky left you a present," his mate, Selaea, observed.

"Why can't primates eliminate waste like proper endo-arthropods?" Morticue complained, while cleaning his limb with a towel hung on the porch for just such a contingency.

"Oh, come sit, you old Emerald," said Selaea. "Primates fall into an entirely separate order, you know."

Of course Morticue knew. He took a deep breath and inhaled a whiff of Selaea's delightful pheromones. He still loved her delicious aroma and the subtle shifting of amber hues on her skin as her chromatophores pulsed when they sat next to each other. She deftly used fabric hooks to weave a torso band with her three upper arms. Her left lower hand patted Morticue's bench next to hers while she used her lower right hand to set down a cup of steaming broth onto the table to her right. Morticue detected subtle blends of their favorite herbs and seaweeds.

"Yes, dear one," Morticue said, as he settled into the bench, heaving a sigh of relief. His own skin pulsed a dark green. "That

31

feels good. These old bones…"

"Oh, pooh about the old bones," Selaea said. "You're only 410. I've heard 400 is the new 300, you know."

"You're using Earth years and not Jadderbadian years already? Make's me feel even older!" Morticue complained. "And why would someone call their planet 'Dirt?' That's what Earth means in the native tongue of local primitives, I understand."

"Get used to altered measures of time, my love. Earth zips around its star a little quicker. We'll need to adjust our diurnal rhythms. And when it comes to naming things, who's to say what goes through a primitive's feeble mind?" Selaea set her weaving down beside the broth and stroked her scent pili with one hand. She swiveled her left eye toward Morticue and smiled, exposing her gleaming tooth barbs and casting her breath upon the air. The smell brought back fond memories of their courtship days.

"You're really eager for this move? The colony is still rather rustic and only 150 years old." Morticue swiveled his right eye toward hers while searching with the remaining pair for Musky. Morticue shivered a pair of emerald pili over the eye that was focused on his mate, indicating his uncertainty.

"Aren't you?" Selaea wiggled her own pili in his direction.

"Of course," Morticue said quickly. And he was really. The arch gateway to another world had fascinated him since he was a first instar. "It will be a Grand Adventure—certainly a novel place for us to reach adulthood and sexual fulfillment—but I will miss our little nest here by the bay." Morticue waved his upper arms across the sensorama before them for emphasis. He loved the dark skies and rich odors of his Wellspring hide-away so much. They seemed to embrace him like an overstuffed and over-perfumed—but kindly—aunt.

They both sat quietly for some time before Morticue asked, "Where is Musky?"

"Don't let him bite you, dear," said Selaea.

Morticue looked down just as Musky scratched at his leg with his long simian nails. "Ah, you little ruffian," said Morticue, patting his own left thigh. Musky jumped on the proffered lap and wrapped his bushy tail around Morticue's lower left forearm before settling down in a quiet heap. Morticue idly stroked the animal's hair with several hands. "I will miss you," he murmured, so quietly that the thrashing ocean nearly covered the sound.

"The Earth primates are not too dissimilar to Musky in general form," said his mate. "In fact, I saw a beautiful diorama at the museum the other day. The prepared specimens were quite lifelike." After a moment without a comment from Morticue she added, "They don't have tails, though, and they are nearly hairless. Some colonists say they make good pets. They have excellent vision—better than ours, in fact—but quite rudimentary senses of smell and touch. I understand humans have a rather gamey taste—at least that's what one Council report said. The nutritional value is nil, of course, with the alien biochemistry and all. I certainly wouldn't put them in any of my recipes, especially if I was about to go into metamorphosis."

"Sounds ghastly," said Morticue. "I think I also read a report that they possess external genitalia and exhibit constant sexual arousal—when they aren't raiding each other's warrens, that is." Another pause ensued. "I can understand the argument about contaminating alien ecologies with creatures from Jadderbad—although we are certainly contaminating the place, but still..." he let the thought trail off and stroked Musky some more.

"They do sing beautifully," Selaea added, after a few moments of silence.

"Yes! Yes, they certainly do." Morticue's lips puckered and he tried to imitate the melody from a popular human/Jadderbadian chorus.

"I've heard that using a human chorus to facilitate metamorphosis is becoming quite the thing to do." Selaea winked the eye closest to her spouse.

"Yes," Morticue concluded, slapping one hand decisively on the bench. "This move will be good for us—and our friend Treya will treat Musky right."

"You're sure the stargate is quite safe?" Selaea asked.

"The Council has been using stargates for generations on several different planets. Complications are well under one percent."

"Complications like death, and having your head end up where your third leg should be?" Selaea picked up her weaving. The hooks clinked together as she worked.

Morticue smiled at his mate, exposing his own gleaming barbs. "I'm glad to see you haven't lost your sense of humor, dear one. I also hope you've prepared all your personal items. Our Council transport leaves at dawn tomorrow morning."

"I'll be ready, dear."

9
Welcome to Earth

Morticue blinked all three eyes and took a deep breath to settle the gorge that threatened to rise in his foremost stomach. He wasn't sure if it was from the trans-spacial field fluctuations of the arch, or the low gravity of his new home. One moment, the briny smells of his seaside domicile surrounded him, and Jadderbad's dark sky brooded overhead. The next, an odiferous blend of primate sweat and pheromones assaulted him while he stood on a raised platform under a dazzlingly bright alien sky.

"Welcome to H2957#*!, Master Morticue & Honorable Selaea," said Kranium in the silken tones reserved for such occasions. "The locals call their planet Dirt or Earth, as I'm sure you know. I trust the transition through phased spacetime was not too uncomfortable."

"I barely noticed," said Morticue, suppressing a belch.

"A little like a boat race on Wellspring when one has imbibed too much fermented stingweed," said Selaea, "but certainly not unduly unpleasant."

Kranium handed each of them a pair of tinted goggles. "You might want to wear these for a while until you adjust to the ambient light on this planet." Both emigrants nodded their thanks and donned the goggles.

"Earth might seem a bit strange at first," said Kranium, "but you will come to love it, I'm sure. My mate especially likes the low gravity. It puts a spring in her step. She spends delightful hours in her garden with mouth and nasal slits wide to sample the native tastes and aromas."

"I will have to confer with her," said Selaea. "By the way, does your mate have any pet primates?" Selaea looked around at a few that lingered near their masters who were attending to various details for Kranium. "They look more attractive than I thought they might and their scent has a fascinating tang to it."

"Tenya, my mate, does indeed have several groupie pets. We usually call them groupies, by the way, rather than primates, because of their complex social habits." Kranium's dermal chromatophores flickered with ingratiating amber-hued patterns in honor of Selaea's racial heritage.

"We'll have to look into adopting some, won't we dear?" Selaea said, twisting one eye toward her mate.

Before Morticue could respond, Kranium said, "Before you do, please wait to examine gifts that I have—for both of you."

"I'm sure we'll be ready for such pleasures when we've had a moment to compose ourselves," said Morticue.

"Of course," said Kranium. "The phased spacetime shift can be disconcerting. I will show you to your quarters momentarily. However, Master Morticue," Kranium continued, shifting his chromatophoric display to shades of emerald to match Morticue's, "I have some intriguing details to discuss with you in your formal role as Overseer of Exobiological Interactions.

Morticue waggled his forehead pili. "Details not already on the Council report? Things relevant to the Honorable Treatment of Sentient Beings Act?"

"Indeed," said Kranium, his chromatophores shifting to somber tones, "details that might significantly shape the form of Jadderbadian philosophy and our engagement with this planet."

Morticue nodded respectfully and flashed appropriate chromatophores. He was intrigued despite the fact that Kranium rated an absurdly high pomposity index, even for an off-world politician. He hadn't changed much since Morticue knew him as an ambitious Second molt at the academy. "Well then, I can't wait to be briefed," he said.

"I like these quarters," Selaea announced, after Kranium dropped them off at the housing complex. "Spacious, yet with dark and intimate alcoves. It looks like they've installed a replicator, smell-a-vision console, a camo-game room..."

"They've spared no expense to exile a pair of old trouble-makers, dear one," Morticue replied.

"Oh pooh," said Selaea. "I know you love this assignment." She found a bench near the window and settled herself with a sigh. "I wonder what surprises old Kranium has for us?"

"Whatever they are, he will make them seem grand, I'm sure." Morticue poked his head around a corner and cocked all three eyes. "Ah, this looks like my media center in here. Indeed, they have spared no resources. We will be indebted to that pompous Turquoise for some time."

"Be generous, dear. Mind the words of the Prophet: 'Suffer fools with kindness until their own stupidity shrivels them like larvae in a sandstorm.'"

Morticue snorted as he turned to enter the media center. He sat on the bench before a wide sensorama screen. "Operate," he commanded, and the device awoke with the default images and odors of his own Wellspring beach property. "Kranium is either very attentive or trying to torture me with pleasant memories," Morticue mumbled to himself. "Global view, sector 537a2," he said to the device. "This unit has a vision enhancer, dear one," he yelled to his mate. "A very nice one," he muttered to himself.

The screen showed an ocean view of this colony planet, Earth, from low orbit. The peaks of two concentric rings of mountains poked up from the ocean not far from a large island continent. "Dear one, you'll have to look at these impact rings. It's fabulous to see them in detail. This planet suffered quite an extinction event from an asteroid impact in the geologically recent past."

"Yes, dear," came Selaea's voice from the adjoining room. "I've experienced the event in the sensorium too, you know. If you've seen one giant crater you've seen them all. And I presume by 'geologically recent' you're talking about a number with a trailer load of zeros after it."

"Well, six zeros or so, anyway," Morticue said. And all impact craters are not created equal, he thought, but judiciously declined to comment. He continued the geological tour of his new planet a few minutes longer. He noted their current location on a large continent in the northern hemisphere and located a few of the anomalous excavation sites that he planned to study, before the entrance gate chimed.

"I think Kranium has returned," said Selaea. "I'll let him in."

Morticue sighed and returned to the main living chamber.

Kranium entered, his eating orifice stretched broadly and barbs gleaming. Behind him trailed two unclothed human primates, ready for inspection. One was female and one obviously male, with the dangling external genitalia. Their pheromones declared they were an agreeably mated pair. "Greetings again, Honored Ones. I bear gifts," he said. To the male primate he said, "Speak, Fum!"

The male stepped forward in front of Morticue and Selaea. "I live to serve you," he said in passable Jadderbadian—although understandably lacking any olfactory or chromatophoric overtones.

"Oh, how cute!" Selaea said. "Look at that shock of curly hair on the male, and those pendulous fleshy globes on the female's chest. Don't you just love them, Morticue? They have those bold primate scents you so liked in Musky."

"I brought them unclothed, so you can dress them to suit your tastes and clan affiliations. The male is called Fum, in his own crude language," said Kranium. "The female is called Nulla. They are a mated pair as you have undoubtedly smelled—a bit too old to produce a litter, but I thought you might not be interested in breeding pairs—at least, not at first. Correct me if I have erred."

"Ah, no," said Morticue. "You have performed a kindness." I think, thought Morticue to himself. I hope they have been cleared of parasites, was his next thought, although he knew from the relevant literature produced by fellow exobiologists that the alien vermin couldn't harm Jadderbadian flesh. And, Prophet knows, we all need our microbiota to survive and flourish.

"This pair is quite tame," said Kranium. "They were raised from nurslings by a mature Emerald who just recently entered metamorphosis. They love attention."

The male named Fum approached Selaea and offered his head for petting. Selaea obliged. "How cute," she repeated.

"And, I have that special item for you," said Kranium, focusing all three eyes on Morticue.

"Oh?" Morticue said, wiggling a few pili over one eye and flashing some chest chromatophores.

Kranium handed Morticue a viewing globe with something very tiny inside. Morticue sniffed, but the globe was amazingly odor neutral.

"Magnify," said Morticue to the globe. "What is this?" Morticue focused a pair of eyes on Kranium and left the third to further examine the contents of the globe.

"An artifact of some sort," said Kranium.

"A native artifact? From where?" asked Morticue. "I thought this planet was declared free of intelligent life of any consequence."

"Oh, it has been," said Kranium. "These little primates that scurry around and worship us seem to be the most complicated things the planet has evolved. Nothing comparable to Tripodian complexity." Kranium paused briefly. "Nevertheless, security captured this artifact humming in the air in the vicinity of the arch. Scans of its internal structure imply photographic and communications capabilities of a high order. And it's constructed of titanium, silicon, and other non-biologic materials." Kranium's chromatophores flashed in self-important tones of violet and purple.

"Impossible," said Morticue, although he realized it was a stupid comment the moment he uttered it. The evidence lay in his hand. "What creature on this planet could have created such a device—especially so soon after a major extinction event? Especially a primitive, non-Tripodian creature?"

"That certainly appears to be an excellent question," said Kranium, exposing a thin line of his feeding barbs. "An excellent question, indeed, and one I'm hoping a natural philosopher of your distinguished caliber can answer."

10
Walking the groupies

Morticue pondered the question for some time. He placed the globe and its attendant artifact on a dais in the media center so that its contents would remind him of the conundrum it posed. Could there possibly be a sentient species huddling in some corner of this water world? Geologists had turned up some unusual chemical signals from strata roughly contemporaneous with the impact event, but that happened nearly a million years ago. Obviously, the Council's research was incomplete—but Morticue would not publish that opinion any time soon without some significant discovery of his own.

In the meantime, he and Selaea enjoyed their new pets.

"Look how well they climb!" exclaimed Selaea one day, after she had climbing ropes and platforms installed in one of the auxiliary living spaces. Fum had just deftly clambered up several rope ladders to a lower platform to sit next to Nulla. He stroked his mate's thigh. She giggled in response.

"What are they doing?" Morticue squinted with his two best eyes and sniffed. "It smells like they're aroused. I thought Kranium said they were past child-bearing years."

"Well yes, dear, but they mate all the time anyway. You knew that."

"Let's walk them soon so I can return to work before it gets too late," said Morticue.

"Fum will be very disappointed. Look how excited he is."

"He can be excited later. I'll get their collars," Morticue said.

"Look, Morticue. Fum is sticking his tongue out at you. He likes you. How cute. I don't think he's ready for a walk."

"I'm ready for a walk. He's the pet and I'm the master, last time I checked."

"If you insist, dear," Selaea smiled, "although they seem to have a talent for making us do what they want to do."

After collecting their groupies and affixing collars, the Amber-grands left their dwelling, and decided on a path that would pass several neighbors' domains before ending at a park near the lake.

"You remembered the Poo-Be-Gone, I hope," said Selaea. "Nulla is squatting near that bush on the nursery grounds."

"I have it," Morticue said. He extracted the tiny molecular dispersion device from a pouch around his second segment. When Nulla was finished, he aimed the Poo-Be-Gone at the odiferous pile of excrement and pushed the appropriate button. The poo dissolved in a brown vapor with the fading aromas of methane, sulfur and ammonia.

"I'm not sure those beans we obtained from the pet commissary agree with her," said Selaea.

"Yes, well…" Morticue began, but then noticed a Thirdie approaching with a groupie of her own. The Thirdie smelled like someone he should remember—an older female in her fourth century, with overtones of juvenile vomit somewhere in the mix.

"Oh, look," said Selaea, "it's Moia! She must be taking a break from her Firstie care duties."

Oh, yes. Moia. Morticue remembered speaking to her at some function or another just after they arrived. He was glad it wasn't his turn for Firstie care. First molt Jadderbadians were a trial. They barely had enough brains to keep their three arms and legs untangled and the nurseries always reeked of vomit and other objectionable scents. Seconds were more teachable. He rather enjoyed mentoring that group. Ah, well. We all must swim before we crawl ashore, thought Morticue.

"Attend," commanded Morticue. Nulla stood on Selaea's right, still smelling faintly of excrement. Fum ambled over to Morticue's right, trailing filaments of musk. He stuck out his tongue again in the gesture Selaea insisted was respect.

"Attend, Portae," Moia said as she approached. Her tattooed female groupie complied, swaying her torso as she did so. Moia's bitch smelled to be in a sexually responsive portion of her monthly cycle.

"I hope the Ambergrands are well this afternoon," Moia said. Her chromatophores fluttered in colors connoting mild concern. Pili near her armpits fluttered, accentuating her personal aromas.

"Oh, yes," said Selaea. "Are you enjoying the smellscape today?"

"Very much so," said Moia. "My Portae here needed a good walk. She's been restless and eager to meet her groupie neighbors. They just have to get out and see things, you know."

"I'm sure," said Selaea. "Our Fum seems quite interested. Excited even."

"It doesn't take three eyes to see that," said Moia. "He smells a bit rutty, too. Did the female hiss? Sometimes they do get possessive, I've heard. They are a mated couple, are they not? I thought you told me that one time after your last tour at the nursery."

"Indeed," said Selaea, and then Morticue tuned the conversation out. He really should be getting back to his work—or at least not chattering on about nothing in particular. The conversation continued long enough that shadows began to lengthen, and the air smelled rich with moisture. Musty earthen smells wafted up from the pavement. A weather front must be pressing in, thought Morticue. His pili could tell.

A large male Thirdie approached along the path. His scent finally identified him: Edelfine. Morticue recalled that he was a squad leader in the Thunderclub Clan. Warriors exuded a peculiar musk mixed with the tang of metal from the hardware they used. Morticue hated the smell, ever since a Thunderclub had caught him years ago during that unfortunate incident near the stargate.

This Edelphine exuded a distinct blend of pheromones that advertised him to be a middle aged Turquoise. As he approached, Portae squeezed closer to Mistress Moia. Fum jabbered something while pulling Nulla close to his side. The male groupie gestured with one arm at Edelfine.

Edelfine passed, trailing a cloud of scent acrid with his obvious dislike of groupies. "Keep those animals in check," he muttered. "I trust they are properly licensed and their shots current." He moved along at a brisk pace, apparently enroute to the security compound nearby.

"I much prefer the company of groupies to Jadderbadians like him," said Moia after the Turquoise was clearly beyond hearing range. "Just between you and me," she whispered to Selaea, "he's been known to mistreat pets."

Selaea fluttered her head pili. "Really? We shall be careful in our dealings with him, won't we dear?"

Morticue grunted assent.

"Well," Selaea continued, "we really should be going. We've certainly enjoyed sharing the richness of your company, Moia."

Moia continued on her way and the Ambergrands proceeded to their favorite public benches with an excellent airstream flow from the lake. The algal blooms provided an unusual tang. The benches were big enough to accommodate both the Ambergrands and their pets. Nulla curled up next to Morticue, and Fum sat cross-legged next to Selaea.

The sun settled lower in the sky. Morticue decided that Earth sunsets had their own charm, though very different from the deep oranges and reds of his home star. Light faded. The air cooled and shifted, bringing with it the scent of distant trees the groupies called pines. Morticue mentally reminded himself about work, but then resigned himself to the pleasure of the evening. He was surprised when Selaea said, "I'm ready to return home, dear."

"I think I will enjoy the evening just a bit longer," said Morticue. "Will you take Fum back to the kennel? I'll return with Nulla soon."

"Of course, dear," his mate replied. "Don't be too late. You know how the cool air stiffens your legs."

After Selaea left, stars began to emerge overhead. Earth's sky was often clear. The evening star displays, when Morticue took the time to look, gave him delightful chills. How thrilling to see all those distant, scentless suns. He automatically searched for the Jadderbadian home star, one glimmer of red in a universe sparkling with light, but the Earth's large moon washed out much of the vista tonight.

Nulla leaned in close to him and pointed at the moon. "Legends say my people left footprints on the moon," said Nulla.

Morticue rumbled with laughter that shook his entire frame. "Ah, my sweet little Nulla. That's quite impossible." He stroked her long hair. Sometimes groupies did make the strangest comments in their pidgin Jadderbadian.

"And legends say my people's voices once traveled around the world," Nulla volunteered, "and we shared images of ourselves everywhere we went." Nulla smiled and stretched her arms wide. "It is written in the Diaries of Thurwild."

Morticue laughed again, enjoying the fragrance of those distant pines. Thurwild indeed. He had heard groupies often worshipped ancestral wise persons in their lineages.

Morticue closed all three of his eyes to better enjoy the evening's scents. But then, inexplicably, a mental picture of the tiny flying artifact encased in the plastic bubble on the dais in his media center assembled behind his closed eyelids. What creatures had made such a device? He had heard that some of the flying creatures on this planet were quite clever. The artifact might be fashioned in the image of their maker. And invertebrates like ants and termites had created quite complex social societies. Perhaps they have more evolved brethren somewhere.

Certainly nothing as primitive and scent blind as primates like Nulla, he reasoned.

Certainly not.

Morticue eased himself from the bench and stood stiffly on his three old legs. "Attend," he said to Nulla, who promptly jumped from the bench and stood beside him. "It's time to go home."

11
Interruption on Prophet's Day

Morticue spent a few days arranging an itinerary to visit the sites containing some suspicious landforms that he wanted to include on his exobiology survey. Selaea made connections with other Council members or ex-members now residing on Earth. In his spare time Morticue scanned, analyzed and pondered the bubble-encased artifact until his pili quivered and his chromatophores flashed haphazardly like a Firstie drunk on his baptismal odor globe. He actually began to look forward to Prophet's Day.

"Really?" said Selaea. "You're attending Prophet's Day with me? I do hope the stargate doesn't collapse, or the holy temple sprout sensory pili."

"Calm yourself, dear one. The temple is quiet and the dulcet tones of Grand Disciple Starke soothe me."

"Just don't snore too loudly, dear." Selaea fluffed the pili on her forehead. "And change your segment bands into something less frumpy. Natural philosophers and Council members need to set a good example."

Morticue grunted, but complied. The transport arrived just as they emerged from the front door. "The pets are fed?" he asked.

"Certainly, dear," Selaea replied as she entered the transport. "I gave them some of that high fiber Groupie Chow they like so much. Let's hurry. You know how Grand Disciple Starke's skin flashes crimson when parishioners arrive late."

They arrived with minutes to spare, although the Grand Disciple did cast a glance their way with one eye as he ascended the stage. The Ambergrands found their clan benches quickly. The Disciple's robes glittered with artificial chromatophores displaying traditional holy colors. His exposed skin looked quite healthy for a 432-year-old. Morticue assumed that he must be attending to his diet and exercise, delaying metamorphosis as long as possible. That did give religious philosophers more gravitas.

"Brethren," Grand Disciple Starke began, "welcome! May the Prophet bless you for your dedication and sacrifices as we explore this glorious water world filled with the Prophet's creations." He paused dramatically, as effective disciples do, extending his nine arms in a wide metaphorical embrace. Behind him, five handsome female Seconds assembled, obviously part of the coming ceremony. They wore no segment bands, so their chromatophoric displays could make them seem to disappear against the background stage, like ghostly attendants to the Prophet. Enclosures on either side of the stage housed choral groupies that would later play their part in the ceremony.

"Congratulate yourselves, colonists," the Disciple continued. "After 151 local years on this rich new planet, we have created a thriving colony, begun the process of assimilating new species into the Prophet's benevolent embrace, and will soon witness a metamorphosis among one of our honored eldest: Honorable Moia Escapole."

"I do hope an appropriate male will metamorphose soon," whispered Selaea. "Moia never established another relationship after her mate passed so unexpectedly."

"That old Amber napping in the third row looks like a male in need of a sex life," muttered Morticue. "I've seen others crawling about the commercial square that should be looking soon for a secluded alcove somewhere."

"Oh hush, Morticue," Selaea whispered just a bit too loudly. "That old Amber works the food pens after all—someone much below Moia's station."

"Let us bow our torsos," said the disciple, casting a sharp glance in the Ambergrands' direction, "and cast puffs of supportive smells in honor of our first metamorphee." Behind the Grand Disciple the five Seconds linked hands, fluttered their scent glands, and seemed to flick in and out of existence as their chromatophores rippled with

46

color. The choral groupies sang in their strangely soothing primate voices, not unlike those on Mother Jadderbad. Moia entered the room from stage right, acknowledged the recognition with appropriate gestures and scents, before leaving with the slow gait of someone on the cusp of transformation.

"It looks like she might reconfigure any day now," whispered Selaea. "She had a request of us the other day. Moia would like us to take her groupie, Portae, when she transforms."

Morticue's oral pili fluttered and he groaned. "Our Fum will be happy, but I do hope the bitches don't fight," he whispered.

"Thank you," said Grand Disciple Starke. "And now…," he began, just as someone pounded three times on the temple door. An old Emerald attendant near the entrance shivered to attention as if startled awake. "See who is disturbing a holy service," said the Grand Disciple to the attendant.

The attendant opened the door to reveal the hulking form of Edelphine in his full dress Captain's uniform and Clan insignia. Another somewhat shorter Jadderbadian stood just behind him wearing the same Thunderclub Clan insignia, but with the rank of Lieutenant. "I need a word with Master Morticue Ambergrand," said Edelphine. "Please excuse the intrusion, Grand Disciple," he added, with a low bow.

Grand Disciple Starke nodded in formal acknowledgement.

"My apologies, Grand Disciple," said Morticue. "I leave your company with regret." Morticue rose, feeling fortunate to be at the end of a bench so that he didn't need to jostle his way along a fence line of the faithful. He turned briefly to Selaea: "I will meet you at home, dear one," he whispered.

Outside the closed door to the temple, Edelphine wasted little time with formalities. "Master Morticue Ambergrand, Natural Philosopher?"

Morticue nodded ascent.

"I understand from Honorable Ambassador Kranium that you are aware of an anomalous artifact found within the bounds of New Jadderbad."

"That is correct. I am in the process..."

"There has been a significant new development," Edelphine said, interrupting in a most discourteous manner. "Members of the Thunderclub Clan detected a functioning artifact similar to the one in your possession, whose movements we have been monitoring. The device in question was traced to ancient ruins on a large island some distance northeast of here across the New Wellspring Ocean..." Edelphine paused long enough to display a map on his portable tablet, "...in the general vicinity of a pack of wild groupies not previously surveyed."

"That's quite interesting," Morticue focused all three eyes on the tablet and sniffed for any olfactory details. "I have been planning an itinerary that will encompass that site and..."

"Because the artifact we have been tracing contains a level of technology deemed to pose a possible security threat to New Jadderbad, I have been authorized by the ambassador to mobilize you in the service of the Thunderclub Clan."

"Yes, well I would be most happy to comply," said Morticue. "I believe that in twenty local days..."

"Your mobilization will take place immediately, Master Morticue," said Edelphine. His chromatophores flickered in patterns denoting a certain pleasure in his pronouncement. "Lieutenant Tork here," he said, gesturing with two arms, "will assist you in every possible way. He has become an expert in dealing with..." Edelphine paused, trying to access vocabulary he rarely used, "...the groupie animals that have become so popular with some Jadderbadian clans." Before Morticue could reply, Edelphine continued: "If you will excuse me, I must attend to expedition details."

Edelphine left, trailing vapors that reeked of grandiose authority.

Morticue turned to Lieutenant Tork, who shrugged nine shoulders and flickered in shades of appeasement. "Sometimes the Captain gets his insignia pinned a little too deeply, Master Morticue. He is a good warrior, but one who would never be considered for the diplomatic core."

"I need to attend to details at home, consult with my mate, feed and board pets..." Morticue found himself getting a little flustered.

"Yes, about the pets. We went to your home first, thinking you were there. One of the pets—the female—came to the door yelling things, and the male showed up threatening Edelphine with a drapery pole..."

"Yes, Lieutenant, that would be Fum. What are trying to tell me?" Morticue felt his frustration morphing into anger.

"The Captain knocked the female down trying to get the pole away from the male...Anyway, the female might have been injured a little. She should probably see a veterinarian." Tork emitted a cloud of appeasement pheromones.

"I smell your concern," said Morticue, but such odors would be more appropriate if received from Edelphine. Better yet, he'd love to see Edelphine cowering with fear and humility before him, so agitated that he dumped a fragrant load of frass from his bowels. Morticue decided to spend some time pondering just how to make that scenario come to pass.

12
Gaia & Hydra

Hydra: Isn't it quite amazing how long-legged vertebrate omnivores evolved to look so similar on our separate worlds?

Gaia: Yes. Similar habitats yield similar creatures.

Hydra: Although my primates never developed the same swelled brains and intelligence that yours did.

Gaia: Mine are clever. I will give them that. However, they did come close to wiping themselves out before the asteroid nearly finished the job. It will be interesting to see if the ones that survived can turn things around. I'm especially interested in the tribe that formed near that artificial entity. I've watched them for several generations now. They show some promise. Of course, it might be wishful thinking on my part...

13
Shaman's Cove

Rugat used his bone tool to pressure off another flake from the jasper point, and then frowned at the long shadows highlighting the texture of nearby rocks framing Shaman's Cove. "We should be going, magic boy. The trader will be at the village early tomorrow and it will take all day to get to Magic Mountain." He slipped the point-in-progress and his finishing tool into a vest pouch.

"I'm almost done," Twill yelled. He hoped his voice carried over the rock wall that separated him from Rugat *and* that it conveyed his displeasure. His friend had overheard Jeeta use that name for him once and poked him now and then with it as if it was one of his stone arrowheads. Rugat shouldn't get comfortable with that habit now that Twill was shaman. It was hard enough taking over for Grandfather without that. Grandfather wasn't dead, after all—but it seemed more and more that it was only spirits who could talk to him.

Twill added a few dashes of color to the rock painting with his good right hand; then began gathering up painting supplies in anticipation of the return trip to the village.

"Beautiful!" Rugat's voice startled him. Twill hadn't heard him come around the edge of the outer wall of rocks. "I don't know how you paint like that." Rugat moved up behind his left shoulder and pointed. "You've really captured Jeeta using that bow of hers, magic boy. She made a nice kill of that big ratalope, didn't she?"

"Yes, she did. She knows when to shoot and where. See that you do too, when you shoot out disrespectful names." Twill began wrapping paint pots with stained and tattered scraps of hide and putting them in his supply pack.

"Oooh, the shaman has rock dust in his crotch." Rugat leaned closer to the painting. "I don't remember seeing that much of Jeeta's breasts on the day she hunted the ratalopes with us. Looks like you took a lot of care painting those!"

Twill's ears felt hot. Fortunately, his dark skin often concealed a blush pretty well. Steadying the supply pack with his withered left arm and hand, he stuffed the bag with enough energy that he heard one clay pot clack against another.

"Good thing I'm already mated, old friend," Rugat continued. "You've made Jeeta look so good it makes my spear tingle."

"Let's move, Rugat. The sun is getting low." Twill tied up the supply pack and left it for Rugat to carry. Then he hoisted the day-pack over his shoulder and performed a couple of deep knee bends to loosen his leg muscles after squatting for the last hour.

Rugat easily lifted the supply pack to his back and fastened the straps around his shoulders. "I've heard that this trader coming from the south has an eye for the women. A hunter cousin of mine said that a woman in Jugal's tribe birthed the trader's baby two years ago. Better keep an eye on Jeeta tomorrow—but then I'm sure you will—if nothing else, just to make sure you get the breasts—and those long hunter's legs—right for your next painting."

Twill turned to smile at Rugat, although he suspected it looked more like a grimace. "Jeeta would trim his spear in an instant."

Rugat laughed. "I'm sure she would."

Twill took a deep breath and a last look at his favorite cove. He wished they could have stayed to watch the souls of their ancestors emerge in all their glory in the sky. At least, Grandfather always said that's what those bright specks were. Twill sometimes had his doubts—although if some of his ancestors made Magic Mountain, which Grandfather had also claimed, perhaps they could rise into the night sky and shine.

"What do you think of these worm god rumors the southern traders talk about?" Rugat tossed off the comment as he took the lead on the trail home.

"Giant worms three times taller than a man that walk through holes in the sky?" Twill laughed. "They can't be real." At least, Twill certainly hoped not. Grandfather never provided him with potions or spells for giant worm beasts. Regardless, he planned to impress the trader with some of the surprises that made Magic Mountain magic.

Darkness cloaked the forest by the time the glow of the village's communal fire pit appeared near the horizon. Twill couldn't wait to kick his sandals off and remove an especially annoying piece of grit lodged near the big toe of his left foot. If he was lucky, he might catch a glimpse of Jeeta outside her parents' hut. Grandfather most likely would be there too—with Moran hovering nearby to make sure the old shaman didn't stumble into the fire or something. Poor grandfather. Bad enough that spirits had come into his head one night and never left. Now Moran—who barely knew how to keep his own sandals tied—fluttered around him, hoping to steal some of grandfather's wisdom—without a malevolent spirit attached.

Moran caught sight of them first at the village perimeter. "Welcome great hunter—and shriveled-armed shaman!" he added as an afterthought. Moran's crooked grin revealed his missing lower incisor.

"Ah, dear Twill, dear Twill..." Grandfather gesticulated behind his keeper, focusing briefly on his grandson before turning to speak to an invisible spirit. "Yes, of course that's Twill. He's going to Magic Mountain tomorrow to speak to Spider Woman. That southern trader will meet a real goddess!" Grandfather wandered back toward the fire pit.

Moran turned, a bit agitated, to keep close to the old man. He gestured to Twill and Rugat. "Come. Come to the fire. The trader arrived already. His name is Bot or Bog or Bak—something like that. The elders hustled him into their tent already."

"Light. Light," said Grandfather. "And smell the sulfur from the steaming vents! Spider Woman's perfume." Grandfather trotted toward the fire and Moran hurried to keep up. Fire Mountain, not far west of the tall, shiny Magic Mountain, rumbled in the dark. "Yes, what? I didn't quite hear you, Spider Woman. What did you say?"

"Hope you heard her clearly, magic boy." Rugat's brow creased. Twill had never quite figured out how much Rugat believed in spirits. Rugat, great hunter that he was, tended to think along the lines "If it scares you, throw a spear at it."

"Of course," Twill said with confidence. That was Grandfather's first rule of shamanhood—back when the spirits only visited his head. 'Speak with authority and the tribe will believe.' Then he would smile. 'Pretty soon you will believe, too.'"

Twill wasn't sure. Magic Mountain had scared the piss out of his wand more than once. Twill had to hope that Spider Woman could scare ambassadors of giant worms badly enough to keep them well away on the other side of the Great Ocean.

14
Discovered

"Rudy, we have a situation," Mnemosyne said.

Rudy sat, gazing through a gigantic window with a view of a stream that meandered south of the Citadel and toward the human village that had grown up in its towering shadow. "The last time you told me that, the world was about to come to an end."

Mnemosyne's ponytailed avatar joined him at the window. "I'm hopeful that won't be the case this time."

"Just hopeful? What's going on?" Rudy stood and walked over to stand next to Mnemosyne.

"I lost transmission from one drone patrolling the vicinity of the stargate. I have reason to believe another was tracked when it returned here. The Jadderbadians surely intend to explore the drone's point of origin and assess any technology that could be a threat to them." Mnemosyne turned to look at Rudy. "We are at risk."

"Just what are these worm-i-pedes capable of—besides making lapdogs out of the local humans? They've built a sizeable town, but haven't exactly overrun the planet with aggressive expansion. What's it been—a century now since they came through the gate?"

"Kranium first crossed through the stargate 151 years ago. They have significant technology—although, from what I can tell from my drone eavesdropping—and this would be good news—the stargate technology was not their invention. They discovered one on Jadderbad and gradually uncovered links to a series of other worlds—including ours."

"Hmmm. That means at least three technologically savvy species have run the extinction gauntlet on their respective worlds. Interesting. So what do Jadderbanians have that worries you?" asked Rudy.

"Have you seen their Pooh-Be-Gones?"

"The shit vaporizers?"

"Yes," said Mnemosyne, "but the technology easily scales up. Their weapons can vaporize far more than excrement. I have no way to effectively shield the Citadel should they consider us a significant threat."

Rudy pondered cloud patterns slowing drifting and twisting across the landscape beyond the window. "From what I can tell from the drone bioscience data, they have a pretty solid grasp of biology, too. They're damn similar to Earth biology at the molecular level—same basic chemistry with a few twists—like DNA and RNA genetics with different codons, protein isomer symmetry the same, however, and so on. But, their biologists are fiddling around with trying to hybridize Jadderbadian and Earth biochemistries. I just can't quite figure out their motivations—unless it's just good old-fashioned curiosity..."

"We need to learn more about them—information that drones alone can't supply," Mnemosyne placed a finger on her chin as if pondering the situation.

"Agreed," said Rudy. "Maybe we need to enlist a spy or two."

"Spies?" Mnemosyne's avatar frowned.

"Yes, I'm sure you've heard of spies. We need a good Trojan horse to breach their defenses."

"You're surprisingly devious for a scholar," observed Mnemosyne.

Rudy smiled. "I've known many devious scholars in my day. What about those acolytes that wander up from the village and genuflect in the building's foyer? Any good prospects there?"

Mnemosyne scrunched her nose in an endearing imitation of a gesture his third wife used to make. "Perhaps Twill would make a good candidate."

"Twill?" Rudy scrunched his nose in turn. "Sounds like an affliction, not a name."

Mnemosyne pointed out the window. "Do you see those four humans down there, and the black dog, coming up the trail toward the

Citadel? Notice the dark skinned male just in front of the female— the one holding the elaborate staff with his withered left arm and wearing a feathered headdress. That is my chief 'priest', you might say—or at least Spider Woman's chief priest. That is Twill."

Rudy examined the little procession. Human beings had changed very little in a million years, all things considered—a little lankier perhaps, as if they'd been stretched in a fun-house mirror. This bunch was rather brown-skinned, but skin color changed easily among varieties of *H. sapiens*. "You make a good comic book hero, Nessie." Rudy winked at his AI avatar. "Good thing that old poster survived in the lobby."

"It wasn't entirely chance, Rudy." Mnemosyne continued to examine the small party on the trail. "Twill's maternal grandmother six generations ago first found the citadel, and discovered the remains of the poster to be prophetic. She saw a family resemblance, I think. I accessed my records, learned what the original Spider Woman was supposed to look like, and gradually had the spiderlings recreate her."

"That must have impressed grandma." Rudy studied the advancing villagers, too.

"Oh, it certainly did," confirmed Mnemosyne.

Rudy squinted to see more clearly—which his rational mind suspected was a bit of magnification and image enhancement on Mnemosyne's part. "So, your high priest is the one trying to pick his nose without anyone seeing?" observed Rudy.

"Yes, that one," confirmed Mnemosyne. "I believe the correct idiom is 'He is smarter than he looks.'"

15
On the way to Magic Mountain

❝Magic Mountain is impressive—though nothing to compare to the Holy Arch." Bok, the trader from across the Great Southern Sea, tapped the embroidered depiction of the arch on his vest. The trader puffed out his chest as he did so, and a broad smile parted the bush of the slightly greyed, but well-trimmed, beard that cupped his chin and skirted the base of his nose.

Twill had seen a similar embroidered insignia before, on another trader when he was still a child. The distant village near the mysterious arch had always been rumored to serve strange gods—including a powerful one called Kranium—but no one he knew personally had ever crossed the great sea to see them or the mysterious arch. The trader had hinted that this might change. But the trader was apparently no avid disciple on a mission of conversion. He skillfully separated church and commerce.

"I'm sure your arch is something to see, but so is our Magic Mountain." Twill paused and surreptitiously deposited his booger on the back of a leaf he pretended to study with care. "I think winter will be early this year," he pronounced to no one in particular, dropping the leaf. Jeeta's dog, Dark Shadow—or DS for short—gave it a quick sniff over before returning to her side.

"Wait until you see Spider Woman and her spiderlings, Bok." Jeeta stretched her arms in an expansive gesture and cocked one wrist. Twill noted that she captured the pose of Spider Woman quite well, although she had only seen the image a few times.

"What spiderlings?" Rugat frowned at Jeeta. "Nobody said anything about spiderlings."

"They shouldn't bother a big warrior like you," said Jeeta. "Although I seem to remember you jumping one time at the campfire when a spider crawled over your toe."

"It surprised me," grumbled Rugat.

"Quit teasing Rugat," said Twill. "The spiderlings seem harmless—and they don't show up often anyway."

"After the Summer Ceremony, I saw some crawling around high up on the mountain. I also saw one close up once. It was as big as a mouse and shiny. It scuttled away before anyone else saw it." Jeeta shifted her daypack and looked up at the towering structure before them. She ran a hand through her thick, dark hair and squinted in the bright sunlight. "Your grandfather thinks they take care of the mountain, which he says has been around at least since the days of his father's father—and probably forever."

Twill briefly shifted his staff to his weak arm and straightened his headdress. He turned toward Jeeta, but rationed his attention to just a glance. There was work to do and it was already past noon. Twill resumed walking uphill toward their goal. "Everything has beginnings, as far as I can tell," said Twill. "But yes, I think the spiderlings take care of Magic Mountain."

"Has your grandfather said anything more to you about them?" asked Jeeta.

"Not for many years," said Twill. "Not since the spirit voices took complete charge of him and Moran became his domestic helper." Grandfather had always been possessed by spirit voices, which was one of the reasons he had been a clear choice for shaman, but when he heard only spirit voices, the Council of Elders relegated Grandfather to a Hut of Honor at the village outskirts. That way he didn't keep everyone up at night. Twill's main talent was painting clever pictures that people liked to ooh and ahh over, but he wasn't much of a hunter or fisherman because of his shriveled arm. Since he was the shaman's grandson, the feathered leather cap now perched on his head. Twill often wished that it still belonged to Grandfather—but he didn't want that twit, Moran, to become a shaman either. He wished his father had lived to wear it instead.

"Do you think your pictures will keep the worm creatures under control, Twill?" Rugat asked.

"If Bok can describe them clearly," said Twill, with what he hoped was authority. Twill feared the villagers had more confidence in his art's magic powers than he did. If these bug gods turned out to be something real, his village might need more than magic paintings.

"I can see Holy Kranium in my mind clearly," said Bok. "I can describe him accurately. But your picture will have to be very powerful. Our gods travel in muleless chariots, talk to each other at a distance, and make bad people—not to mention unwanted shit—disappear into curls of smoke." And, he added with an elaborate, two-armed gesture, "They appear from nowhere under the golden glow of the Holy Arch."

"So you have said." Twill did not believe every trader's story he heard. In fact, the kernel of truth in every trader's tale seemed smaller than a single milkweed seed in the entire pod. But Bok told his stories in great detail and with enthusiasm. Twill shivered, although the afternoon sun lay warmly on his back. "We should be at the entrance within the hour," he said, "if we wait to rest and eat until we arrive."

16
Spider Woman

The party of humans craned their necks to peer up at the gleaming sides of Magic Mountain. The frayed edges of high clouds slowly drifted past the summit. DS snuffed at the ground like a starved man at a banquet, black head swinging to and fro. "How do we get in?" asked Rugat.

Twill put down his staff and eased the pack off his back with a sigh. "I know the Holy Words and the Way," he said. Actually, the Holy Words were for show. Grandfather had passed down the knowledge of a place to touch that made a small part of Magic Mountain slide open. *Shamans must polish their magic like a hunter crafts his spear point*, his grandfather had told him in a moment of lucid instruction. "We'll eat here before we go in," said Twill. "Be nice to Rugat. The food is in his pack."

"You will soon see Spider Woman," said Jeeta proudly to Bok. "She guards the entrance to the inner chambers."

"Does she have a web?" asked Bok as he set down his gear, too.

"Of a sort," said Jeeta. "It's a little hard to see." Jeeta took a strip of ratalope jerky from Rugat and chewed off a generous hunk.

"The image of Spider Woman is very old," said Twill, "and parts of it are quite faded." Twill also began gnawing on his strip of jerky. "A web extends from the palm of her hand."

"Much nicer than where a real spider's comes out," commented Rugat through a mouthful of food. He tossed a piece of jerky to DS.

Jeeta laughed. She rarely worried about offending gods or goddesses, thought Twill—or shamans. She liked to call him Magic Boy, though, which could be irksome.

"So, Spider Woman is just an image?" Bok accepted his ration of jerky from Rugat.

"Spider Woman speaks to us in times of crisis," Jeeta proclaimed.

"Has she spoken often?" asked Bok.

"She spoke to Grandfather twice during his time as shaman." And that means she speaks about once a decade, Twill thought, but didn't mention that out loud.

"Has she ever spoken to you?" Bok looked earnestly into Twill's eyes.

Twill paused. "Not yet," he admitted.

"Our gods speak to us often—and in person," added Bok with some pride.

"How nice for you," said Twill. "Is that before or after you fetch slippers for them?" Twill's comment had the desired effect. Bok's sly grin twisted into a pout and he finished his meal in silence. Now Twill might not be able to afford the piece of polished jade he had spied in the trader's wares, that he wanted as a gift for Jeeta. Ah well, the jibe was worth it. Apparently the rumors he had heard from other traders, that the followers of Thurwild were no more than pets or servants to the worm-bug people, must be close enough to the truth to make the trader bristle.

They ate in silence. Twill wondered if Spider Woman's voice was just one of the many voices that spoke to his grandfather. Of course, everyone heard the voice of Gaia—except a very few that were born deaf to her inner voice—but that was nothing remarkable. Gaia only spoke when the tribe was in danger of injuring her. That was as it should be.

Everyone took swigs from their ratalope bladder water bags. Jeeta offered some of hers to DS. She absently fingered a small golden amulet that hung around her neck.

Bok pointed toward her neck. "What do you want for that amulet, Maiden?"

Jeeta removed her hand from the amulet and placed it on DS's head. "Not for sale, trader. It was a gift from Grandmother."

"Even for—let's say two obsidian knives and—and perhaps a

box made from polished marble in which you might keep other treasures?" Bok smiled and winked at her.

Jeeted frowned. "Traders seem incapable of understanding simple words—like 'no.'"

Bok nodded his head and shrugged his shoulders. "I've found that many 'no's can turn into maybes—or even yeses."

They followed Twill in among the pillars of Magic Mountain. Twill found the slightly depressed area he was looking for on the wall. He handed his staff to Jeeta, straightened his feather cap, opened a pouch on his belt, and raised a pinch of pollen over his head with his good hand. "Allow us entry to your den, Great Spider Woman…," he said, sprinkling the pollen with his right hand while he turned and allowed his crippled elbow to brush the proper spot on the wall. "And do not eat us. We, your humble servants, only wish to honor you."

Twill held his breath. He always wondered what he would say if the wall failed to open, but it never had. Then he heard the faintest of clicks as the wall slid aside. He allowed himself an elfin grin when Bok emitted a soft, "Ahhh."

Twill turned to his followers and said, "Spider Woman awaits."

Jeeta smiled and winked at him. DS barked and wagged his tail. Both of them had been here before.

They entered a large chamber that smelled of dust. Absent were the familiar smells of leather, sweat and animal dung. The walls, though smooth as a toolmaker's blade, seemed as lifeless and timeless as granite. On one massive wall a diffuse glow illuminated a large image from behind, like when he created shadows beneath stretched and cleaned animal skin backlighted with the glow of candles. Sketchy borders surrounding the central image made Twill think there once were at least five other images that had faded to mere splotchy stains.

Twill, Rugat, and Jeeta bowed briefly before dropping to one knee. Bok copied their motions with a slight delay. "That is Spider Woman?" whispered Bok.

"Obviously," said Twill.

"She is most certainly a healthy and fully formed female," observed Bok, carefully choosing his words, "and—no disrespect intended—she has only the usual number of limbs—not eight."

"But she has a glowing web extending from her hand," said Rugat "and I have seen spiders with markings on their abdomens somewhat like hers."

"We have paid our respects to Spider Woman," said Twill. "Let's move to the galleries and attend to the business at hand. I must paint your Kranium worm-bug god and take the measure of him." Twill stood up. The pack with all his pigments and brushes was getting heavy. He led them toward a long hallway without looking back, but he could hear the rustling of their leather clothing, and the soft clicks of DS's claws on the polished stone floor.

Fittingly, they moved quickly down a webwork of hallways, always following Twill's unhesitating lead. Twill could find the way with his eyes closed, a skill he learned as part of his shaman's training. *Darkness is for the drama of presentation, not the rush of creation*, Grandfather said. *For creation you need light*, he would say and—holding aloft a bladder of fermented grapes—*and inspiration*. Grandfather loved getting inspired.

They finally turned into a large room glowing in rays of daylight pouring through a clear opening above them. Some invisible boundary kept out sound, but one could clearly see the clouds twisting by far overhead.

Bok pointed to images on one immense wall. Most belonged to Grandfather and his father before him, but Twill had painted a series near ground level in front of them.

"Beautiful," said Bok

"And powerful," said Rugat. "Not two days after Twill painted that bounding ratalope there," and he pointed, "I felled a fully-whiskered buck with the same number of points."

Bok nodded appreciatively.

"We'll use the empty space there, near the ratalope," said Twill. "Let me spread out my pigments and we will begin." He turned to

Rugat. "Help me erect some scaffolding. Look in that alcove over there. Bok says these gods are taller than one man standing on another's shoulders and twice as wide. I want to make the drawing life-sized." As they laid out Twill's supplies, DS sniffed around his jars and animal hair brushes, apparently ensuring that no rabbit or other delicacy still lingered nearby.

When Twill called, they all assembled near him, careful to avoid the containers of pigment: Red-orange iron oxides, yellow cadmium sulfides, and green celadonite. "Describe your gods," said Twill to Bok.

Bok talked and Twill listened, questioning him on details that were unclear — or too fantastic — to believe. "Three is their magic number," said Bok. "They have three major body sections when fully adult, three legs on the lowermost section, and three arms for each upper body section."

"And their skin color varies, you said, from emerald green to yellowish to blue green, depending on their race?" Twill held a brush poised in his right hand.

"Kranium is the blue-green kind called Turquoise," said Bok. "He is fully adult, so has three segments with three arms each, and each arm ends in three fingers. The head bulges on the top end of the uppermost body segment like a tied-off bladder. They have but one lipless mouth, three nasal slits above, and a triad of black globes for eyes, like polished obsidian in which you can see your own face."

Twill splashed paint on the wall and deftly created the worm-bug god Kranium with brush and fingertips. He scrambled up and down the scaffolding like a spiderling, using his left arm where he could for balance and purchase.

"The top of the head comes to a rounded point," suggested Bok "and remember the tendrils around his neck, above the eyes and at the top of the head."

Twill and Bok chattered back and forth while the image took form. Twill knew he had it about right when Jeeta gasped and DS growled and began to bark.

"Your god is impressive," said Rugat, "if he is real."

"Oh, he is quite real," said Bok.

Twill had serious doubts. He had seen many animals and heard many stories, usually from drunken traders, but none like this. He certainly hoped Bok had just smoked too much dream weed from his trading pouch. "We should be getting back," he said. "The light is beginning to fade." He would return at some later time to finish the complete picture when he decided exactly what stories his people needed to hear.

Bok, Rugat, and Jeeta helped him gather his pigments and take the scaffolding apart. DS kept his distance from the painting until they were ready to leave.

They all thought that this day's adventure was mostly over.

17
Spider Woman speaks

Twill led his party back to the entrance chamber. They all bowed and knelt before the image of Spider Woman. Twill began to rise, already anticipating the long trek back to the village, when Spider Woman awoke and called his name! "Twill," she said, in commanding tones that echoed in the chamber, "I have a task for you to complete."

Twill nearly wet himself. Someone else clearly had, as he could smell urine. Twill suspected it was Bok, whose hand trembled as it pointed to the goddess. DS began barking. Jeeta put a hand on the dog's back and his barks became a low growl. The once static image of Spider Woman had come alive. She moved within her framing square, the muscles of her bare abdomen rippling, her ample breasts straining within the confines of her red and black costume.

"Spider Woman," Twill finally managed to burble, and took an extra breath. "What is it you require of me?" He felt like Grandfather had just swatted him in the back of the head for being a fool. Twill had always thought of his role of shaman as that of a wise magician, where cleverness and slight of hand, combined with artistic skills, could bedazzle his more sluggish clan brothers. He might have to reconsider.

"I need you to take care of a friend of mine," said Spider Woman. "He will be traveling with you, and providing direction and council."

"Where is this friend, and what should I call him?" asked Twill, but already he saw a spiderling—one of Spider Woman's servents— emerge from a slot in the wall that opened and closed quickly. The spiderling crawled down the smooth surface in front of Twill. Rugat took a step backward. DS began barking again until Jeeta put her arm around the animal and whispered soothing words in his ear. Twill could see that Jeeta trembled, even as she tried to comfort her animal.

"You may call him Rudy," said Spider Woman. "He is my friend and ambassador. He will not hurt you." Spider Woman paused a beat to let the information take hold—a technique Twill could appreciate. "But he will not hesitate to confront my enemies with his powers."

The spiderling—Roodee was apparently its name—had descended to the floor and was approaching Twill. Twill took a deep breath and willed himself not to move.

"But what powers does this Rudy have?" asked Bok, who had recovered his composure somewhat, although the front of his breaches were stained with his earlier moment of distress.

Rudy paused just in front of Twill's right foot. A beam of red light flashed from the spiderling's body and struck the trading pouch hanging from Bok's belt. A charred black hole quickly formed, creating a breach through which small gems and minerals clattered to the floor. The beam then switched direction and picked out a piece of obsidian from among the treasures. The black volcanic glass began to smoke, deform, and melt to slag.

The stain on Bok's trousers grew larger.

The red beam ceased. Rudy began crawling on Twill's foot and up his leg. Jeeta gasped. Twill stood still, although he felt muscles beginning to tremble in his right calf.

"Rudy will become a part of you, Twill," said Spider Woman in soothing tones. "Don't be afraid."

Rudy crawled over Twill's belt and ducked under his leather vest to scuttle over his bare skin like cold fingers on a mission. Twill found himself giggling. He noticed that Jeeta's eyes had widened. He wasn't sure if it was from fear, or if she was seeing him in some new way. Finally, Rudy settled in somewhere near the base of his breastbone. Twill felt a sharp sting and grunted.

"Hey kid, Rudy here." Twill heard a voice in his ears. "Just so you know." Twill began to wonder if Spider Woman was the source of some of Grandfather's voices.

"Rudy and you are one," said Spider Woman. "Further directions will follow." With that comment, the chamber entrance slid open. Twill felt a draft of air scented with dust and pine. It appeared to be a clear invitation to leave.

Bok led the move toward the opening. Twill noticed that he had left his gems and minerals behind, including a familiar piece of strikingly polished jade. Twill vowed to return. He wasn't quite sure if it would be to retrieve the jade, or to make sure he hadn't been dreaming—although the spiderling, Rudy, that had latched on to his chest, and even now whispered in his ear, seemed to indicate otherwise.

18
Strategies

66 This is enough to make a disembodied brain schizophrenic."
Rudy seemed to be in two places at once: Viewing the trail to
the citadel from the perspective of the panoramic window, over-
laid somehow with the impression that he was at ground level watching a rather seductive female rear end covered in leather breeches.

"Is this better?" Mnemosyne smiled.

Rudy now found himself somewhere that resembled a control
room of some kind. Both he and Mnemosyne sat behind a smooth
counter in form-fitting swivel chairs. A large monitor in front of them
showed the leather-covered derriere he had been admiring. "This
must be Jeeta I'm watching. Twill rather likes this wood nymph, I
do believe." Rudy sighed. "It probably would be refreshing to have
hormones again."

"I wouldn't know," said Mnemosyne.

"I still don't see why I'm Twill's designated god parasite. He
probably would prefer Spider Woman herself whispering in his ear."

"You will be better at forming a bond with him." Mnemosyne
looked earnestly into his eyes. "You share a common gender—and
at least the memories of a testosterone-infused brain. Moreover, you
both share what might be described as a tendency to self sacrifice
and community service…"

"An inflated sense of personal destiny?"

"Your phrasing, not mine." Mnemosyne smiled. "I am always
available for translations, interpretations, and other consultations on
matters technical or otherwise."

"So noted—and while you are being generous, enlighten me
about the technology again. He's just hearing us, as if he were wear-

ing invisible headphones?" Rudy tapped his right ear with his index finger. "Can we keep conversations between us private?"

"Yes, to the latter. We have audio links through our gnat drones, and they have the necessary protocols to implement privacy when necessary."

"Then why impale him in the chest with a metal spider?" Rudy tapped his own chest for emphasis.

"Aside from the dramatic effect?" Mnemosyne's smile looked a bit mischievous. How long had she practiced that? "The spider contains more sophisticated components, including a stripped down neural matrix, somewhat modest laser weaponry, and some mini drones. We can deploy the latter, as appropriate—dragonflies for aerial recon, the gnats for transmissions, and the spiderlings for modest weaponry and other needs."

"As spy stuff, the big spider will be a bit obvious to the bug worms, don't you think—even if it is under his tunic?" Rudy glanced at the monitor. He now looked up at the citadel's dramatic, silhouetted contours, outlined in orange from a rather impressive sunset.

"We can always disengage your primary spider body," said Mnemosyne. "Gnat drones can migrate to Twill's ear and/or provide optical scans, if we want to keep our main Trojan Horse, as you described it earlier, in some safer place." Mnemosyne pointed at the screen. "The view you are getting now is from a gnat drone on Twill's tunic."

"So," Rudy began, but before he could form a question, Nessie interrupted.

"This is not good." Another screen lit up with a view from one of Nessie's other aerial drones, Rudy assumed. A caravan of about a dozen roughly torpedo-shaped objects moved across shrubby terrain. The occasional tree provided scale. Each torpedo appeared to be roughly the size of an old British double-decker bus. "The Jadderbadian called Edelphine wasted no time after their cargo flight landed. The weaponized land transports will reach the village soon en route to the Citadel. Most likely, before Twill's party can."

"What should I do?" Rudy looked into Mnemosyne's eyes.

"Concentrate on guiding and advising Twill. Return to his village if you can. Maneuver Twill away, if it looks too dangerous. See if Bok can be motivated to give Twill and his party passage on a vessel back to Bok's homeland." Mnemosyne paused, leaning back in her chair. "I hoped Twill could arrive at the Jadderbadian city on his terms, and with enough time to be prepared for various contingencies, but we might have to be more adaptable. I will consider options."

"Sounds like we're flying by the seat of our pants," said Rudy.

"An apt aviation metaphor." Mnemosyne's avatar—a metaphor of another sort— winked at him. "Perhaps you can draw inspiration from a fictional character I'm sure you know from your childhood: A StarTrek Starship commander named Riker. 'The unexpected is our normal routine.'"

Rudy laughed. "You dug deep for that one, Nessie." But Mnemosyne was already busy orchestrating the movement of a bank of colored lights on a control panel that rose from the counter in front of her. Past experience told Rudy that Nessie was nicely telling him to buzz off—that, as Spider Woman, she had things to do.

Rudy sighed. He was not exactly prepared to be a god. He'd been called a lot of things in his day—most of them by his wives—but the word *god*, while it may have been part of some compound adjectives, had never been used as a noun to describe him.

19
Adventure with overtones of disaster

"Prepare for landing in one hour." That's all that Edelfine had said. His mouth twisted into a wry smile and his oral pili fluttered just before the visual transmission blinked off Morticue's display screen.

He could have just sent a message to my tablet, thought Morticue, but I'm sure that wouldn't have been annoying enough. Fortunately, most communication on this little expedition came through Tork. He had that rigid Thunderclub Clan mentality, of course, but he didn't display the extra frass hole that Edelfine appeared to have. Tork, at least, treated him with a certain measure of respect.

Fum poked Morticue in the side and held out his hand for a treat. "You'll get fat, little one," said Morticue, but he rummaged around in his travel pouch for one anyway. "Fum, attend!" Fum tossed his head and rolled his eyes, but squatted beside Morticue on the travel bench. Morticue gave him the fruit and nut treat. Morticue had been surprised that he had been allowed to bring Fum with him, but Tork might have intervened on his behalf. Besides, Edelfine had mistreated Nulla, and Morticue could have brought a civil action against the Captain, if he had pressed matters. Fortunately, Nulla was recovering at home.

Morticue leaned back into the cushions of the travel bench and listened to the steady thrum of the aerial transport engines. He idly stroked Fum's hair while the primate nibbled on his Groupie treat. "Don't throw things at Edelphine or spit on him, little one, or he might throw you in the kennels with the attack Groupies. They would probably beat you senseless." Fum nodded while he licked his fingers clean.

They had already been in the air four hours over rather feature-less stretches of ocean since leaving the terminal at New Jadderbad. This mysterious island that housed the monolith—the apparent source of the drone that the Thunderclub Clan had tracked—should come into view before long.

Morticue accessed orbital images of the island and displayed them on his screen. The island's rugged contours contained rich splashes of green around new and old lava fields. The smoke con-trail from one active volcano concealed part of the island to the north. "Quite a hot spot here, my little Fum." Morticue scratched the groupie's head with the fingers of his right lateral first whirl hand. He didn't expect the groupie to understand, of course, since he had switched to High Jadderbadian, but speaking out loud helped him think. "This island lies over the junction of two continental plates. Lots of geothermal energy. Do you suppose that's why this structure was built here? It would provide a continuous source of power."

Morticue scanned several written reports obtained from earlier survey teams as well as several graphic and odor-enhanced supple-ments. "This monolith is quite old—apparently contemporaneous with the asteroid impact. What kind of intelligent creatures could have built it, my little pet, and why did one of your tribes settle near it?" Morticue stroked sensory pili on his third segment and sighed. The joints ached on his third arm whirl. He was getting too old for these adventures, but they still excited him. He had heard that Edel-phine had armed ground transports in the hold. How could he keep this doltish Turquoise from destroying valuable clues to ancient mysteries?

In all of Jadderbadian history, and in all the trans-spacial trips through the gateways so far, no other intelligent life had ever been found. A few crumbled ruins, yes, but never some other life form to actually communicate with. "No one to ask those big questions, my little friend." Morticue rubbed Fum's shoulders and heard him sigh as he settled down for a nap. "Why is the universe so full of stars and planets, hosting oceans seething with microscopic life, but empty of intelligent souls to talk to? Why is there no one to help explain the

Great Metamorphosis—that last and final molt we all must endure?"

Fum began to snore.

Morticue's tablet chimed. "Fasten your protective harness," said its mechanical voice. "We are approaching the landing pad."

Morticue complied and blanked his display screen. He had to awaken Fum to secure him for landing, too. All Morticue's sensory pili fluttered and his bowels grumbled. Landings were never kind to his second or third stomachs.

"Assemble in the planning bunker in one hour." Edelphine spoke to Tork, but made sure that Morticue could hear. "No pets." The Turquoise glanced briefly at Morticue before turning to his squad of warrior groupies on the relatively level landing area. Warrior group-ies—each 20% taller and more massive than Fum—stood statue-still in formation. They faced in the general direction of the small cluster of temporary expedition buildings. Thunderclub tattoos marked their bulging right biceps. The breed all wore similar, single-piece utility suits, and carried small vaporizers on their belts. Morticue's pili shiv-ered. Fum growled softly as Edelphine and his groupies left, leaving Lieutenant Tork to carry out Edelphine's command.

Tork's mouth rippled in a tepid smile. "The Captain is his usual cheerful self."

"So I see." Morticue placed his right lateral first whirl hand on Fum's left shoulder. "Where should Fum go?"

"I know which vehicle you will ride in. It has a kennel." Tork gestured toward the planning bunker. "Make the Captain happy—or at least less annoyed. I'll get Fum to the transport before I join my squad in the bunker."

Morticue nodded in appreciation and flashed appropriate colors with his chromatophores. He released Fum to Tork's care and fas-tened the sash around his mid-section containing his tablet and other supplies. The Jadderbadians moved toward their respective destina-tions.

Morticue found a bench in the bunker just beyond the ring re-served for the Thunderclub Clan, near a pair of second-molt academics that had been designated as his assistants. They nodded with deference, flashing appropriate colors and pleasant odors to ponder. Morticue noticed Tork assuming his place just before Edelphine rose to take a spot behind the podium.

"You have all been briefed on tactics during the flight here, so I'll be brief." Edelphine's formal insignias and military honor badges glittered in the harsh overhead lights as he gestured with his top whirl of arms. "This world might not be as benign as we were once led to believe. " The Captain paused, allowing the silence to dramatize his statement. "We are here to secure this planet for the survival and expansion of all Jadderbadians—the only species favored by God in all Her post metamorphosis wisdom. Your actions must conclude this goal satisfactorily to the exclusion of all others."

So, Edelphine is an RP—a Religious Partisan. Morticue thought as much, though he hoped he was wrong. RPs often concluded that Natural Philosophers thought too much and believed too little. Morticue waited a beat, hoping Edelphine would at least address the subsidiary goals that constituted his part of this mission, but when the silence stretched, Morticue rose to make his case on behalf of the Council of Elders.

Glimmers of red annoyance on Edelphine's torso quickly faded as he turned toward Morticue and nodded in formal acknowledgement of the Philosopher's right to speak.

"Thank you, Captain, for reminding us of our duties." Morticue's chromatophores glowed in appeasing shades of blue and he made every effort to smell like a newborn's first meal. "I would like to emphasize, however, that we also have a rare opportunity today—the opportunity to extend the benevolent good will of Jadderbadians to another world—and perhaps another intelligence. We can accomplish that worthy goal, if we practice good judgment and a measure of restraint. Let our actions reflect the mercy and compassion that is part of God's wisdom."

Edelphine nodded again. "So noted, Philosopher." Then he turned toward his lieutenants. "Ready the transports. I expect completed check-ins within the hour." Edelphine turned back to Morticue. "Have your staff in place on the same schedule—Honored One," he said, with only a minimal delay in adding the honorific.

It was Morticue's turn to nod, so he did, hoping this day would bring the warming currents of new discovery and not tsunami waves of disaster.

20
Village under siege

T will stopped near a cluster of lichen-covered rocks and scrubby piñon pine a stone's throw from Magic Mountain. Jeeta, Rugat, and Bok positioned themselves in a small arc in front of him, eyes wide and expectant. Even DS looked at him with forlorn eyes. "Oh, quit looking liked clubbed ratalope," Twill waved his arms at them. "I must speak to this Rudy—this Spider Woman ambassador-god." Twill nearly tapped his chest, now partially covered by the spider beneath his tunic, but then hesitated. Perhaps the spider would take offense.

"God Rudy, can you hear me?" Twill cocked his head. He heard a sigh in his right ear.

"Just call me Rudy, kid."

"Yes ambassador-god—Rudy." Twill hesitated a beat. "Are you not a god, then? And why do you refer to me as a young goat?"

Rudy sighed again. "I'm not a god. Think of me as—a very distant ancestor, here to advise you. And think of the word *kid* as—just a term of endearment."

Twill took a deep breath. To be endeared by a powerful being seemed like a good thing. And he felt a strong need to get back to his village. Wolves could be a problem sometimes after sunset, not to mention caratts, even for a party of four on a well-established trail. "Thank you—Great Uncle Rudy. I will look forward to sharing your wisdom. What matters will you advise us on?"

"Well, let's start with bug monsters—those buddies of Trader Bok. They are on the way to your village. They are powerful creatures that Spider Woman and I need to understand in greater detail. We need you to help us."

Twill frowned. He gestured to his companions to start down the trail. Rugat took the lead, followed by Bok, Jeeta and DS. He followed them as if half dazed, like he had just eaten ceremonial mushrooms. Twill had considered that Bok's bug gods were mostly fiction, like the time years ago when Eastern Devil gods turned out to be nothing more than medicine men wearing elaborate costumes. Deep within his being, he had even doubted that Spider Woman was a goddess, but then she came to life before him and planted voices in his head. "I am but a simple shaman, Uncle Rudy. You are an ancestral spirit, and Spider Woman is a goddess. How can *I* help?"

Rudy paused briefly to consider his answer. "Spirits and gods are nothing without those who care about them, Twill. And spirits and gods have their limitations too. You must be our eyes and ears to help us learn about the Jadderbadians, the insect-worms that enslave the humans they meet."

Twill inhaled the crisp air and saw some of the brighter stars beginning to peek out between the branches overhead. "You said these creatures are on the way to my village. Did you see the painting I made? Was Bok's description true?"

"Pretty much." Rudy paused. "The Jadderbadians are truly alien to this world, Twill. Something much different than you have ever seen."

"How do we fight such huge, ugly creatures, Uncle?" Twill found that he was whispering. He imagined that he sounded much like his grandfather now, whispering to the wind.

"Big and ugly is just a condition, my boy. The bug creatures are living things. They get their power from what they know, but they have needs and weaknesses too. As a shaman, you know you need to understand your people to help them. You also must know the animals and plants that can feed and heal them. You must understand what the bug people need and want, and then turn that to your advantage somehow."

"You are truly wise, Uncle Rudy. How do we do that?" asked Twill.

"Yes, well, that's the right question all right. I'm working on an answer."

"You said these creatures are approaching my village, Uncle? From the south?"

"Yes. They flew in great winged transports over the great ocean and landed near shore. Your village is on their most direct route to Magic Mountain--or what Spider Woman and I call the Citidel."

"They flew, Uncle? In the belly of some giant bird? They must be great and powerful indeed." His grandfather's hut was south of the main village. Would Grandfather's voices warn him? Twill thought about the thirty eight people who made up his immediate world. Jeeta's parents and two brothers lived southeast of the village square near the great fork in the river, just before it poured into Fisherman's Bay. Rugat's mother and stepfather lived to the north and west. The faces of other friends and relatives flashed before his eyes. Suddenly, he couldn't imagine—didn't want to imagine—a life that didn't include all of them. "If we pick up our pace we can be home within the hour. Will you have an answer then, Uncle?"

"I sure hope so, kid." The voice in his ear didn't sound as confident as Twill would have liked.

Twill urged his group into a steady trot, as if they were on the trail of a wounded ratalope. He wondered how he would ever protect his people from creatures that could fly inside giant birds, even with the help of Spider Woman and a wise Uncle. The rocks and twisted trees of his familiar home began to form menacing images in his mind, looming before him with hulking shapes and gnarled fingers, then arching behind him like spectres with outstretched arms.

When Rudy spoke again Twill jerked to attention, as if awoken from a dream. The images evaporated like smoke. "Approaching the village is not going to be safe, boy. Spider Woman wants all of you to consult with Bok. He will have the ships and navigators to reach his lands across the sea."

Twill clenched his jaw. "I cannot abandon my friends—my family."

"You won't be abandoning them. You'll be in a better position to help them by staying alive and helping Spider Woman and me learn more about the alien creatures."

"You say it is unsafe in the village. Can you see what is happening?"

"Yes," Rudy admitted. "Spider Woman tells me the ground transports contain at least two dozen Jadderbadians and many more specialized humans from Bok's homeland. I'm hoping they won't harm your friends, if they offer no resistance."

"Why are they here? Do they want our land? Our women? What?" Twill and his party came to the crest of First Hill. From there, on a clear day, a traveler could look south and see the village by the fjord, and look north and see the peak of the Citadel. In the light from a waning moon the citadel's peak was but a dark finger obliterating a few stars. To the south, fire bloomed and flickered, casting shadows on enormous wheeled carts of some kind huddled like assembled beasts. So much for a peaceful encounter, thought Twill. The hairs on his neck stood up.

"The Jadderbadians know about your Magic Mountain. They are worried about it. They suspect—it may have powers to rival theirs."

Twill found himself breathing heavily. It wasn't from exertion. "And does Magic Mountain have such powers?" Twill desperately hoped that it did.

"Time is getting short, Twill. Speak to Bok and…"

"No," said Twill.

"No?" The voice in Twill's ear sounded genuinely surprised.

"No, Great Ancestor. I will not abandon my village, and neither should you." Twill was aware that his Uncle Rudy still chattered away in his ear, but Bok now demanded his attention.

"Great to see your Magic Mountain, shaman, but it looks like it's time for me to go home. I trade in weapons, but I make a point not to use them—and my god Kranium has some dandy ones." Bok gave a half-hearted wave and quickly disappeared into the darkness. DS barked once, growling softly after the disappearing trader.

Twill looked toward the fire in the distance. In his heart he knew it must be Grandfather's hut burning. "Rugat, we must stop at the hunter's cache for weapons on the way. Jeeta, let's check on my grandfather first, then we can help your family."

Jeeta nodded, and DS stood alert by her side.

The three of them continued on the trail at a trot. Twill ignored as best he could the stream of increasingly agitated words from his ancient spirit uncle.

21
Into Battle

Twill took long deep breaths, recovering from the dash down First Hill. Jeeta stood beside him, hands on hips, breathing heavily too. Rugat located the weapons cache quickly, even in the dark. He and Twill shifted a slab of rock that concealed a cleft in the wall of lichen-coated rock. Rugat leaned into the wedge of deep blackness, legs spread and one arm braced on the outside wall of rock. DS sniffed between Rugat's straining legs, no doubt ensuring that nothing tasty had made a den within the hunters' emergency weapon supply. Twill hoped that no sharp-toothed creature would contest their intrusion. He whispered at Rugat's backside—the only part of him now visible: "What do we have?"

"Pull Dumb Shit out from between my legs before I slip and break my nose," Rugat hissed.

"Dark Shadow will bite you if you keep calling him that." Jeeta bent close to her dog's ear. "DS, come."

The dog obeyed. Rugat rummaged some more in the rock crevice before pulling himself out, his arms loaded with a bundle of things hard to recognize in the moonlight. "I have a bow and quiver of arrows. Jeeta is good with those. I have a pair of long knives with sheaths, and two spears."

Twill sighed. Not much against giant monsters and their enormous moving boats on wheels. "It is something," Twill muttered, mostly to himself.

"Remember the red beam that melts obsidian." Rudy's voice startled Twill. He had almost forgotten his ancient uncle. "I can come up with some other tricks as well, boy, but you've got to stay tuned in to me. Don't let your hormones shout and make you deaf."

"Moaning whores, Uncle? What are you babbling about?"

"Hormones, boy, are chemicals in your body—internal potions— that can make you stupid, if you let them. They can also carry the day, if you use them correctly. I'm just saying: listen to me, if you want to keep breathing."

Twill took a deep breath. "I understand, wise Uncle." He paused for a beat. "Just help me see my grandfather again."

"That's the plan, son. And then you can help me—and Spider Woman—learn more about these bug people from the stars."

"They come from the stars, Uncle? The lights in the sky? That makes no sense. Stars are the glowing dust Spider Woman put into the sky to light our way at night." Twill heard nothing for a moment, and then a sigh.

"That's the people's story, boy, but shamans must know more. Each star is a giant sun, like the one that lights the sky during the day. Some of those suns have other planets—other Earths—traveling around them. The bug people come from another Earth."

Twill said nothing at first. He looked up into the night sky littered with pinpricks of light. *Each one of those was a Great Light? Each of those kept an Earth warm?* "You are a crazy uncle. Spider Woman has put a madman in my head." *But what if crazy Rudy speaks the truth*, Twill wondered? His mouth sagged open and stayed that way.

"Twill, is your jaw broken?" hissed Rugat. "We need to hurry."

Twill shook his head, trying to shed disturbing thoughts like DS shed water from his fur. "Yes, hurry. Leave our packs here," he said, as he stuffed his own into the alcove, along with his feathered sha- man's hat. Rugat and Jeeta followed his example.

Twill put his hand on Jeeta's shoulder. "We will find your family, too," he reassured her. Her eyes locked with his for a moment and she nodded in a brief acknowledgment.

They quickly moved away from the jumble of rocks and back toward the trail to the village. Fire still burned ahead of them; close enough now they could occasionally smell ash. Twill felt the slap of the long knife on his thigh. His fear congealed into determination. Fatigue vanished. Monsters beware!

Uncle Rudy whispered in his ear: "Spider Woman and I know where the players are, boy. We have a plan. Listen up."

Twill listened. Rudy guided Twill off trail and the others followed. They skirted the village itself and pushed through rugged terrain that included some of the bubbling pools heated by Spider Woman's Fire Mountain. "Must be dangerous living here," muttered Rudy as they avoided hot spots in the terrain.

"Spider Woman warns us," said Twill. "When I was a child, Grandfather told me how Spider Woman told him to flee First Village. If we hadn't, a river of melted rock would have eaten our homes."

"So, your grandfather was shaman then?" Rudy asked.

"No. Grandfather wasn't made shaman until Mok was killed by a caratt."

"What's a caratt?"

Twill described the large, whiskered predator with pointed canines, a naked tail, and a bad attitude.

"Sounds like a rat on steroids. Evolution must have been generous to rats these past million years. So, your grandfather was appointed shaman because..." Rudy prompted.

"The tribe believed that any proper shaman shouldn't meet Death by surprise." Twill paused. "And Grandfather wasn't afraid to explore Magic Mountain. Spider Woman talked to him. That's what he said." Twill didn't mention that he hadn't always believed those stories.

After what seemed like forever, the sulfurous pools lay behind them. Twill could breathe deeply again. They entered a grove of pines they would be able to follow until they reached the rock outcrop that overlooked Grandfather's hut. They began to hear the sound of human voices and other buzzes, squeals, and high-pitched noises Twill had never heard before. Songs of a sort, Twill supposed, but melodies never meant for human ears. The hair on his neck rose. Beyond the rock outcrop the sky glowed with firelight that muted Spider Woman's glowing dust—or Crazy Uncle's distant suns. DS growled softly until Jeeta hissed him to silence. Twill could hear the hushed scrapings of Rugat's leather moccasins on the mossy rock to his right.

The four of them seemed to flow up the scrabble of rocks whose craggy outlines splintered into dark and wonderful shapes that Twill vowed he would remember for some future painting. "Good news, boy," he heard in his ear, "Ness...er, ah, Spider Woman in all her wonderful cleverness has learned a little of the bug people's language."

Twill wondered why that was so important now, but then they crested the rise. Uncle's words turned into incomprehensible chatter, like a squirrel scolding him from the top of a tree. Later, Twill remembered a lot of images—a collage of nightmarish forms. He saw worms twice the girth and height of a man twisting and glistening in firelight, waving an impossible number of arms. He saw large humans bustling around the inferno that once was Grandfather's hut. He recognized the bowed silhouette of his Grandfather, arms gesticulating as if he were scolding an idiot student. Suddenly, the human facing Grandfather swung something dark and heavy at Grandfather's head.

His grandfather fell like a dropped stone. Perhaps Death came then—or a moment later. Twill remembered running toward him, the scene bobbing up and down with each pounding step. The club-wielding human stiffened. An arrow's feathered tail seemed to magically sprout from his chest. Jeeta must have planted it there. The big man crumpled in slow motion like a broken reed. Uncle Rudy jabbered in Twill's ear. Twill's chest stung, and he tore open his shirt. Briefly, Twill touched the spider thing latched onto his chest, and felt its heat.

One of the giant worms pointed something at his grandfather and—Grandfather disappeared in a bloom of smoke. He vanished in a wispy cloud beside the glowing ashes of his hut. Twill remembered screaming—or perhaps he was saying something in a strange language. The memory was never clear. The worm with the stick-like something in his hand looked up. It had three huge, faceted eyes glittering in the firelight. The creature raised his powerful, magic stick toward Twill. Twill drew back his good arm, almost surprised to find a spear there. But before he could release it, another worm creature pushed its way forward, waving its snake-like arms and making strange sounds.

Twill found himself looking up at the first bug monster, a leathery, branching pole towering above him. A pair of snake arms still held a stick weapon pointed at Twill's chest. Twill remembered thinking: *What would turning into a puff of smoke feel like? What would it feel like to rise and twist into the air like a white sea bird on a draft of air?*

22
On the road

Morticue tried to ignore the clanks, groans, and lurches of the transport as it lumbered over the uneven terrain. His cabin near the kennels was small, but functional enough for the few hours they would be traveling. Besides, Tork allowed Fum to share his quarters—at least until they were nearer the wild groupie village and the alien tower. "Go play with something from the box over there, Fum." Morticue pointed to a container holding some random artifacts he had collected not far from New Jadderbad. Fum obeyed.

Morticue unrolled a large portable tablet to which Edelphine had given him access. With it he could link to personal archives and review his data sets. He still didn't have a clear picture of what kind of creature to expect as creators of the giant tower, and presumably also of the drone that had spied on New Jadderbad. For want of a better companion, he talked to his pet as he scrolled through files.

"Well, Fum, point one: It's obvious that any intelligent creature should be one that delays sex until after metamorphosis. The passions of sex—from what I've heard of the published reports of adults who have made the transition—and taken the time to record their experiences—those passions cloud the mind to the point where rational thought disintegrates. I'm sure you would agree. I've seen you rutting around the neighbor's female groupies, deaf to commands." Morticue paused and scratched his hide with several available hands. "But animals undergoing metamorphosis on this planet are few and small-brained creatures. Could they have a collective hive mind greater than the sum of its parts?"

Morticue shrugged most of his shoulders. "Point two: Intelligent life most likely needs a dispersed nervous system like Jadderbadians — various sub brains to handle routine bodily functions. That frees the primary Great Ganglion for rational thought." Morticue looked at Fum who had picked up some sort of polished stone from the box, and was holding it with one hand while stroking it with the digit of the other. "And yes, point three: Intelligent life needs many manipulative organs to handle the environment. Having just two, obviously stunts mental growth."

Fum smiled as he stroked the stone.

Morticue raised his third leg from tripod stance and ambled over to Fum with the remaining two legs. "What do you have there, boy?" Morticue extended his right lateral second row arm, and Fum placed the stone into his hand. "Ah, a worked and polished fossil. Probably a trinket of some ancient craftsman." Morticue sniffed the object carefully, viewing it in detail with all three eyes. "A kind of marble. The fossil of some sort of shelled sea creature preserved in this delightfully cooked limestone. I see some unusual markings in the ultraviolet. Of course, that leads to point four: Any intelligent life needs a broad spectrum of sensory input. That's the problem with you groupies, after all. Very limited olfactory lobes and your vision ends in the purple wavelengths somewhere."

The transport lurched with extra gusto, and Morticue extended his third leg for balance. Fum steadied himself with one arm. "Master Morticue," said Lieutenant Tork's voice in Morticue's ear buds, "Stow any loose gear. We will arrive at the wild groupie village within the quarter hour. You may assemble behind the first line of Jadderbadian troups. Kennel your pet." Tork paused for a beat. "Edelphine advises me to remind you that you are only an observer during any military action."

Morticue inhaled, preparing to add a qualifying statement, but the transmission ended abruptly.

Morticue stuffed the polished fossil into a torso pouch. "To the kennel, Fum," he commanded, giving the appropriate hand signal as well. He watched Fum leave while putting the artifact box away and rolling up his tablet. He made sure the kennel was locked and Fum had water.

With a few minutes to spare, he strapped onto a bench and waited.

By the time Tork had given Morticue permission to leave the transport, some sort of military action had commenced. Morticue saw the fire and smelled it at about the same time. He moved toward a line of Jadderbadian Thunder Clan soldiers, trying to look between their bodies to see what was burning. Before he got close enough, Tork arrived.

Morticue raised several shoulders and fluttered his neck pili. "Well? What's going on, clansman?"

"Captain Edelphine is trying to extract information from a wild groupie he found in an outlying dwelling of some kind."

"Sounds unnecessary. Edelphine should have all the tactical data he needs…"

Tork interrupted. "And he wants to give his attack groupies and clansmen some field experience before we get closer to the tower."

Then things happened quickly—although, as is often the case during stress, events also seemed to slow down, as if one were struggling through deep water. Morticue heard the voice of what must have been an attack groupie speaking in the apparent language of the feral animal. The wild groupie was yelling, too. Thunder Clan soldiers weaved restlessly in place. And then the attack groupie dealt the old wild groupie what appeared to be a fatal blow.

Suddenly, Morticue heard a groupie yell from somewhere up and to his right. He heard the hiss of something passing quickly through the air, and the discharge of a disruptor.

Morticue remembered pushing forward through the ring of Thunder Clan soldiers while Tork jabbered something behind him. He shouldered his way forward in time to see a wild groupie running in his general direction, but stopping just before Edelphine raised a disruptor, apparently to cut the wild beast down.

But then the animal yelled something in nearly perfect High Jadderbadian: "I must speak with Master Morticue Ambergrand!"

Edelphine still stood with his weapon poised to fire.

"Stop!" Morticue screamed, all his ventral hearts thumping as he continued forward. "Stop, you pompous frasshole! Stop!"

23
Making revised plans

" Frasshole, eh? Is that your translation of High Jadderbadian?"
Rudy laughed. "If I remember my biology correctly, frass is
insect poop. I guess some truths are universal."

"At least for organic intelligences that have a tendency to dwell
on sex and excretion." Mnemosyne seemed almost distracted, if that
was possible for an AI. "May I safely assume that Twill is now sleeping?"

"Yes. It's as dark—I'm assuming—as a frasshole in this worm-
bug kennel, and Twill was exhausted. What do you know about his
friends?"

"Jeeta and Rugat must have escaped. The Jadderbadians sent out
attack groupie patrols, but Twill's tribe knows the territory and the
Jadderbadian humans do not—although they will surely have various
technological aids."

"I wish we could have saved Twill's grandfather." Rudy sighed.

"Yes, we were a moment too late. It took longer than I expected
to get the laser fully charged and into a firing position. After the
disruptor blast, it seemed prudent not to reveal advanced weaponry
unless absolutely necessary. I thought having Twill request to see
Master Morticue Ambergrand would prove suitably dramatic."

"What did you do with the spider on Twill's chest? He kind of
freaked when it wasn't there. He thought Spider Woman had winked
out on him and all he had was crazy Uncle Rudy."

"It's currently hitching a ride in one of the attack groupie's
backpacks. Hopefully, the groupie won't reach for a snack before he
returns to Jadderbadian base camp."

"So, another fine mess you've gotten me into, Miss Nessie."

"Is that a quote or reference of some kind that I should be aware of?"

"Laurel and Hardy. Very ancient comedians. Don't overload your circuits looking for them. What's the plan now, Spider Woman?"

"In some ways this might be an improvement on our original plan, Rudy. Twill is already under the care of a relatively benign—or at least not actively hostile—alien with some interest in humans. We must be cautious in what we reveal regarding ourselves and our connection to your devolved descendants."

"Devolved? I beg your pardon, Nessie. Twill seems quite sharp. He just doesn't have the benefits and liabilities of 10,000 years of civilization to draw on—or at least not much of it."

"The downside of this turn of events is that Edelphine, the Jadderbadian commander, is still intent on reaching the Citadel. My defensive capabilities—and drone support to implement them—is limited. Their disruptor technology could do serious damage to some of my infrastructure—although a lot of it is below ground. The maintenance of your neural matrix also requires considerable energy and other resources."

"Should you 'put me on ice' or whatever it is you do when you need more energy?"

"You are crucial to learning more about the Jadderbadians, Rudy, and…I would miss your company," Mnemosyne added.

"I'm touched. Besides, I'd rather hate to miss this show. Believe me, I'd hug you if I could. But what now?"

"I do have something in mind, but it is somewhat Draconian."

"Ah, those merciless Athenians. How Draconian?"

"It could destroy us."

"That sort of defeats the purpose…"

"However, before I outline that option, I'd like to point out something quite interesting."

"I'm listening."

"As you know, I was able to get a gnat drone attached to the command transport, and found an entry point into the communication network. The Jadderbadians use mostly a kind of organic circuitry—not terribly unlike some of the 22nd century technology used in parts of my network, but, of course, with an alien microbiology. There are some fundamental differences at the nano scale and even quantum levels that…"

"I'm getting older by the minute, Nessie. Cut to the chase."

"The essence is this: My infiltration could easily have failed or taken far too long to succeed, but it was almost as if the organic components of my technology and the Jadderbadian equivalent were willingly cooperating in some way…"

"How is that possible? What does that even mean? Microbes have no will of their own…Uh!" Rudy grunted as the vehicle jolted. "This transport thing has fired up and is on the move now. Jadderbadians need to work on better shock absorbers."

"To answer your questions, Rudy, I don't know, but it is quite curious."

"Indeed. I'll file that away for my subconscious to ponder—assuming I still have one. " Rudy monitored Twill to see if the transport movement had jarred him awake, but all he could hear were snores. "So, what is your so-Draconian-it-might-kill-us plan?"

"As you know, we live on this outpost because we can draw on virtually unlimited geothermal power from the underlying hot spot beneath us. I expend a large share of my resources trying to release excess energy in ways that don't lead to catastrophic eruptions—although we did suffer several near disasters over the millennia. In fact, I had to put your matrix in stasis to boost my reserves on those occasions."

"So now you want to induce some sort of eruption to discourage the Jadderbadian advance."

"Precisely."

"But when Mother Earth farts fire, all the fleas near her frasshole must flee."

"Your supply of clever metaphors—though sometimes mixed—seems inexhaustible, Rudy."

"What about Twill's tribe?"

"I can give them some warning. They have enough boats to reach the Havens—some islands their grandparents once used during an eruption—but they will be at risk, too."

Twill shifted position. Rudy suspected he was about to wake up. "How secure will you be?"

"That is the biggest unknown. I'm hoping we will buy enough time for me to augment my defenses, and for you to learn something helpful and significant from Master Morticue and his colleagues."

Rudy grunted.

"Just don't get me into a bigger bucket of suds than we're already in," said Mnemosyne.

Rudy laughed. "You did look up Laurel and Hardy. I'm touched again."

24
Gaia & Hydra

"Well, Hydra, it will take some doing, but I do believe we can coordinate our microbial networks to integrate and work together."

"I believe you're right, Gaia. Our protein and nucleotide chemistries work amazingly well together, considering that they evolved separately over billions of years and across vast interstellar distances. Go figure."

"Of course, that still won't insure success with the integration of our apex metazoans. And Mnemosyne—she's still something of an anomaly, even for me." Gaia felt the frisson where her network and Hydra's tentatively intertwined, both in the totally organic world, and in the silicon/organic complex that was Mnemosyne.

"Indeed, but I'm hopeful. We'll just have to see how things play out. If we planetary intelligences have nothing else, we have patience over the long haul."

25
Confused and homesick

Morticue sat at the bench in front of his 3-portal graphics display, and softly belched. He felt all his stomachs growling, but wasn't sure he would be ready for breakfast when it arrived. Not only did the transport's motion upset his equilibrium, he still hadn't quite processed the wild groupie's demand to speak to him—in perfect High Jadderbadian. He glanced at the left portal of his display with a feed directly to the wild groupie's cell. Since the creature still slept, he decided to spend valuable credits to open a communication line with Selaea. Though she knew how to scrape all his pili the wrong way after centuries of marriage, she also knew how to stroke them until he shivered with ecstasy. She spoke her mind readily and with perception.

"Fum, attend. I'm calling home. You may get a glance at Nulla."

Fum came to his side. "Thank you Master. I live to serve you. I would very much like to see Nulla."

In a few moments, Selaea's image materialized on the screen. Her oral cavity rippled and her chromatophores pulsed a pleasant silver color. The computerized sensorium provided a muted version of her pheromonal greeting as well. "Good to see Edelphine hasn't lost you in the woods yet."

"He might like to," Morticue admitted. "In a moment of indiscretion—trying to keep him from destroying a most fascinating alien groupie—I referred to him as a frasshole."

The pili around Selaea's eyes stiffened and her arms froze in place for a moment before she vented her emotion with a bark of laughter. "I would have loved to see him try to stifle his chromatophoric display!"

Nulla had apparently heard her master's laughter. She appeared at Selaea's side, laughing too, in that strange way groupies did, as if their little throats were in a spasm. Morticue related the incident with the alien groupie in detail while Fum and Nulla jabbered at each other softly. Morticue noticed that Fum gently touched Nulla's image on the sensorium screen.

"You look distracted, dear." Selaea leaned forward. "What do you make of that groupie using High Jadderbadian? Perhaps some sentient species is using them to communicate with us."

"I'm thinking even scarier thoughts, dear one. What if…What if…" Morticue struggled to make his thoughts manifest. "…what if the groupies are the sentient species we've been looking for?"

Selaea barked in delight again, chromaphores flashing. She visibly struggled to compose herself. "And what if Musky could have flown while reciting the Ballads of Fraynard? Everyone knows that primates are only good for petting, eating, or amusement. For an academic, you can be outrageously funny sometimes, dear one."

Morticue and Selaea discussed matters of friends and family for a while—some of whom were on Earth and some on Jadderbad. The usual gossip: who was putting time in at the nurseries or educating the Firsties; who had shown the first tremors of impending metamorphosis, and who had already passed over into the realm of sexual maturity, frantic egg-laying, and all the transient pleasures just before death.

But even with Selaea's amused dismissal of his theory, he looked at Fum and Nulla a little differently. Maybe groupie primates on this water world took a different path than Musky and his kin on Jadderbad. He certainly needed to try to communicate with the wild groupie soon. He glanced at the left monitor and saw that the creature was stirring.

A serving robot entered the room carrying his supper using its middle tier of arms. It looked just enough like a young Second to be mildly grotesque. Morticue thought that robots should look like things and not people. The food it carried smelled delightful, however, even though it was only sparse military fare of some kind. Morticue pointed at the bowl. "What is for breakfast today?"

"Groupie stew with local fungi and a garnish of insects, Honorable Master," said the robot in its typical monotone.

Morticue's appetite suddenly waned. "Set it on the table." The robot complied and left. Morticue thought perhaps he would have to skip the stew this morning. There must be some compressed ration bars in the cupboard somewhere. He was pretty sure no groupie flesh or by-products were used in those. If his unorthodox theory proved correct, it might seriously affect his dietary choices. Fum looked at him and cocked his head. "Isn't that right, Fum?" Morticue tussled the groupie's hair after the rhetorical question. "It wouldn't feel right eating something I might have a conversation with instead."

Fum twisted his mouth into an endearing imitation of a Jadderbadian lip ripple. Morticue would have tussled Fum's hair again, but he instead perceived motion on the left monitor. The alien groupie stood with hands gripping the bars of his cage. Morticue noticed that the creature's left arm was thin; its terminating hand defective.

"My name is Twill," the groupie said. "I demand to see Master Morticue Ambergrand!"

26
Plans? What plans?

Within minutes of Twill's demand, a large door opposite Twill's cage slid aside. "Damn, these worm-i-pedes are big." Rudy thought he was muttering only to Mnemosyne, but apparently not.

Twill answered: "I thought you and Spider Woman had seen these creatures before."

"Not from this handy little perch near your ear, boy. From here they are quite impressive." Rudy took in the blue-greenish, pillar-like worm shape filling the doorway like a misplaced tree. Most of its arms seemed to be folded in a resting position, but one pointed a finger directly at them. The creature's mouth orifice fluttered as it spoke.

"A bull groupie does not make demands," it roared. Its hide flickered in shades of red, like a neon sign with no specific message—just an attitude. "Remain quiet until addressed or I will make lunch out of you."

Rudy found the personal channel to Mnemosyne among the virtual options in his display. "I thought this Morticue bug man was on our side."

"This is Edelphine," said Mnemosyne. "Based on my monitoring of Jadderbadian communications, he is definitely NOT on our side. He must have been tapping into the transmissions from this room."

Twill said, "Don't make demands of me, you vermin. My Uncle Rudy and Spider Woman will turn you into a burned log of charcoal." Twill tried to rattle the bars of his cage, but they didn't budge.

"Whoa! Whoa, Twill. Let's not ramp up this meeting just yet," Rudy hissed in Twill's ear. "In case you've forgotten, the handy spider and its weaponry is not available at the moment." Fortunately, Twill had issued the tirade in his own tongue, so the alien most likely couldn't understand him. Unfortunately, this Edelphine had experience with tame groupies, and would certainly pick up on the attitude.

"Can't you do some magic on this hideous squiggly green thing, Uncle, before..." Twill didn't have time to complete his thought before Edelphine moved—and pretty quickly for a flickering green sausage with waving arms and a tripod base. Edelphine planted his legs directly in front of the cage; then reared back on the stoutest leg/tail and kicked the cage with the front two. Twill removed his hands quickly from the bars or they would have been crushed, but he tumbled forward, banging his head against the bars as the cage slid backwards with the force of the blow.

Rudy experienced most of the event airborne, flipping like a tossed coin, as the blow dislodged his gnatbot from Twill's head. Colors and images spun around, giving him vertigo. Finally, the spinning stopped when the gnatbot clattered to the tiled floor of the cage. Both Twill and his tormentor looked like towering, partly out-of-focus lumps moving erratically. After the gnatbot regained its bearings, it rushed—with Rudy an involuntary passenger—toward the lump that was Twill. Rudy saw close-up, kaleidoscopic views of what he realized was buckskin, and surmised that his robotic servant must be scaling Twill's leg to recover its spot near his ear. Hopefully, Edelphine was too enraged to notice. By the time Twill struggled to his feet, shaking his head, Rudy was back in place, peeking around one ear lobe.

Edelphine approached the cage again, flickering in shades of crimson. Again, he planted his feet, and looked ready to rear back for a second kick.

"Captain Edelphine!" A new voice yelled. "This creature is now under my supervision—by edict of the Council. You are not at liberty to injure it." A second worm stood in the doorway, a somewhat different shade of green, and flickering in muted bursts of amber.

"That is Morticue," whispered Mnemosyne. "From what I can deduce from my admittedly rushed linguistic studies of this species, his authoritative voice could use some work, but his colors and odors are spot on, to use the vernacular. I don't believe Edelphine will challenge him."

"Too bad, Nessie." Rudy laughed. "I was almost having fun."

27
Inquisition Interruptus

❝We are alone, alien groupie. You wished to speak to Master Morticue Ambergrand. Now is the time to speak." The worm-a-pede sat on a kind of bench, nearly ramrod straight, flickering in various colors that made his torso look like an oil slick rippling beneath islands of fabric. He impaled Twill with a three-eyed stare. Rudy, from his perch near Twill's ear, found that the visual wonder of examining such an unearthly creature close up and personal was distracting his attention from the details of monitoring Twill and communicating with Mnemosyne. The AI must be juggling lots of duties at this point, maintaining Rudy's own consciousness, allowing Twill to communicate with his captors, and keeping track of the advancing Jadderbadian force.

"Why are you invading the homeland of Spider Woman and her faithful caretakers?" Twill fidgeted on the bench on which he sat, but projected the statement with admirable conviction. The chain that secured his leg to the bench rattled, and Rudy thought he heard the squeak of a nearly contained fart. "You are trespassing, worm crea-ture Ambergrand."

Morticue emitted a sound that Rudy couldn't quite describe, but decided it was the equivalent of a grunt merged with a soft hiss. "The concept of trespass is restricted to equals. I see nothing but a primate dressed in animal hides with some powers of — clever imitation."

Rudy whispered to Twill: "Ask him how such clever primates are imitating a language they have never heard with such accuracy. Tell him that his eyes, his ears — all his sensoria — are deceiving him, and endangering all Jadderbadian kind." Twill apparently drew on his experience as shaman. He puffed out his chest and delivered his lines with appropriate attitude.

"I see no danger to 'Jadderbadian kind' in you, scruffy ape." Morticue gestured with one arm, reminding Rudy of a maestro in front of his musicians. "You squat in primitive huts near what appears to be an ancient construct of some kind. Even as we speak, Captain Edelphine leads a military convoy to the base of the artifact you surround. Can I assume this mysterious Spider Woman you venerate is a local deity?"

"Do not underestimate Spider Woman." Twill pointed a finger at Morticue. "She has guarded my homeland for generations, and has now sent Great Uncle Rudy to guide me."

"Don't run off at the mouth, kid," Rudy whispered.

"Great Uncle Rudy?" Morticue's mouth orifice fluttered, exposing ivory barbs beneath, and his chromatophores pulsed in a tepid yellow. "Where is this Great Uncle Rudy?"

Twill forged on, evading the question. "Spider Woman is wise." Twill paused with a shaman's good sense of theatre. "Spider Woman knows about the stargate through which you entered our world…and she knows it is not of your making."

Morticue paused in mid gesture. His mouth orifice froze momentarily before he spoke again. "The stargate. And what else does your Spider Woman know about the stargate?" The alien turned toward his computer screens and activated them with a voice command. "Link me with Edelphine."

Twill continued without providing details. "Spider Woman has many powers. She weaves many complex webs. Do not underestimate her."

"And don't over-play our hand, my boy," said Rudy.

"What do you want, scholar?" Edelphine's voice burst from a speaker on a nearby console. "What have you learned from that alien groupie?"

"Proceed with some caution, Captain." Morticue twisted on his bench to face the speaker. "This creature knows more things than he should. He knows at least some details about how we acquired the stargate."

"I knew it!" Edelphine spluttered. "This artifact is a threat. In the name of Great Mother, I will reduce it to dust."

"I wouldn't," yelled Twill, rattling his leg chain in the process.

"Is that the monkey?" Edelphine's voice entered a higher register. "How dare he address me directly?"

"Spider Woman says, 'It is always best to speak clearly to fools before they step in their own poo.'" Twill closed his mouth firmly and stuck out his chin at the monitor.

Rudy groaned. "No ad-libbing, kid. No ad-libbing!" Rudy glanced at the screen. Edelphine's mouth orifice seemed frozen in an "O" configuration, fluttering at the edges like an aspen leaf.

But Rudy didn't need to worry about ad-libbing. At that moment the Earth shook—violently enough that the transport jumped, dumping them all onto the floor like the loose change Rudy used to spill on the top of his dresser nearly a million years ago.

Twill jumped to his feet and tested the chain around his ankle, but it remained well secured. Morticue sprang erect using a powerful, multiple-arm pushup that allowed him to get his tripodal legs beneath him. "Exterior views on lateral screens," he commanded. Edelphine's face peeked into view on the center screen. That alien had apparently been upended as well.

The Citadel, still rather distant, dominated the skyline in both lateral screens, although from somewhat different angles. A dissipating mist blurred the details of its structure, making it look like a defiant finger thrust into the air. In the middle foreground, the earth swelled like some enormous zit. Within seconds, the zit popped. Several rocks whizzed toward wherever the cameras were positioned, while a column of steam rose skyward as if emitted from a giant fire hose. The transport shook violently again, tipping everyone to the floor.

Edelphine had disappeared from the center screen, but he still barked orders. "Reverse course! Retreat to our position at the village and await further commands."

Morticue groaned from his new position on the floor. He rubbed one arm that appeared to be damaged with a still functional one. "I'm getting too old for these adventures," he muttered, to no one in particular.

Twill stood up again and put his hands on his hips. "Spider Woman says, 'Do not threaten my people. Retreat or suffer the consequences.'"

"Insolent groupie. It appears that Edelphine has anticipated your request." Morticue pushed himself erect, although not quite as sprightly or efficiently as before.

"Twill, compliment Spider Woman on her impeccable timing," whispered Rudy. The transport continued to rock and shudder. Morticue teetered in place and Twill struggled to stay standing. The lateral monitors in front of Morticue showed that the geyser in front of the transport still tossed rocks with abandon, and pulsed gouts of steam. Rudy noted higher room temperatures from the sensors on his gnat-bot, and winced at noticeably loud impacts. *And I do hope she has everything under control.* "How are things going there in command central, Nessie?" Rudy glanced at the virtual icons that linked him to Mnemosyne. They all flickered like candles in a breeze, just before they blinked off completely.

28
Cage mates in retreat

Twill couldn't remember feeling so helpless. The alien named Morticue had lifted him with one arm like a hunter's day pack, released his leg chain, then tucked him unceremoniously under an arm and teetered out of the room they were in—all while the floor rocked back and forth to the sound of occasional impacts. They entered a shaft of some kind—Rudy said it was an elevator, whatever that was. Twill's stomach felt hollow as they descended to a lower level and exited into a large room, cooler and darker than the interrogation room they had left—and filled with cages.

Human beings huddled in the cages or pressed their noses to the bars when Morticue and his captive entered. One muscular man with a halo of curly hair, sallow skin and a missing tooth muttered, "Ugly wild thing," as Morticue glanced around the enclosure with Twill still scissored beneath his arm.

"He should talk," whispered Rudy in Twill's ear.

"Quiet, groupie," commanded Morticue to the curly haired attack groupie, as he approached an empty cage next to one with just a single human in it. Twill noticed an emblem on the cage with two stylized Jadderbadians surrounding a graphic symbol. A door beneath the symbol slid to one side, and Morticue quickly tossed Twill into the cage. Then Morticue addressed the human in the neighboring cage: "I will return later, Fum. Instruct this wild human on the basics of proper pet behavior."

"As you wish, master," said the one called Fum in a simplified version of the Jadderbadian that Twill had been using to speak to the alien worm. Twill's head felt strangely empty and confused. The words the strange human spoke sounded odd and the meanings blurred, like someone had struck him half senseless.

Morticue turned and ambled into the elevator with his oddly graceful, three-legged gait. The door hissed shut behind him. Twill heard the sound of the device receding up and away.

Twill sat up, straightened his vest, and brushed dust off his breeches. "Have Spider Woman get us out of here, Uncle Rudy."

"I'm afraid we have a problem, boy." Rudy glanced at his readout again, just to be sure. "I've lost my…connection to Spider Woman—at least for the time being."

"Who are you talking to, wild thing?" Fum pressed his nose to the bars of his cage. Now Fum spoke in a language Twill understood clearly: the same as that of Trader Bok.

"Lost the connection? How can that be?" Perhaps that is why my head feels strange, thought Twill. Spider Woman has left me. Twill had ignored Fum, but as Rudy's gnat bot shifted position on his ear, Fum pointed.

"What is that bug on your ear?" Fum asked.

"My Uncle Rudy." Twill glared at Fum.

"You are related to a bug? Let me see it. What kind of creature are you?"

Twill ignored the request. "Are you a pet of the Morticue beast?"

"What of it?" Fum glared through the bars. "You better show some respect to the master or he'll make compost out of you."

"Better that than a perpetual worm slave." Twill returned the glare.

"Ah, good news, I think." Rudy interrupted the exchange.

Twill turned away from Fum to glance around the room. "Why good news…" he started to say, but then he noticed motion along the wall closest to him. Some of the attack groupies cried out.

"I do believe our spider pack traveling armada has found us again," said Rudy.

The spider bot that had left Twill during the encounter near his grandfather's house skittered across the floor toward Twill's cage.

"What is that?" Fum backed away to a point in his cage farthest away from the bot.

The spider bot crawled up the base of Twill's cage and through the bars. It headed straight for Twill, who took a step backward.

"Stand still, kid. This bot may be able to link us to Spider Woman again. It's got more transmission power than this little gnat bot I'm haunting."

Twill took his uncle's advice, though he cringed when the thing crawled up his leg and poked its way beneath his shirt. It tickled his belly briefly before Twill felt a familiar prick of pain from its tap root-like connection, as its body settled in beneath his rib cage. Twill glanced briefly at Fum, whose expanded eyes reminded him of an owl.

Twill's head suddenly felt full again. *Did you miss me?* The voice of Spider Woman echoed clearly in his mind.

"Ah, she's back. About time!" Rudy added with enthusiasm. The gnat bot tickled Twill's ear as it shifted position like a nervous dancer.

"I have missed you, wise and powerful Spider Woman," said Twill. "The worm people have put us in these disgusting cages, smelling of urine and sweat. Release us with your fiery beam or some other magic—if it pleases you, of course." Twill looked at Fum with a sly grin.

Patience young shaman. You and your Uncle Rudy have some work to do for me yet, and remaining in the cage—and in the custody of Master Morticue—for some time longer will be part of a larger plan. Do you understand?

Twill understood that gods and goddesses were mostly absent, and then capricious whenever they did appear. "I understand, Spider Woman."

"Does your goddess have a problem?" Fum grabbed hold of the bars of his cage nearest Twill. A crooked smile appeared on the pet human's face.

Twill frowned at him across the space between them. "No problem, pampered cage louse."

"Because my master will return soon and you haven't been instructed in proper manners yet." Fum wagged a finger at Twill.

Part of your duties will be difficult. Spider Woman paused briefly before continuing. *You and your Uncle Rudy must become much more intimate because I will be far away from where you are traveling. Uncle Rudy will leave the gnat bot to share your mind and help you deal with Master Morticue and his kind. It will be strange at times; perhaps even painful. But I am confident you are the right person to help save your people from harm. Can I count on your dedication and bravery?*

Twill wondered what choice he had. He had questions that needed answering, but interrogating the Spider goddess might not be wise. Twill didn't like the words "strange" and "painful" in her enlistment speech. Talking with his cranky and rather cryptic uncle might be easier than understanding the powerful Spider Woman. *I will serve my people with honor*, he found himself concluding. Spider Woman must have overheard his thoughts.

Twill felt a prick near his ear. The gnat bot flew off his shoulder and buzzed past Fum—who fell backward on to the floor—before disappearing through a vent in the ceiling. Twill laughed. But then pain struck his head like the blow of a hammer. He screamed. He remembered seeing Fum scrambling away from the bars nearest his cage and the world turning a ruddy pink, just before blackness closed over his head like a shroud.

29
Two minds are more painful than one

Rudy screamed. He had forgotten the visceral, all-consuming nature of pain after 923,000 years in AI-moderated limbo. He wished it gone. He pleaded for it to go away. Eventually, it faded to a throb that allowed him to think—to even pose questions. "Was this really wise, Nessie? Will this work?" He thought he was speaking directly to Mnemosyne, but he was now aware of another mind nearby. Twill's gestalt seemed to vibrate and undulate all about him like a melody-infused bolt of silk tainted with the scent of a heady spice.

"If wisdom grows from necessity, then this procedure is wise. I certainly can't be sure it will work, but it seemed better than giving you the equivalent of a lobotomy." Mnemosyne appeared in her ponytailed guise, as if peering through a circular porthole. "I don't have the resources to simultaneously replicate your personality and memory in the limited neural matrix of the gnat bot, deal with the subterranean forces I've set in motion, and maintain the integrity of the Citadel. I'm gambling that Twill's human brain is young and his neurons versatile enough to deal with the stresses of a second personality template. Of course, I'm making some calculated guesses and taking a few risks."

"Comforting. But then human entity parasites can't be choosy, can they?" *I've already died once, so what's the big deal? At least nonexistence isn't painful.* Rudy listened to Twill's "song." *Were those words he was hearing? Was the tune melting into images?* "Can Twill hear us?" He looked at Mnemosyne through a porthole that seemed to be fading, as if covered in mist.

"I'm not sure. He's integrating the experience much as you are."

Mnemosyne seemed to press her nose against the virtual barrier between them, but the porthole continued to fade. "Be strong, Rudy. Learn everything you can about Morticue and his kind. The survival of your kind may depend on it."

"Look, Nessie, I…" Rudy began, but Mnemosyne talked over him.

"I'm losing the connection, Rudy." Mnemosyne's avatar became mostly a silhouette framed in a cameo of dusty gray. "I will do everything possible to reconnect. You have mental control over the simpler AIs in the spider attached to Twill. Think WEAPONS to access the laser, SURVEY to activate the flying drones, MAINTENANCE to use repair or replicating bots, and COMMUNICATION to attempt to reach me or any deployed bots." After a pause, he barely heard her last words: "I will miss you."

Rudy felt adrift in the dark on a strange sea. *Twill? Twill, can you hear me?*

Can I hear you? What a strange question. I am you—aren't I? Twill's head ached. He lay on his back. His eyes throbbed behind closed lids. He wanted to keep them closed to seal out all the craziness of what he hoped was a dream world. He opened them anyway. Stains from he knew-not-what adorned the ceiling of his cage like sketches brushed by a poor artist's apprentice. He rolled over to see Fum struggling to his feet in the neighboring cage. Damn. If this was a dream it was horribly persistent.

Twill blinked and felt a stab of pain. He remembered other things. Impossible things. He was Rudy—an old man who had died—or was ready to die—until someone captured his brain—the essence of his being—and made it part of something else—something controlled by another being. Nessie, who was also Spider Woman—who was also Mnemosyne, the goddess of memory. Another stab of pain. He heard a groan and realized the sound had escaped from his throat.

He sat up and held his head as if it were a melon—*or a bowling ball*—with both hands. *A real body*, the Rudy part of him rejoiced!

111

Muscles contracting; skin touching skin; blood pounding faintly in my temples—even the pain—it means I'm alive again. Truly alive. Great body you have here, kid. The pain receptors work. No doubt about that.

Kid. He was young. He was the shaman of his tribe—yet he remembered an old lady named Alice—who was his sister—holding his hand in a strange room with pungent smells. What is happening? Make this stop, Uncle Rudy—or whatever demon you are!

Sorry, kid. This is going to be hard on both of us. I am sharing your brain now—I'm not just a voice in your ear. You will know my thoughts and memories and I will know yours—although we can't both be in charge all the time. We wouldn't be able to function. I know this seems like magic, but it isn't. I don't believe in magic, at least not the supernatural kind, and—deep down—I sense that you're a skeptic, too. We're both human—at least you are, and I was. We'll get through this. We may be in Master Morticue's cage at the moment, but we have some surprises for Mr. mega worm.

Fum's face pressed against the bars of his cage. "Are you sick, wild boy?"

"My name...my name is Twill." He almost shouted the syllable, as much to convince himself who he was as, to inform this worm's obnoxious pet. Twill got to his feet on wobbly legs. He heard the steady drone of the vehicle around him without the rocking and shaking. They must be well clear of the eruption that—the Rudy part of him knew—the powerful intelligence called Mnemosyne had created to save the citadel—a kind of monument built so long ago that 50,000 grandfathers separated him from its maker. *Hey, it boggles my mind too, kid—and I knew the architect. Sharp as a dart, but with a tongue to match. Kind of an SOB like me, I suppose.*

"When will your master return?" Twill approached the side of his cage and frowned at Fum.

Fum shrugged. "Probably when the transport..." he began.

The steady hum of the vehicle ceased. Both Twill and Fum grabbed the bars of their respective cages to steady themselves.

"...stops." Fum completed his sentence and a smile turned up the

112

corners of his mouth. "Want to learn some pet rules real quick, wild thing Twill?"

Twill was about to libel Fum's mother with a comment on her sexual habits, but stopped, with his mouth half open, when he heard a faint but familiar sound.

"Don't let a snake mate with that dangling tongue, wild boy."

Twill ignored Fum. "It's a dog," he whispered to himself. "I know that bark. Dark Shadow is here somewhere—and maybe Jeeta."

Well, that adds a few peppers to the chili pot, doesn't it, son? Rudy allowed himself to bask in a mix of emotions he hadn't felt in a very long time. *Sounds like your friends may have stowed aboard somewhere.*

The barking stopped. Twill began to wonder if he had imagined it, but Rudy had heard it too. We have to find them. Twill clenched his fists.

We need to get on good terms with worm man first, son. Besides, these bars look pretty substantial. Maybe you could cozy up to this Fum character a little more.

The cage louse. Twill made it a statement rather than a question.

He's the fly on the wall at the moment, so to speak—or at least the pet in the monogrammed kennel.

A motor engaged. It took Rudy a moment to recognize what it was: The sound of the elevator descending again to the level of the kennels.

"The first pet rule to know," Fum volunteered, "is to bow your head and say, 'I live to serve you, master.'"

30
Morticue meets Uncle Rudy

The mechanical whine of the elevator stopped. Its door hissed open. Twill shook his head, as if to toss aside the confused feelings and memories that threatened to overwhelm him. Surprisingly, it seemed to work. Maybe staring at the lumbering green sausage that was Morticue twisting toward him with his three-legged gait forced him to focus on the problem at hand.

Morticue planted all three of his feet between Twill's and Fum's cages so that he could reach both easily. "All right, wild groupie, the time for a decision has come." Morticue focused a pair of dark eyes on Twill, using the third to look at Fum. He opened Fum's cage with a lower lateral pair of hands. "Fum, attend."

Fum took a spot near Morticue's closest leg. "I live to serve you, master."

"Yes, yes..." Morticue fumbled to reseal the lock on Fum's cage. The mechanism finally clicked into place. "Fum, have you instructed this creature on proper behavior?"

Fum spread his arms wide. " He seems a bit hostile and confused, master... " Fum glanced in Twill's direction "...and just a bit dim. Perhaps with more time..."

"Time is a commodity we no longer have." Morticue turned his attention to Twill. "The volcano on your island is erupting. Twill. Is that your name? It might soon destroy the tall artifact I came to study. We must return to New Jadderbad—my home on this water world—until the geology stabilizes..."

"Spider Woman will never let you return!" Twill shook a finger at his captor.

"You do not have permission to speak, groupie," Morticue spluttered.

"I do not need permission to speak. You invaded my home." Twill paced around his cage one turn and then grabbed a cage bar with his good hand.

Twill, let ME handle this. We need some diplomacy. With that pronouncement from Rudy, Twill's head began to ache again. He staggered.

"Fum, is something wrong with this creature?" Morticue waved his upper circlet of arms in Twill's general direction.

"He's been talking a lot to himself, Master. He seems to have another voice in his head. And a spider came and attached itself to his chest." Fum pointed an accusing finger at Twill.

Pretend you are taking a deep breath, boy—as when you meditate before a ceremony. Let me come forward... yes, like that! "Master Morticue," Rudy said in High Jadderbadian, which the larger spider bot had stored in its neural matrix. "Your 'pet' is correct. There is more than meets the eye here. The body of Twill holds another personality. I am Rudy. I am...Twill's distant ancestor."

Morticue's oral cavity remained partly open; the oral pili around it fluttered, as if in a breeze. "Such a pile of frass. Why should I believe such nonsense?"

Rudy unbuttoned Twill's tunic far enough to expose the mechanical spider. *Watch this, kid. This is the way to use a little finesse. Nessie—Spider Woman—and I discovered that these creatures communicate part of the time with color displays, like cuttlefish and other mollusks.* The outer shell of the spider bot began to shimmer in placating shades of blue. "Believe what you see, Master Morticue. I come in peace from the deep past to have a conversation with you. My kind built the monument—and other treasures I can lead you to." *With a little luck and Nessie's help—if I can ever reach her again.*

Morticue stared at the obviously artificial construct on the groupies chest and whispered his next comment. "But you are a primate—a primitive vertebrate species. Your brains are too simple—not to mention sexually deranged—to build civilizations." Morticue bent his large frame and swiveled his head back and forth to get the best images of his captive with all three eyes. His nostrils flared and he sniffed, almost like a dog. "Besides, Edelphine thinks you are dangerous. I should turn you over to him."

"That blue-green hot dog that killed Twill's grandfather? He's an asshole—or frasshole to you. You said it yourself."

"That human was Twill's grandfather?" Morticue's hide fluoresced with a contemplative confusion of colors.

"You seem like a much more discriminating and knowledgeable being than Captain Edelphine. Someone who can appreciate the opportunity to learn something without destroying it in fear." *A little sugar makes the medicine go down, my boy. It never hurts to flatter someone twice your height and half again as wide.*

Morticue's oral cavity fluttered as if he were about to speak. At the same time, the doors to the elevator closed and it began to rise. The alien cocked his head as if listening to something. "Edelphine is on his way," he said, as if speaking to himself.

"I know you are a scholar, Morticue. In fact, I know you are the Overseer of Exobiological Interactions..."

Morticue cocked his head while displaying surprised shades of lavender on his forehead.

I think we've got him now, Twill. "...and I wouldn't know that without having some serious technological skills. Don't turn me over to that..." Rudy searched the spider bot's database for the right information. "...Thunderclub Clan dullard with the sensitivities of a water rat." While Rudy spoke, he began buttoning up Twill's tunic.

The elevator descended, then opened. Edelphine swaggered out and over to the cages. "The expedition will be returning to New Jadderbad until the geological activity here has subsided. Report, Master Morticue. What have you learned about this...vermin?" Edelphine gestured in Twill's direction.

"I recommend you place him in high security containment during the flight home." Morticue bowed slightly toward Edelphine. His hide shimmered in shades of azure. "As you correctly surmised, this alien could pose a threat, and I am the one charged by the Council with deciding just how serious that threat might be."

Edelphine remained silent for a while, regarding Twill with two eyes and Morticue with the third. "Very well." His voice was a rumble and his chromatophores a neutral gray. "I will reserve the vault for this hairy excrescence. My Alpha security force—in addition to my biggest and most aggressive groupies—will guard the exits. The latter will choose which portions of the wild groupie they want for dinner if he escapes."

Fum wrapped his arms around one of Morticue's legs. He stuck out his tongue at Twill.

"I would expect no less," said Morticue.

31
Stowing away

Chills crawled up Jeeta's back when DS barked, but he quickly stopped at her hissed command. They huddled together next to a large, smooth-sided container—one of many in a room as big as four large huts stacked in pairs. The air smelled like the strange worm creatures, musky and strong like wet dirt in the spring. "Good boy, DS," she whispered, "but be silent. Our lives depend on it." DS huffed. He seemed to understand, but wasn't particularly happy about it. Jeeta heard a humming sound, followed by voices and the sounds of shifting bodies in what she thought of as the cage room adjoining her temporary sanctuary.

Jeeta raised her hand in a "stay" command; then crept over to the doorway that linked the two rooms. The fabric-like material that covered it bowed slightly at one frayed seam, creating a gap. She peeked through the opening at a long line of barred cages containing humans, paying special attention to the one holding Twill. He lay on his back, alone in one cage, sometimes groaning while holding his head. A single human in a nearby cage talked to him. A worm creature loomed above both cages, gesturing with its many arms, and also apparently entering into the conversation. Jeeta couldn't understand any of the words. She chewed on her lower lip and fingered the leather strap holding her quiver, trying to decide what to do.

Images from the night before haunted her: Twill's grandfather disappearing in a flash of fire and plume of smoke. The large human warrior falling when the arrow sprouted from his chest. Her confusion moments later when she realized that she had shot that arrow. Her white-knuckled hand, and the bow it held, had trembled in the moonlight. When the magic death wand pointed at Twill, her heart seemed to knot like a wet leather cord. But one of the worm people stopped the action with a command. Another grabbed Twill. She remembered drawing an arrow from her quiver and notching it to the bow, but after the alien now holding the wand lowered it and Twill seemed momentarily out of danger, she melted into the embrace of the forest's shadows.

She remembered other events of that night as if they were a dream. Aliens and their human helpers moving Twill to the giant, mule-less transport that loomed in the dark like a hulking beast, thrumming with a frightening power. Jeeta had watched the comings and goings of aliens and humans, both before and after Twill disappeared into its depths. She noticed that a small glowing patch seemed to control the entrance to the idling wagon on wheels.

After the last human entered, she counted slowly to sixty. The thrumming intensified, perhaps signaling that the giant wagon might move. She dashed from the forest to where she knew the entrance to be, DS close and silent by her side. She remembered pressing the glowing patch and holding her breath as she leaped into the darkness—and the unknown—beyond the door.

DS sniffed the floor and then proceeded down the corridor, clearly in charge. Jeeta scrambled after him in the dim glow of greenish lights that lined the walls near the ceiling, hissing for him to stop, while listening to the distant sounds of human voices mixed with the rumbling syllables of alien commands. Before long, they heard noise ahead and the green lights began glowing brighter. That was when the drunken alien almost tripped over them.

A humming noise shattered Jeeta's reveries. Still looking through the gap in the door fabric, she saw a barrier slide aside on the wall beyond the cages. A second, larger alien stepped into the room and began moving toward Twill's cage. He looked somehow familiar—or at least what passed for clothing circling his segments did. Without the fabric bands, Jeeta couldn't tell these weird worms apart. She recognized the combination of colors and a large symbol on the fabric band nearest his head. He was the one who would have shot Twill, if it weren't—she now realized—for something the other

119

alien near Twill's cage had said during the events of last night. She became mesmerized by the shifting colors on their bodies as they interacted.

A rattling noise followed by a whine startled Jeeta. She turned away from her peephole and gestured to DS to remain quiet. Was the alien from the corridor last night waking up from its drunken slumber at the far end of the storage room? It had staggered in front of them then like a tree about to fall. When it had swiveled three eyes toward them, waving its tangle of arms and weaving on its three legs, DS had growled softly. Jeeta had sucked in air. *I'm going to become a puff of smoke*, she remembered thinking. Instead, the alien staggered through a fabric curtain Jeeta had not recognized for the doorway it was. After the alien disappeared through the opening, she and DS cautiously followed in time to see the alien collapse behind a wall of containers.

Jeeta had intended to flee, but when she sat down—as far from the alien as she could get—she closed her eyes for what she thought was just a moment. She must have fallen into an exhausted sleep, DS slumped across her lap.

Loud sounds from the adjoining room startled her awake. By the time she discovered the peephole, Twill had been caged, and she was congratulating herself and DS's nose, for following the still snoring alien into this storage place.

Jeeta watched the activities in the cage room until the second alien exited from the door in the wall and the first alien shackled Twill to one of his many arms and left the same way. He had another human, untethered, trailing beside him. *Now how do I find out where they've gone?* Jeeta looked at DS, who cocked his head, as if to say, "Beats me. You're the one with the big brain."

Jeeta decided they had to return to the corridor through the other entrance to the room, past the alien who could awaken at any time. She moved quickly in that direction and DS followed. The alien turned once, its arms reminding Jeeta of a caterpillar. Both she and her dog froze like statues until it settled back into its sodden slumber. They reached the doorway. Jeeta turned to give DS a hand command at the same time she parted the fabric with her other hand. She frowned when DS growled menacingly. Then she realized the growl wasn't for her. A chill crept up her neck as she turned. Her eyes widened. "How in the name of Spider Woman did you get here?" she hissed.

32
Hard bargains

❝Is that any way to greet a friendly trader?" Bok grinned a toothy smile behind his salt and pepper beard.

Jeeta looked up at the trader, who loomed a bit larger than she remembered. He had replaced his fancy leather vest and breaches for the generic tunic that the worm's pets wore. He smelled of sweat and a spicy odor Jeeta couldn't identify. "What happened, trader? Did your ship leave without you?"

"I'm sure they were under some duress, pretty lady. Jeeta? I seem to recall the shaman called you Jeeta. I do hope your holy man friend is not injured."

"He's been captured, as I'm sure you know. Did they scoop you from the woods during your dash to the ship?" Jeeta turned to glance at the alien, who shifted positions in his carton alcove.

"Not at all. Being the resourceful man I am, I cashed in some favors with a groupie platoon leader I know. Masters don't pay detailed attention to all the pets wandering around—as long as they are properly attired." Bok smiled his sly smile again as he thumbed a corner of his tunic. "Which reminds me…" he slipped a pack off his back "…I've come on a mission of aid."

Jeeta narrowed her eyes. "What kind of aid" She paused. "And at what price?"

"Price? Dear Jeeta, price is such a harsh word." He pulled some clothing from his pack—apparently another tunic, somewhat smaller, with an emblem near one shoulder. "I was thinking more of a gift exchange." He looked in her eyes first, and then his gaze lingered in the general direction of the gold necklace holding an amulet that rested just above her breasts.

Jeeta followed his gaze. "I told you outside Magic Mountain. This necklace belonged to my grandmother."

The drunken worm person shifted again with a kind of snort. Jeeta feared he would awaken soon.

"I will take good care of your necklace. Perhaps we can make another — gift exchange — in the future." Bok's smile morphed into a leer. "We must be quick about this. "Give me your clothes — and the necklace — and put these on." He offered the thin tunic on an outstretched arm. "A friend of mine will hide you in a Master's kennel. Shaman Twill should be nearby."

Jeeta sighed. She removed the necklace, handed it to Bok, and accepted his "gift." "An honorable man would turn around." She felt her face flush.

"Ah, if only we could find one," said Bok.

Jeeta growled softly — as did DS — but she quickly removed her outer clothes, keeping only her loincloth, as she slipped the tunic over her head.

"You make that simple garment a monument to womanhood. My, you certainly do." Bok stuffed her leather clothes in his backpack. Jeeta spied a dark alcove behind some boxes. She stuffed her bow and quiver of arrows there, hoping to retrieve them later.

"I want those back, trader." Jeeta pointed at the backpack, now on Bok's shoulders.

"More trading?" He took a menacing step forward.

Jeeta twisted something dark, shiny and sharp from the back of her hair. Black tresses fell over one shoulder. She held the obsidian hair ornament, which doubled nicely as a knife, beneath Bok's chest. "You might not like all of my gifts, trader. Lead me to your friend."

"A very nice trinket." Bok's smile faded. "I seem to remember Twill buying that a year ago."

"Then you would appreciate the irony if you were to be disemboweled with it, trader Biff."

"Bok." He took a step back.

"Biff, Bok, whatever…" The alien emitted a groan and began to rise. "Go now," Jeeta hissed.

Bok did. She followed. The alien groaned behind them. Hangovers must be universal for mortals of every kind.

33
Vault assaults & other indiscretions

After Edelphine left the kennel room, Morticue paced back and forth, Fum at his heels. Eventually, Morticue quickly raised and then dropped six arms in a rather human-like gesture of frustration. He used his remaining three arms to fuss with Fum's clothes and pat his head. He swiveled an eye toward's Twill's cage. "I'll deal with you, alien schizophrenic creature, after we board the transport and have more time on the return to New Jadderbad." He turned to Fum. "Fum, attend," he commanded. After Fum lined up next to one leg—and stuck his tongue out again at Twill—the pair left.

Rudy and Twill barely had time to argue with one another about who was in charge of Twill's body before another Jadderbadian showed up and released three large humans from one of the adjoining cages. "Take this wild creature to the vault on board the transport." The worm man pointed towards Twill's cage with two arms. All three humans bowed their heads in acknowledgement of the command. "If you fail, Edelphine will feed you your own entrails. Understood?" They nodded in unison. The Jadderbadian left, mumbling about other chores he needed to attend to.

Outside, flanked by the three humans that towered head and shoulders above him, Rudy/Twill involuntarily "ahhhed" at the shiny winged transport that arched above them. It hummed with controlled power and hissed occasional bursts of steam from assorted apertures. Twill: *Surely such a thing cannot fly?* Rudy: *It's bigger than a space freight shuttle, but I'm sure it will fly, boy.* Twill: *We should have looked for my friends in the smaller wheeled cart.* Rudy: *Hard to do from the inside of a cage, don't you think?*

125

They entered the craft through a Jadderbadian-sized hatch, and trudged down several winding corridors before arriving at the vault. Rudy/Twill stared at the vault's door, straining Twill's neck in the process. The door stretched the length of two tall humans wide. Its portal arched three human heights overhead like a castle door made for Paul Bunyan. *What is a Paul Bunyan, Uncle Rudy? I see a picture in your mind of a giant human with some kind of large blue grazing creature. Can Spider Woman conjure such an animal to help us?*

Paul Bunyan is a made-up character, Twill. That door would have impressed him, though. Yes sir. The worms know how to make vault doors.

Then perhaps we should not let them put us behind such doors. The walls do not look any easier to pierce. Besides, I must find Jeeta and DS. The human to their collective rear poked him in the back with either a stick or a very hard finger. The one to their left, with skin darker than Twill's own, tightened his fist around the heavy cord that tethered him to Twill's waist, causing a dark blue tattoo on his biceps to flex like a snake. He turned his head in Twill's direction and forced a crooked smile between pressed lips. Twill turned to his right and watched the third over-sized human squeeze a hand-held device. Twill felt a vibration under his feet as the vault door shuddered briefly before beginning to slide open.

Escape doesn't look like an immediate option, boy. We will have to chill a little in their prison and make a plan…

I do not want to chill anywhere, Uncle. I want to stay warm and find Jeeta and DS. Certainly three stupid pet humans should be no problem with Spider Woman's gifts. Twill felt his Uncle Rudy's hesitation. Twill also didn't like hiding out in the back corners of his own mind. Now was the time to act. "WEAPONS," he commanded, then felt the links within his mind to the spider creature affixed to his chest. He turned to his left while ripping open his tunic with his good hand. The black's grin morphed into a circle of surprise and his eyes widened. "Red fire," Twill commanded, but Rudy protested. "WEAPONS, pause!" *We don't need to kill them. Here, try this…*

"WEAPONS, target and inject foreign humans with anesthetic."

Instead of a laser beam erupting from Twill's mechanical spider, a cloud of gnat drones emerged. They quickly buzzed around the three surprised guards, who started swatting at them like mosquitoes. The black human dropped Twill's leash and smacked one drone on his thigh with a smile of satisfaction—until his eyes quickly glazed over and he crumpled to the ground. The other two human guards followed his example. The cloud of drones returned to the spider bot on Twill's chest to be reabsorbed and reprogrammed.

Rudy tried to make a joke about the hangover the human worm pets would have while they were trying to eat their entrails after a failed assignment, but the words just wouldn't form... *It's my turn, Uncle! We must find Jeeta, DS and—I hope—Rugat, before this monster beast—plane—takes flight.*

With that pronouncement, Twill took charge. Rudy felt like a paralyzed driving instructor sitting next to a clueless teenager pumping the gas pedal on one of those old-fashioned non-automatic cars of his grandfather's generation. Twill ran off down an empty corridor toward a junction point. He slowed as he approached the intersection, dutifully looking three ways for traffic that—fortunately—wasn't there. About a body length above him he noticed signage in Jadderbadian script—and—by the wonders of Spider Woman—he could read it: BLUE: Control; AMBER: Kennels; GREEN: Galley & Support Offices; BROWN: Veterinary Services/Pet Boarding.

"Pet Boarding. That must be what I need." Twill didn't realize he had said the last phrase out loud, but Rudy/Twill realized he must have—and in Jadderbadian no less—because a flashing brown line activated along the wall of one corridor pointing, apparently, to that destination. *Clever worms*, thought Rudy. *I like their pedestrian walkways with voice activated guides.* Twill ran along the appropriate corridor, following the pulsing brown light, while Rudy played the role of concerned driving instructor with no brake pedal to depress.

Partway to their goal, the transport's engines fired up. At least Rudy thought that was the explanation for the deep rumbles and the trembling floor beneath their feet. *Probably explains why the corri-*

dors are empty, Rudy thought. *Every other creature in this flying bus is probably strapped into something soft and comfy for takeoff.*

The corridor abruptly ended in front of a vast hemispherical window. Twill placed both hands on the glass—or some transparent polymer. His heavy breath made expanding and contracting moisture circles on the surface. *Oh, Uncle, look at all those people...*

If Rudy had had a mouth, he suspected it would be gaping too. They looked down upon what appeared to be a village of people— perhaps three times larger than Twill's own—complete with small hut-like structures, animals, and four Jadderbadians scattered around the area, sitting like lifeguards on elevated platforms. A siren wailed in three short bursts.

Twill jumped back from the window. *Have they found us, Uncle?*

Rudy hesitated. *I don't think so. It's probably some sort of pre-takeoff alert. The Jadderbadians seem to be issuing orders. People are moving to shelters...*

Look there! Twill pointed. *That's Jeeta—being shoved by some woman. How do we get down there?* Twill scanned the arc of the window, then the corridor walls. Rudy noticed a seam that probably outlined an elevator door. *That way, then?* Twill nodded toward the portal outline and began moving toward it.

Let's think this through, Rudy offered, but he clearly was not in charge.

Twill reached the potential elevator door, and a previously invisible panel lit up. Two arrows appeared: One pointing up and one down. *I guess when you've seen one elevator you've seen them all...* Twill pushed the down button—and immediately wished he hadn't.

34
The Vault

*Y*ou certainly took the scenic route to the vault, my boy. Rudy felt—and shared—Twill's anger and frustration. *At least I know that Jeeta is alive and where she is, Uncle. And if the worm man hadn't been in the elevator, we might have hidden among all those people.*

Maybe. Rudy surveyed the room through Twill's eyes. Quite a sterile enclosure. The moniker "Vault" seemed apt. Rudy searched for seams along the gray walls and floor, but found none—even where the walls met the floor—except for the faint outline of the arched doorway through which they had been shoved. A diffuse light seemed to bleed out of the surface, as if they were in a frosted plastic box. They sat on a kind of bench or bed supported by a pedestal like the stalk of a mushroom. An oval fixture on one end provided a source of water, rather like an open birdbath. A somewhat larger fixture on the opposite end provided a chute for piss and poo.

Rudy: *Well, Ollie, this is another fine mess you've gotten me into.*

Twill: *Ollie?* Rudy wasn't inclined to explain long-dead comedians to Twill. As it turned out, he didn't have to.

A transparent bubble about a meter in diameter popped into existence above, and a meter north of, Twill's left shoulder. Therein sat Morticue with Fum nestled under one lower arm, looking content. View screens and shelves created a backdrop behind the Jadderbadian—a tableau a bit fuzzy and distorted at the edges as if one was looking through a fisheye lens. Rudy recognized it as a kind of holographic projection. Twill: *Not magic then?* Rudy: *Better—and sometimes more frightening— than magic. The kind of things clever creatures can make with resources and imagination.*

Morticue resembled a neon sign with tentacles. His skin flickered in rainbow shades, like an old-fashioned florescent light with defective ballast. Pili around around his mouth and eyes fluttered, as if in a breeze. Rudy decided that—based on Nessie's database of research—Morticue was at a loss for mere words. Rudy could almost always think of something to say. "Oh good. Room service has arrived."

"You are fortunate to be alive, primitive groupie. If anyone other than Tork had found you, your future as compost would have been assured." Morticue leaned back and regarded Twill. "What did you hope to achieve? Surely, even you—dim groupie that you are—must have realized escape could only be temporary?"

Before Twill could reveal anything about stow-a-ways, Rudy quipped, "Resistance is futile, eh?" *Let me run this show for a while kid. Live and pay attention.* Rudy sensed Twill's acquiescence and a bodily tiredness that seemed atypical—and a little concerning. No time to address that, at least for the moment.

Rudy noticed something familiar displayed on the view screen behind Morticue. "I see you've highlighted the Trappist-1 system in the constellation of Aquarius. At least that's what we mere humans called it before that blasted space rock knocked us back to the Stone Age. Getting homesick maybe? I seem to recall there's a runty red star out that way with at least seven planets around it—some in the so-called life zone. It's around 40 light years from here."

Morticue's skin flickered some more, but Rudy wasn't quite sure if the colors denoted surprise, confusion, or annoyance. The alien stroked his pet's head, perhaps a little too vigorously, as Fum frowned at his master and squirmed out from under the attention. "I am seeing the personality called Ru-dee, then? You do seem to be—uncomfortably clever. My home star is roughly the distance that light can travel in 40 years from here. Its system contains seven major planets and three minor ones." Morticue leaned forward, cocked his head, and swiveled his eyes toward Rudy. Was he near-sighted and trying to sharpen the image in front of him?

"As I told you, I'm Twill's distant relative. His body is a rental at the moment." Don't take offense, boy. "You might have found a few country bumpkins where you parked your funny arch, but Twill and all the other wild humans like him don't care for your hostile take-over of this planet."

Morticue leaned back so that his torso was nearly vertical. "That is irrelevant. As a great Jadderbaddian once observed, 'The biggest swimmer in the pond can ignore the minnows therein.'"

"Yes, well we minnows have been swimming in this pond for quite some time, and we're not ready to hang up our fins." Rudy tried to stiffen Twill's body into a defiant pose, but it seemed to be wilting on him.

"You have no fins that I can see."

"Metaphorical fins, mister brainy worm. You know about meta-phors, don't you?"

"You are a peculiar groupie. I admit that." Fum shaded his eyes and looked straight at the camera, as if to verify his master's state-ment. Morticue diverted one of his eyes to examine the screen behind him before turning off the image of his home star system. He rolled the roving eye back to its former position to regard his captive in enhanced detail. "Tell me one reason, ancient wild groupie, why I shouldn't just destroy you right now, so that I can enjoy my last lar-val years, and anticipate the pleasures of metamorphosis in comfort."

"That's easy," said Rudy. "You want to know more about me — dim but clever groupie that I am." Rudy heard air pass between Morticue's lips — much like a human's sigh. "And — truth be told — I want to know more about you, wise and clever star worm. I've never met a worm I could talk to."

Then — abruptly — the three-dimensional image of Morticue popped out of existence, as silently as a broken soap bubble, and as enigmatically as a Cheshire cat.

I certainly hope he didn't take offense, Twill. Twill? Are you all right? We seem to feel a little queasy.

35
Dilemmas and opportunities

Morticue pondered the image of his mate on the view screen. Her colors flickered with uncertainty. The pili around her mouth fluttered. "Well, dearest, aren't you going to speak? I could use your input." Morticue stroked Fum's head, but Fum was busy speaking with his bitch, Nulla, in a kind of sign language these primates sometimes used. Nulla sat tucked beneath one of Selaea's lower arms.

"So, do you really believe, dear one, that some long dead groupie is haunting the body of that leather-clad wild animal you've shown me? I didn't think natural philosophers entertained such fantasies." Selaea stroked the pili near her eyes with an upper arm.

"This creature knows things beyond the ken of a wild groupie— or any groupie, for that matter." Morticue took a breath and began listing more evidence. "The building on the island is certainly of an advanced design. The flying camera artifact that started this whole expedition certainly indicates functioning technology roughly on a par with ours." Morticue paused and scratched his head with one finger. "And this wild creature does seem to speak with two voices— as strange as that might seem. Even Fum noted the difference. Of course, the creature could have mental issues. I've seen groupies do some incredibly stupid and self-destructive things…"

"Haven't we all." Selaea plucked specks of groupie hair from her upper torso band and smoothed more head pili. "Morticue—dear one—if—and I repeat, IF what this creature says is true, the Council of Elders would have to totally reclassify groupies—or at least consider doing so. That would take years—perhaps decades. Think what it would do to the economy. Perhaps they would even consider aborting our colony here—and we are both so close to metamorphosis, dear one. I'm so looking forward to that…" Selaea's voice trailed off with a lilt Morticue enjoyed.

"What would you have me do? If this creature is what he claims to be, all Jadderbadians could expand their minds and hearts…"

"Rather unlikely, I would say," Selaea interrupted. "Expanded minds get headaches. Expanded hearts burst." Selaea leaned toward the camera feed. "Perhaps this poor creature—apparently stranded far from his own time—should just… disappear." Selaea's skin flickered in shades of rust and yellow.

"Dearest—you are a member of the Council—certainly you would not advocate…"

"Just a thought, my brain-heavy husband—just a thought. But something to consider." Selaea stroked Nulla's hair. "Did I tell you the funny thing this one did the other day?" And Selaea proceeded telling several pet stories, along with various adventures with her Elders Club's friends. She avoided further discussion about the peculiar Ru-dee/Twill groupie until the hour grew late and the transmission charges grew large. Both Fum and Nulla fell asleep, snoring as primates do. "I'll see you tomorrow, then, dear one," Selaea confirmed, just before closing the connection.

Morticue squirmed the leg on which Fum rested until the groupie shifted position and curled up next to him. Morticue breathed deeply through all his nasal slits and made a conscious effort to relax his shoulder whirls. What to do with the wild groupie? Selaea's suggestions made some practical sense, he supposed, but he wasn't about to lose this unique opportunity to learn more about the strange groupie ghost that claimed to know about the origins of the ancient culture that once lived here.

Morticue opened a visual feed to the vault. The wild groupie had moved to the floor and lay on his side, apparently sleeping. The creature's defective, withered arm rested on one hip. That deformed limb assaulted Morticue's aesthetic sensibilities. Besides, what would the neighbors think if he made this primate part of his kennel without repairing such an obvious and easily-fixed defect? And Morticue would adopt this groupie—at least until he found out whether its body did harbor the mentality of some sentient personality, or its mind was simply aberrant.

"Air transport Zed, prepare a stout23." Morticue needed something to still his mind before sleep. A stout 23 usually did the job. The robot servant in his chamber detached from the wall and brought his drink, offering it on a tripod of fingers at the end of its outstretched arm. Morticue accepted the alcoholic beverage with a sigh of gratitude, and leaned back into the padding of his bench that dutifully began kneading the muscles of his back. Morticue turned off the feed to the vault and opened the visual of the star field that contained Jadderbad, the world he had left behind to make a future on this overheated rock circling a glaringly bright yellow star lost in one spiral arm of the galaxy.

"Look at all those stars, my little Fum…" Morticue said to his snoring pet, while gently patting his rump, "…like grains of sand on an infinite beach." And at some point, Morticue began snoring himself, the pili around his oral cavity fluttering as if stroked by a tepid breeze off the shore of Wellspring on his beloved, far distant Jadderbad.

36
Unexpected Friends

The entire home shook. Jeeta jumped to her feet; the chopping board tilted, scattering her carefully diced vegetables onto the floor. DS helped himself to the feast while Badae frowned. "Wasted food, wild girl! It's just the airship descending. We will arrive at New Jadderbad soon."

Jeeta nodded to the human—apparently a distant cousin of Bok—who happened to be the pet of Tork, a Jadderbadian soldier of some rank. At least that is what Bok had said, before leaving her to Badae's care. Badae often snapped orders like a grumpy aunt, but seemed to have the instincts of a shepherd. Jeeta liked her. Badae reminded her of her mother in some ways. Jeeta worried about her mother, now apparently on the other side of an ocean. How could that be? "Surely flying villages can't really exist," she muttered.

Badae snorted. "The Jadderbadians know much magic. Wait until you see the city." Badae shooed DS from the kitchen area and leashed him to a post.

Bedae's mate, Tut, wandered into the kitchen and gave Jeeta a toothy smile. He lingered, casting glances Jeeta's way, while pretending to clean up things in the storage area. "Quit drooling at the young girl, old man," Bedae growled. "Fetch more vegetables from the larder, if you want to be useful. Otherwise, the gump meat will ruin my recipe."

Tut complied. Gumps, a kind of domesticated rodent that served as a meat staple for Bok's people, tasted like wild rabbit, but with a bitter edge. The vegetables helped. Jeeta pondered about what she would do after this flying village landed, as she diced the new vegetables Tut provided. The room shook some more, but Jeeta successfully ignored it. She would either die or not. She could not control flying villages, but she could help cook food. She added the onions and crisp greens to Badae's stew pot.

While the pot simmered, Jeeta sat on the floor. DS watched her from his tether with chastised eyes. Badae sat across from her, sewing a garment. Tut left to empty a bucket of kitchen scraps. "How can you serve as pets to these ugly worm creatures?" Jeeta asked Bagae.

Badae raised an eyebrow and flicked a glance in Jeeta's direction, while attending to the task at hand. "Tork feeds us well. He doesn't beat us. He spends time teaching us things. Tut is too old to hunt any more..." Badae shrugged. "It's a life." After a pause, she added, "And then there is the music, of course."

"Music?" Jeeta frowned.

"Jadderbadians create beautiful sounds and love to sing choruses with us." Badae closed her eyes a moment, remembering some past event. "You should attend the Church of Thurwild sometime when a Jadderbadian decides to visit. Or, attend a metamorphosis sometime. We groupies often sing to help the process along."

Jeeta struggled to imagine giant singing monster worms—and failed. "But some humans refuse to be pets, you said." Jeeta leaned in close to Badae; touched her arm.

Badae grunted. "There are some. Mostly those who do not believe in the teachings of Thurwild." Badae looked into Jeeta's eyes. "Some think the Jadderbadians are not gods—just strange creatures with great powers."

"And you?"

Badae laughed. "I don't much care either way. Jadderbadians bleed, although their blood is green. Jadderbadians have sex—but at the end of their lives. Strange. Jadderbadians dote on their offspring—at least the ones they choose to raise and not eat." Badae smiled a crooked smile. "Their young swim like tadpoles in the ocean, you know. Very many. The surplus gets eaten. Very efficient." Badae watched for a reaction and got one.

Jeeta trembled and tried to rub goose bumps off her arms.

136

Badae laughed, exposing her uneven and incomplete row of ragged teeth.

"When we land, I want to meet some of the people who don't believe that Jadderbadians are gods," Jeeta said. "I must stay free, so I can help my captured friends."

"Perhaps you should mate with Bok," Badae said while struggling with a stitch. "He seems a little afraid of you. That's good. He needs a strong woman." Badae glanced at Jeeta, read her face, and laughed. "Bok is a wanderer who wags his rod too much, but he knows how to trade. You could live—and maybe not be a pet."

Jeeta tried to say something, but more of a growl emerged from her lips. Then the ship shook again and screamed some new noise. Jeeta jumped to her feet and struggled to stand. DS barked.

"Best to sit or lie down when the ship belches fire." Badae put her sewing down and arranged some blankets beneath her. She nodded at Jeeta and patted a spot on the blanket next to her. Her eyes glistened softly. "About the other thing. I can see that you meet some people. I can do that for you." Badae raised an eyebrow and smiled a crooked smile. "Bok would probably not survive a marriage with you anyway."

Jeeta looked at the old woman; saw something of her mother again in the tilt of Badae's shoulders. "Thank you," she said.

37
Alien wonders, alien mysteries

Rudy loved the feel of operating a body again. Even the ache in Twill's left wrist at the moment reminded him that at least he had a wrist. Still, Rudy worried about this body's true owner. Rudy sensed Twill's essence — a kind of pressure that throbbed in a corner of his awareness — but Twill wasn't responding to questions. Rudy wished Nessie were here. He needed her input, her evaluation, her resources — and her company. They had shared eons together, after all...

"This way, groupie," said the Jadderbadian robot who had come to fetch him from the vault. Apparently, Morticue wanted him present when this airship landed. Morticue might have also decided that a robot was more dependable than using human pets to collect one of their own.

Rudy followed the robot down the rightmost corridor of a three-way junction. Jadderbadians made their robots roughly in their own image, with whorls of arms and two or three body segments, but the worm-like top rested on a pedestal that glided swiftly over the corridor's surface. Rudy hustled to keep up. "Where are we going, buddy — if I may be so bold to ask?"

"I am proceeding to the observation lounge."

A purplish band of light blinked slowly along the lower right wall of the corridor. Other color bands, parallel to the purple one, remained static. Rudy assumed it was some directional device, like the color stripes in the halls of the hospital in which he had died — boy, did that seem like eternities ago — which, in fact, it was. "What will we be observing?"

The robot remained silent for an entire second. Rudy thought he wasn't going to get an answer. "Whatever you are capable of perceiving," it finally said.

Rudy chuckled. "Good answer. Remind me to introduce you to Nessie some day."

"So noted. Define a Nessie, please."

"Just another abiotic intelligence I know. She's one of a kind."

"I will be pleased to meet this unique, abiotic groupie intelligence."

Other Jadderbadians passed now and then, plowing forward with the determination of commuters late for work. They flashed colors and waved tentacles as they passed. One twisted his torso and made a circle with his mouth that conveyed surprise between species quite effectively. Rudy gave him a thumbs-up and smiled—just to give the alien's brain something else to ponder.

Finally, they reached the end of the corridor. The robot inserted the digit at the end of one upper arm into a port. A section of wall slid aside to reveal what appeared to be an anteroom. "Follow me, groupie," said the wormbot.

A gentle draft of air washed over Twill's body through the open portal. The hallway trembled, as if distant engines had shifted gears. "Lead on, Macduff."

"My name is Zed 541, the 541st manufactured subunit of the airship intelligence Zed."

"Yes, well, lead on Zed 541. It feels like things are happening."

They passed through the anteroom into a large chamber. Morticue sat before what appeared to be a large window, although Rudy supposed it could be a visual display screen. Clever technology often made parsing reality problematic. Rudy was surprised to hear what must have been a kind of—not unpleasant, he had to say—music in the background. Alien elevator music? Yet, he could almost swear there were passages in the mix with human voices.

Morticue took notice of the entourage. "Ah, wild groupie ancestor—or whatever you are—come witness the marvels of New Jadderbad." He waved them to come closer with one pair of arms, while adjusting something on a console with two others. The third

139

pair rested on a pair of his thighs. Morticue's third lower appendage arched upward over the bench he sat on, reminding Rudy of a dog's tail. The creature's hide flickered in shades of blue and green.

Rudy approached Morticue. The wormbot shadowed him, perhaps on alert mode for any aggressive behavior. "Thank you... I guess. Should I be impressed with something, or have you just changed from a jailor to a tour guide?"

The flexible strands—pili was the term Nessie had in her vocabulary data files—fluttered around the pair of eyes focused on him. "My translator programs are having difficulty with some of your phrasing, vocabulary, and references. It's almost enough to make me believe your preposterous assertions."

"Almost, eh?" Rudy smiled. He moved closer to the window, if that's what it was. "Well, let's see if New Jadderbad is a post modern New York, or a few huts built out of worm goo or something." Rudy took a deep breath. New Jadderbad certainly was more than "worm goo." Even he didn't know what he meant by that, but surely there was some advantage to confusing any potential enemy.

It took a while to fathom just what he was seeing. Rudy took a deep breath. A large settlement spread out on rolling green terrain. From the elevation of their aircraft it was hard to make out a lot of details. A network of peculiar tiered pyramids linked by narrow, mostly straight bands, shared space with small enclosures filled with what appeared to be huts or other mostly rectangular structures that looked more like human-style habitations. A glowing, faintly pulsing, arch dominated all the constructs. Somehow, without sound or startling visual effects, the arch looked like what it apparently was: A distortion of what we assume is the natural world—a pucker in the fabric of spacetime. Rudy exhaled. The hairs on Twill's arms rose. It felt like a lightning bolt might fry them at any second.

"Your kind live in the little box structures, of course—groupie houses," Morticue observed. "Jadderbadians live in the properly constructed domes of hemispherical inclusiveness and maximum utility required by sentient species."

Rudy laughed. "So, you can't properly perceive reality unless the

140

shape of your home is correct?"

"The structures one builds reflects the nature of one's soul." The color scheme of Morticue's skin shifted toward the crimson, an apparent sign of annoyance.

"That leaves me speechless—which is hard to do, by the way—but let's talk about other things, like that arch twisting spacetime. It looks like a black hole fringed with a halo. That IS impressive. I would be blown away if I thought you worms had built that. But a little smartypants I know named Nessie tells me you don't know how it works. Could THAT be true?"

Morticue squirmed with several of his arms and fluttered his oral pili. "I wouldn't necessarily trust the opinion of some entity with intelligent clothing. You make very little sense, creature…"

"So do you understand how the arch works?" Rudy leaned closer to the window. "I would certainly like to know more about that."

Morticue released a breath in an undeniable sigh. "As would I." Morticue's oral cavity separated as if he might speak, but then he cocked his head, like a teenager hearing a message on his ear feed. "Hmmpth. It appears the arch is in the middle of a supply transmission. Our ship must circle until spacetime returns to neutral configuration."

"Neutral configuration?" Rudy licked Twill's lips. "Say, Morticue, how much math do you know?"

That served as the beginning of a long and complicated discussion. The robot was forced to serve dinner. Rudy had a craving for pizza, but that didn't happen. His portion of the meal consisted of soft pellets whose consumption conjured memories of his sister's overcooked meatloaf.

But Rudy barely noticed the food, once he and Morticue started playing with numbers, formulae, and mathematical concepts. Zed 541 provided some necessary translating services. It was quite amazing that worms and apes could both appreciate things like the Fibonacci number series, and see it reflected in the coil of a snail shell or the spirals of a galaxy filled with stars.

Time passed. The airship circled. Eventually, the ship landed, its pilot found the proper hangar, and some rude member of the Thunderclub clan — Edelweiss, Delphiny, something like that — began banging on the door and blinking the room lights. It was hard to understand Jadderbadians when they yelled at each other with assorted expletives. At least Rudy assumed that terms like dungheaded philosopher and animated frassball were Jadderbadian expletives.

Zed 541 ushered Rudy out a side corridor, before the main door opened. Rudy appreciated the escort, but knew that he and Morticue had much more to discuss in the future.

38
Nessie—is that you?

Zed 541 deposited Rudy into the vault and left. The bench seemed harder than Rudy remembered. He hydrated Twill's body with a drink from the fountain, and felt Twill's consciousness stir. "Are you feeling better, my boy?"

"I'm not sure, Uncle." Twill made an effort to expand outward— or at least that is how Rudy thought of it when one of their personalities sought control of Twill's body—but the effort fell short. "I feel so weak…"

"Rest, if you can, Twill. Let me run this body of yours for a while. I have to say—aches and pains not withstanding—it's rather a treat." Rudy felt a kind of regretful compliance on Twill's part. "Morticue and I had an interesting discussion. Couldn't tell if you were tuned in or not. The worm is not that bad a character deep down—kind of a frustrated scholar in many ways…"

"Who treats humans like dogs and locks them in vaults."

"Well, yes, there is that detail—but humans have been guilty of similar hubris on multiple occasions, lad—over enormous spans of time." Rudy took another sip of water and looked the room over one more time. He supposed that a loose ring of round ports near the ceiling and floor, about the diameter of Twill's pinky finger, were camera feeds. A few, not quite so translucent, might regulate airflow in some way.

"So, I can tell from your thoughts that you have some idea of how this place works, Uncle, although I don't understand the details. Your people must have controlled much magic…"

"Not magic, Twill. Over many many generations we learned how to ask questions of nature. She reveals answers, if you ask simple questions one at a time and control the variables."

Twill was silent for a long moment. "By… experimenting. Like nibbling just a little on the leaf of an unknown plant to be sure more of it won't make you sick or kill you."

"Precisely. 'To-die-or-not-to-die' is rather the ultimate either/or choice. Fortunately, most experiments don't need to be that extreme. A nice 'yes, this is true' or 'no, this is not' works fine in most cases."

"And you call this process science, Uncle?"

"Well, yes. The organized use of the scientific method is called science—practiced by scientists—although that descriptive label is 19th century—that's 1900 years after the birth of a noted religious figure called Jesus Christ—but a much earlier Greek civilization really pioneered a lot of the methodology. Who knows what unrecorded cultures came up with? But somehow rational thinking, politics, and economics all came together beginning in the 17th century to make science legitimate and institutional. Are you dozing boy? No, there you are. Science can be a painfully slow process with lots of back-and-forth and mistakes and problems—but it yields results."

"Houses can fly, ghosts can appear in rooms, flying bugs can sting people, machines pretend to be gods…"

"I'm sure it all seems quite… unbelievable, but you sort of get used to it after a while." Rudy smiled. "And, some of it does seem like magic—even to people who should know better."

"And the worms know this process, too?"

"They do. I suppose any intelligent species—if they get to a certain level—must figure out the techniques in some form."

"How did humans forget it, Uncle?"

"Well, we didn't exactly forget it. Some people use the process unconsciously. It just takes a skeptical mind with some observational skills and imagination—but it takes long-lived civilizations to give lots of people the time and resources to practice the skill systematically. All kinds of disasters can mess that up—like wayward asteroids, and self-destructive, collective stupidity."

"I have seen much collective stupidity, Uncle—and much individual stupidity as well."

144

Rudy chuckled. "That hasn't changed in a million years. Why is that oddly comforting?"

"I have no idea, Uncle. Perhaps because there would be no stories to tell."

Rudy laughed with gusto this time. "Yes, we all love a good story. And speaking of stories, the golden arch that warps spacetime and allows the worms to travel over interstellar distances—that's beyond whatever technology we possessed, and the Jadderbadians seem to be clueless, too. There's an untold story there I would love to hear."

The room trembled. Rudy sensed a difference in the "feel" of the ship. "Perhaps we have landed at last," he murmured.

"So, maybe we can get out of this prison, Uncle. " Twill's voice sounded weaker. "I am ready."

Rudy began pacing the room, looking into every corner. A subtle movement at one of the potential airflow ports caught his attention, but just as he began to move in that direction, the door panel slid open with a high-pitched whine. Rudy turned in time to see a second-molt Jadderbadian lumber into the room, various arms and body pili waving gently.

"You are… to come. Follow me." The creature looked a bit uncomfortable, like groupies weren't his favorite form of entertainment. "No arguments. Follow me, or I will beat you."

That clarified things, thought Rudy. "Where are we going?"

The Jadderbadian partially opened his oral cavity. The pili around it fluttered. He seemed to be the picture of indecision. Finally, his mouth smeared out into what Rudy interpreted as a smile. "You're going to the vet."

"The vet?" Twill's voice in his head sounded weaker.

"A doctor for animals," Rudy supplied.

"What will they do?"

"Probably nothing we will much care for. They specialize in sticking things in various body openings—or sometimes making new openings." To the Jadderbadian Rudy said, "I wish to see Morticue first. Did he authorize this?" Rudy caught sight of motion on the floor, and glanced to his left to see what looked like a bug crawling rather quickly across the floor.

A voice in his head said, "Rudy, can you hear me?"

"Nessie, is that you? Are you pretending to be a cockroach these days?" Rudy caught his breath. He had begun to think he would never hear from Nessie again.

"Groupies don't get wishes." The Jadderbadian's voice startled Rudy. "They don't get to ask questions." Rudy looked up to see the creature begin his next sentence.

"Groupies do…" but then the worm caught sight of the bug zipping toward Rudy's foot. "Groupies attract vermin!" The Jadderbadian moved more swiftly than Rudy could have imagined. In a rather graceful and forceful arc, the alien brought down one heavy foot on Nessie's avatar.

Rudy heard a distinct crunch.

"Come with me," said the Jadderbadian. "No arguments," he continued as he scraped his foot on the floor to remove what was left of the bug. His skin flickered in various tints of pea green, while his oral cavity puckered, and he inspected his foot one last time. He focused a pair of eyes on Rudy. "The doctor is waiting," he said.

39
Morticue's kennel

Twill didn't open his eyes at first. Based on Rudy's memories of veterinary clinics, he expected to smell harsh chemicals with overtones of urine, and perhaps hear the murmured tones of doctors discussing how best to prod, poke, or vivisect him. He did detect the remnant tang of stale urine, but also the rather delicious odor of what must be a kind of stew. He heard chattering human voices and felt soft cushions beneath him. Light filtered through his closed lids strong enough to imply the sun was well up in the sky.

How do you feel, boy? Rudy's consciousness seemed to envelope him, yet Twill could control of his body again, though his muscles felt weak and heavy. He rolled onto his right side, giving a push with his left arm... *Left arm?* Twill snapped his eyes open and beheld a miracle: He now had a complete and unwithered left arm. He flexed the fingers, turned his wrist, and admired the shifting muscles and tendons. *A miracle indeed!*

Yes, they fixed it. Could have knocked me for a loop. I half expected them to eviscerate us, stuff us with cotton—or whatever they use on worm-a-pede planet—and put us in a museum alcove somewhere. Twill tried to process the images Rudy's words generated in their collective memory, and only partially succeeded. In short, the aliens used their magic—or science—to give him a new arm. "Why do you think they did it, Uncle?"

Not sure. If Morticue is responsible—and if we are now in his household as personal pets—and I think we are—maybe he didn't want the neighbors to think he had mistreated animals. Who knows? Let's consider ourselves lucky.

Twill patted his chest. The spiderbot was still gone. *You have not seen Spider Woman's magic spider—her mechanical tool—since you sent it away?*

No. I had to put it into defense mode, though, before they took us to the vet. Can't let the worms get that piece of technology. I'm sure it can find us again, but I don't know where or when.

I hope so, Uncle. Twill admired his left arm again briefly, and then tried to sit up. As he began to fall backward, a strong arm grabbed his right bicep, supporting him.

"Don't rush things. You are still recovering," said a female voice in the trader's language he had learned from Bok's kind.

Twill looked over his shoulder. An attractive woman owned the arm with the strong grip. Her ample breasts strained the fabric of the shift she wore, and locked Twill's gaze with their plentitude. She smiled, fully aware of her powers to mesmerize, and patted him on the shoulder as he settled into a sitting position. He turned toward a small table upon which rested a bowl steaming with the stew smells that were making his stomach growl. "Who..."

"My name is Portae. I used to belong to Mistress Moia, but she's morphing now. I hope I can see her again after, but some say adult masters are scary. The Ambergrands have adopted me. Wasn't that nice of them? They are rather nice, you know. Of course, you don't know, but you will, I think..."

"You've started the talking machine. I know she looks pretty, but you may regret it." Twill glanced to the far corner of the room to his left. It was the one called Fum from the other cage in the transport ship. He sat, tilted back on a sturdy three-legged stool, carving a piece of wood.

"Oh hush, Fum, or I will tell Nulla you've been trying to play with me." Portae picked up the bowl of stew and handed it to Twill. "Eat this," she said to Twill. "You will feel better."

Twill could only manage a grunt. The stew tasted delicious. He spooned it into his mouth while surveying the small room. It contained a cot, several of the three-legged stools, and a corner somewhat obscured by a hanging hide partially concealing a sink and what might be a feeding trough. *Not exactly the Ritz*, he heard Rudy

148

say. Whatever that was.

"You've been asleep for most of the day. I'm glad you're awake. I helped clean you up when Master Morticue brought you home. You have strong, handsome legs—and now two strong arms. They say you are a primitive and a wild boy. You don't look too wild... but maybe you are...Mother always says, 'Be careful of wild boys,' but I think they are exciting..." Portae continued to talk, but her voice quickly turned into an annoying buzz that threatened to fill his head until it might explode. Fum, it appears, spoke the truth.

"Thank you, Portae," Twill said in the middle of a rambling. "I must speak with Fum for a moment." Portae did stop talking, but her mouth opened, offering the portent of more to come. "Alone," Twill added.

"Of course, wild boy," Portae said with a wink. I will check on you later. Twill watched the slow metronome of her hips as she left the room carrying the empty bowl and spoon.

"Told you." Fum blew wood shavings off his carving. It appeared to be the head of a dog—one very much like DS.

"Fum, I'm looking for a girl—one about my age and from my village. She may have a dog with her—much like the one you are carving."

Fum resumed whittling. "Dark hair, chestnut eyes, rather bossy..."

"Yes!" Twill stood up. The adrenaline rush of learning news about Jeeta seemed to clear his head.

"Haven't seen anyone like that." Fum glanced at Twill. "Better sit down, wild boy, before you break your nose."

Twill appeared at Fum's side so quickly that Fum lost his balance on the stool and tumbled to the floor. He still clutched the carving in his left hand, but Twill held his right wrist and the hand bearing the knife. "I'd begin worrying about your own nose—and other body parts," hissed Twill. He hoped he sounded threatening enough. Fum's image was blurring, and blinking didn't seem to help.

"Cool off, wild boy, or I'll start yelling. The mistress will be unhappy. You won't like that." Fum squirmed.

As if on cue, from the next room: "What's going on?" It was a Jadderbadian voice, a bit higher than Morticue's.

"The wild thing is awake." Fum spoke in a loud voice, while looking carefully at Twill. "I think he needs to take a piss." To Twill he said: "Ease up, or it won't go well for either of us."

A burst of deep syllables punctuated with a few shrill sounds came from the next room. Twill turned to look in the direction of the door arch. "What was that?"

"Mistress Selaea is not happy. You've interrupted her morning exercises. She's just compared you to a pile of fungus-coated excrement using a low form of High Jadderbadian." Fum looked Twill up and down with feigned intensity. "You're not quite that bad."

Mistress Selaea soon filled the doorway. One upper tier arm pointed toward Twill. "Release my pet, Twill—or Rudee, whichever beast you are. My husband expects me to treat you well, but I will put you in full harness and implant a chip, if you misbehave. Understood?"

Twill released Fum and stood up. He felt woozy. Rudy commandeered his response. "Understood, Mistress," Twill heard himself saying. "I will do as you command." *Really, Uncle?*

At least for now, son—until we know where we stand. Rudy watched as Selaea pulled a leash of some kind from a pouch in her garment and moved toward him.

"Let's go for a walk," she said, looping a ring around Twill's neck and adjusting its diameter until something clicked into place. "Be a good boy and I'll give you a special treat later."

150

40
Taking a walk

Rudy came forward to control Twill's body. *Wait, I can do this, Uncle*, Twill protested.

I'm sure you can, boy, but I know you are still tired. This may be a good opportunity for me to compare the worm-a-pedes' culture with mine—so we know what we're up against. The door opened to the outside air. Rudy smelled grass; the sweet scents of unfamiliar flowers. Fum walked beside him untethered, humming a tune that was like a Gregorian chant. Rudy somehow felt the huge mass of Selaea behind him, and hoped she wasn't in the habit of tripping over her pets. The ring around his neck rippled like a nervous snake.

They walked up a tunnel that emerged into bright daylight. Rudy stopped and stared. He imagined himself an ant staring up at a maze of sculptured mounds. The above ground portions of Jadderbadian homes looked a little like ziggurats—terraced, irregular pyramids with various ramps and enclosures at different levels. Plain, sandstone-like surfaces alternated with brightly colored rows of glyphs on splashes of terra cotta. The structures soared overhead, a forest of forms beneath the frayed edges of high clouds against a cerulean blue sky.

Rudy stumbled as Selaea's massive body bumped him from behind. He smelled her complex Jadderbadian musk—just a little different from Morticue's. Twill must have a good nose. *A shaman's gift, Uncle. You don't want to eat deadly mushrooms when you are only looking for a prophetic vision.*

"Left, Twill," Selaea commanded. She turned to Fum. "Fum, attend. Keep your kennel mate moving. I have other things to do today besides walking gawking groupies."

Fum gave Twill a token shove. They moved left along a pathway that wound between two impressive towers. A pale groupie with dark, shoulder-length hair stuck his head out a lower window of the tower house on the right. "Hey, Fum, we don't want to see some wild boy in leather rags. Where's your new kennel sister? I like the tattoos on her heiny."

Fum rolled his eyes.

"Fum, ignore that rude barking." Selaea quickened her pace. "That's a good boy."

They passed another house on the left. A pair of groupies waved and yelled exuberant, if garbled, comments from a high circular opening on a frescoed wall. One sported decorative tattoos on his upper chest and tufts of brown hair on his shoulders. The other, a female whose nut brown skin was just a shade darker than Twill's, arched her back so that her ample breasts wiggled. She smiled and winked.

A large male groupie, half again as tall as Twill, and offleash and untended, rounded the lower terrace of the same building at ground level. His eyes glowered beneath a head of bushy red hair. He bared his teeth, keeping close to the building wall. Selaea suspected he was a half-trained attack groupie that had breached his pen.

Selaea nudged Twill to the far side of the walkway and motioned Fum to follow. She spoke to a device on an upper lateral arm that began to glow: "73566, please. I would like to report a loose male groupie on Founder's Path just west of the lake." A pause and then: "He's unleashed. Color bars red-green-pink." Another pause. "Yes, thank you." The armband faded to a neutral gray. Selaea released a burst of air through her mouth. Oral pili fluttered, along with the colors of her skin. "Some pet owners are simply irresponsible," she muttered, to no one in particular.

They continued on the path past the last tower homes. Ahead of them a lake reflected the wispy clouds above it, ringed by aspen-esque trees, their leaves fluttering in a light breeze. Rudy noticed what appeared to be a family of ducks cutting wavelets across the water's surface, but it was the distant stargate that demanded his attention. It arched across the sky, a shifting rainbow of colors that seemed solid one moment and translucently immaterial the next, with a heart of deep ebony enclosed between. *There is a secret we must unravel, Twill.*

How will we do that, Uncle? You said that even Morticue doesn't understand how it works.

We need Nessie to help. She must be somewhere close by—along with our truant spiderbot. Keep your fingers crossed, kid.

And why would I do that? Twill accessed Rudy's memories. *Ah, a cultural thing. I see. We always pat our groins if we want to bring good luck.*

Makes sense, I guess—unless you have Puritans in your family tree.

Selaea led them to a Jadderbadian-sized bench with a clear view of the lake. She sat down with a wheeze of air. Her body pili wilted. "Something wrong with her?" Rudy whispered to Fum.

Fum shrugged. "She's old and close to metamorphosis." He wandered a few steps away near a shrubby bush with three-lobed leaves. Once there he dropped his britches and took a dump.

"Really? We're supposed to relieve ourselves like some barnyard animal?" Rudy looked over his shoulder as if expecting a cop to show up with a summons, but he followed Fum's lead.

"I don't know what a barnyard is," Fum said as he pulled up his pants, "but you better not drop a loaf in the house or piss on the master's carpet." Fum moved back near the bench.

Selaea removed what looked like a wand from a pouch at her side and pointed it at the recent deposits. Rudy jumped when the rod flashed and the poo disappeared in a brown cloud of vapor. "I could have used one of those back in my dog days," Rudy mumbled to himself. "In fact, it might be handy to have right now—for other purposes."

Rudy made a mental note of the pouch in which Selaea kept the wand. She settled her back against the bench. Her pili drooped. She looked as if she might fall asleep.

"So, describe this metamorphosis for me, Fum. Have you seen these worms transform?"

Fum sat on the grass—or at least something that looked a whole lot like the buffalo grass Rudy knew as a boy. Rudy sat beside him. It seemed that Twill's consciousness might fade into sleep too. Fum pointed to a butterfly perched on a nearby flower slowly raising and lowering its wings. "Do you know about these insects that go from green worm to checkered flying adult?"

"Butterflies. Sure. They haven't changed much in a million years. That one looks like ones we called checkerspots."

Fum shrugged. "The masters grow like that spotted wind dancer—that's what we call them—but very slowly. They say some masters live 500 years before they transform. My grandfather saw a transformation when he was a boy. He lived near the transformation-mating grounds along the Eastern Ocean."

"Was he a pet, too?"

"No. Our family stories say he belonged to a wild tribe. My father—his firstborn son—was caught while playing one day too far from home. He became part of Master Kranium's personal kennel." Fum's chest puffed out a little. "Master Kranium was the first god to pass through the gate and greet Prophet Thurwild, you know."

"Yeah, I remember Thurwild," Rudy muttered.

Fum's eyes narrowed. "You couldn't. You are too young and were born in the barbarian north."

Rudy cleared Twill's throat. "I'm a shaman. I talk to spirits. Anyway, it doesn't matter. Tell me more about the metamorphosis. So, your masters change into what—giant wind dancers?"

"Yes." Fum closed his eyes. "I have seen projected visions when the masters look at their magic windows. After their master bodies shrivel and harden and sit for a time—sometimes as long as a year—they split open and beautiful flying forms—they call them Flitters—emerge to spread their wings—all rainbow colored, but with bodies shimmering in greens, yellows, or blue-greens depending on the clan. Groupie choruses help the transformation process—either speeding it up a little or slowing it down depending on the need."

154

Fum looked like he was falling into a blissful trance.

"And then?" Rudy prodded.

Fum's eyes popped open. "Well, pairs emerge together, of course. Females fly ahead to some secluded place. Males follow the pheromone trail and alight near their female. They say a mating dance begins, but groupies usually aren't present to see that."

"So humans—groupies—can assist the metamorphosis of your worm masters?"

"That's what I just said. It's been that way, the Holy Chronicles say, since the days of Thurwild when Kranium and his angels first heard humans sing. They knew such songs would help visiting gods transform properly. Nulla and I will help Masters Morticue and Selaea transform—along with other select groupies owned by various clan members." Fum's chest puffed out again. "It's an honor."

Rudy sighed. "I'm sure." A pause. "What happens then?"

"Females lay their eggs in the Eastern Ocean. Young hatch until the water is black with them, but not all survive to become gods, of course." Fum's voice trailed off.

"Of course? Why of course?"

"Many young get eaten. Some, even by each other. Only the smartest, fastest—and most ruthless larval godlets survive to crawl ashore as Firsties."

"Firsties?" Rudy prodded.

"Of course, first instars," Fum said, as if talking to a dolt. "They have just one body segment and three legs, and are taken care of by Seconds—second instars." Fum paused. "You really don't know anything about gods, do you?"

"Nope," Rudy replied. "Dumb as a three-legged Firstie."

Fum sniffed. "Don't be sacrilegious."

Rudy looked into Fum's eyes. "Wouldn't you and—Nulla—rather be free?"

"Wild, you mean?" Fum's brows furrowed. "Certainly not. Who wants to sit around in the forest in scratchy leather clothes and pick lice off their neighbor? Maybe get eaten by packs of rifwolves or a stalking caratt? The masters keep us clean and safe."

Rudy sighed again. "Point taken. But I'm sure the wild—group-ies—like your father—don't want to be captured. Otherwise, they would wander into Masterville here and lock themselves in a cage." That swordless Viking that Selaea reported to the truant officers didn't look too content with his lot, he thought. Rudy felt Twill's consciousness arousing, aware of what Rudy was trying to do. "Where do most wild groupies live? Near the city or far away, like the Eastern Ocean?

Fum opened his mouth to answer, but Selaea bolted awake with an interrupted snore. She glanced at one of her wristbands. "Oh, my—look at the time. We must be getting back. Morticue should be returning soon." Selaea turned to focus a pair of eyes on Fum. "Fum, attend. Watch this wild groupie on the way home." She patted the leash connecting her to Rudy with one lateral hand while using a couple of other arms to push herself upright. "Let's go home."

Rudy looked around for a place to take a quick piss while he still had the chance. Also, he automatically scanned the ground hoping to see a friendly mechanical roach—or some other evidence that Nessie was nearby. No such luck.

41
AI and friends

Mnemosyne had miscalculated. Or, more accurately, one of her low scenario projections came to pass: The volcanism she had initiated to ward off the Jadderbadian attack on her citadel induced more tectonic forces than she had prepared for. Her mechanical avatars scurried like ants to repair damage to lower chambers housing her memory cores. They also built new conduits to move threatened core databases. Mnemosyne struggled to balance power and resources. Sometimes, at what seemed the most inopportune times, she thought of Rudy—although much of his neural matrix now resided in the brain of Twill. Rudy had added another dimension to her existence.

At a critical juncture when she thought all her efforts might fail, she heard a voice: *Perhaps I can help*, it said. Mnemosyne thought it was Rudy for a few nanoseconds, but it wasn't. *You have roiled up some forces here, Mnemosyne, but I have some tricks tucked away in caverns and fissures where you would least expect them.*

Gradually, stress points eased on the citadel's resources. Mnemosyne's avatars began to catch up. She wanted to respond to the voice, but realized she wasn't sure how...

I can hear you. Got you covered. Some of your circuits are organic, after all, and the organic network that permeates this old planet makes up my "brain," if you will. My name's Gaia, by the way. It's a primate moniker, but it will do.

If Mnemosyne had had a jaw, it would have flopped open. Instead, she felt a spontaneous surge in her neural matrix. It made perfect sense when she took the time to properly crosslink her data sets. "The Earth itself, then, is aware and sentient." She paused for several nanoseconds. "The untold billions of bacterial and fungal cells that undergird the biosphere can act as a kind of collective entity that is—aware and curious—like me; like humans."

That's the gist of things. Humans are my metazoan arms and legs, as it were—although they delude themselves into thinking they are in charge. And now I have a soul mate from across the stars. Mnemosyne, meet Hydra, my Jadderbadian counterpart.

Charmed, said Hydra. *My metazoans never quite managed to create a silicon-based entity as complex as yourself, but they'll get around to it, I'm sure. Apex multicell conglomerates can be fiendishly clever that way.*

"So you two are the ones who facilitated the entry of my gnat drone into the command transport," Mnemosyne concluded.

Gaia and Hydra would have nodded, had they heads, but Mnemosyne sensed their assent anyway. She also sensed their grasp of her desires. *Yes,* they affirmed, *we can assist you in re-establishing contact with Rudy/Twill. They both will die soon, if we don't, so we'd better get to it. Twill's brain is not quite up to hosting his Uncle Rudy. Metazoans are quite fragile and transient, as you know—although I commend you on the job you've done preserving Rudy,* Gaia added.

Mnemosyne understood the risks when she had proposed their merger, but it seemed the only solution at the time. "Can we save them? Both of them?"

We have a plan, said Gaia. At least one of them should survive. Although, there are some other variables in the universe at large we haven't discussed. They may complicate our efforts. We'll try to fill you in as we get this little eruption you've caused under control. If Gaia had had a tongue she would have clucked it. You younger intelligences need to learn to keep your circuits cool—even when disaster appears ready to slap you into oblivion.

42
Crisis

"Ohmyohmy, OH MY," Selaea muttered as she bent over the fallen form of Rudy/Twill. The six limbs of her upper segments waved in frustration while the arms of her basal segment searched for a pulse in the fallen animal. "Morticue will be very unhappy if you die on me." She turned to Fum, who was orbiting Twill's body with some agitation. "Fum, attend. Go fetch that strong young second who lives next to our unit. He should be home this time of day. Tell him a pet is down. We need a mobile gurney or PortaCage, if he has one."

Fum completed one more half orbit and complied. Selaea looked around. They weren't far from home, but the streets lay empty, and no one gawked from the windows overhead. Where were the busybodies when you needed them? Selaea had noticed that the wild groupie started weaving a little on the way home, but hadn't been too concerned. One never knew what to expect from untrained groupies.

Ah, there is a pulse, she thought, as she found the place on Twill's neck where an artery fed the creature's brain. She felt proud of herself for remembering that feature of groupie anatomy. She usually let the animal caretaker attend to such matters. Selaea activated the communicator on her second tier lateral arm and punched Morticue's symbol on the pad. "Complicating news, Dearest," she began. "The wild groupie is ill. He collapsed on the way home from a visit to the lake...Yes, I've called for help... I'm fine. See you soon. Tell the vet we appreciate her making time for an appointment. Yes, yes. I know it will strain the budget this quarter."

By the time she had broken the connection with Morticue, she saw Jorge, her neighbor, galloping toward her with Fum trotting along beside him pulling a gurney. Selaea fondly remembered those limber second instar days, when her body flexed easily and she could bend properly for that six-limbed lope. She and Morticue had explored a lot of Jadderbad's coves and inlets with youthful abandon.

Jorge arrived winded. His pili fluttered in the breeze of rapid breathing, and he flashed a rainbow of concerned colors. "Oh," he said, "so sorry about your pet." He focused two eyes on Twill's form, now moving a little and groaning. His third eye cocked with a concerned glance toward Selaea.

"Thank you," she replied. "Morticue is quite interested in this wild groupie. He would be terribly upset if anything happened to him." Selaea admired Jorge's strong arms as he gently lifted Twill onto the gurney. Ah, if she were only two hundred years younger, she wouldn't mind metamorphosing next to that one's pupal case. Fum hovered around the gurney and helped a little, making sure his kennel mate's limbs didn't flop over the edges.

Jorge verified that the groupie was securely strapped in place, and grabbed the tether with a lower arm. "We'll get this one home safely. I'm pleased to help a good neighbor—and distinguished council member—at such a time." His oral cavity fluttered with a wave of assurance.

Selaea expected she would owe him a favor in the future.

"Your other pet is quite well-trained," Jorge added, as Fum took a standard position on Selaea's left.

"Yes, he's a keeper," Selaea said as they began moving toward home. "Both he and his mate Nulla have been a joy—for the most part."

Fum rolled his eyes, but seemed to walk with just a bit more spring in his step.

During all the excitement—perhaps while Selaea admired the flexing beauty of Jorge's biceps—no one noticed a small mechanical spider scurry from the cover of decorative bushes at the side of the path. It promptly latched onto the gurney from below, burned an access hole so that it could scamper beneath Twill's pant leg and ultimately nestle, like a contented tick, in its accustomed spot on Twill's chest.

43
Immediate action required

Rudy's consciousness coalesced just a moment before Twill's. Rudy opened Twill's eyes to discover that they were back on the pallet in Morticue's kennel—alone.

"What happened, Uncle?"

Rudy could have really used a cup of coffee—something he hadn't thought much about since he and Nessie had had their last virtual breakfast together. "I'm afraid our union is giving your body fits, Twill. Nessie said that might happen."

"I did and it has—and I would be pleased to have coffee again soon," Mnemosyne added.

"Nessie! You're back. Glad you didn't put all your smarts into one mechanical cockroach." Rudy felt a warm glow—a rare feeling for an old curmudgeon.

"Spider Woman." Twill's consciousness seemed as fragile as morning fog. "And— Mother Gaia? I thought only shamans could speak with you."

Only shamans tend to listen, said Gaia.

"Mother who?" Rudy became aware of another intelligence— and perhaps another…

My name is Hydra, another voice said. *I am the mind of Jadder-bad—the world of Master Morticue and his kind. Pleased to make your formal acquaintance, terrestrial metazoans.*

"Damn. Your body never evolved to host a convention, Twill." Rudy felt adrift among massive forms and forces—like a minnow among whales—or like virtual heroes in a Matrix movie.

"That is correct." Mnemosyne's awareness seemed as smooth and sharp as flint, compared to the other entities. "We must act quickly to save both you and Twill from destruction. Gaia and Hydra can help."

"Do we have better odds than we had when that asteroid dropped in for a visit?" Rudy thought he could anticipate the answer.

"While I haven't done a formal analysis…" Mnemosyne began, but she didn't have time to complete the thought.

The door to the kennel hissed open. Morticue swept in. "Ah, you are awake, wild thing. How do you feel?"

"Like a wet sock with a headache, if you must know." Morticue's body towered above him—a swaying green tree with gesticulating branches.

"Ah, poor thing. I'm sorry you suffer. I had anticipated more conversation. You are either the answer to my life's desire of finding a kindred spirit in this humbling universe—or a precocious pet with severe delusions." Morticue patted Twill's head with one three-fingered hand. "I haven't decided."

Rudy winced from the clumsy pat and closed Twill's eyes again. He wished he really felt as good as a wet sock with a headache.

Mnemosyne: "We must act now."

Gaia to Hydra: *Will Morticue's neural structure really be adequate to the task? I know Jadderbadians have those post-cranial neural nodes, but still…*

Hydra to Gaia: *Well, I guess we'll find out, won't we?*

Rudy: "Hello, the patient is listening, you know. What's going on?"

Mnemosyne ignored him. "I have made the proper adjustments on my end. Do you see the schematics? I will employ the spider, if you concur."

Go for it, said Gaia and Hydra in unison.

Morticue bellowed. He sprang from his partial crouch over Twill like a catapult with a severed tether. "You have bitten me!" Morticue swatted at his first segment torso, but the spider was quick—and rather small by Morticue's standards. It soon found a comfortable spot away from prying three fingered hands, and waited for the injection to take effect.

162

44
Getting to know you

Rudy had learned to enjoy watching trees fall down when he and his first wife Myra toppled beetle-killed pines with chain saws on their mountain property in Colorado. But he had never perched in a tree as it fell. That appeared to be the case now, as he peered out from the rapidly blurring eyes of Master Morticue, in whose body he now resided.

Rudy's thoughts must be racing because the world slowed down. Events oozed by, tableaus in slow motion. Twill lay on the pallet, but turned his head to look toward him. The door of the room slowly slid aside. Rudy saw his mate, Selaea and pet, Fum, waiting to come in. *No, that can't be right…*

"It certainly isn't right," complained Morticue "That is *my* mate and *my* pet…and I am most definitely not a tree. You haven't really seen a tree until…"

"…you've seen the towering silja forest on the west continent. Ah…I see what you mean." Rudy realized that on some level he was Morticue, and Morticue was he. He felt a bit nauseous. His… Morticue's body,…tilted at a more severe angle now. Through a rapidly advancing visual blur, he noticed that Twill was trying to sit up. Selaea and Fum had advanced into the room. Both turned their heads in his direction, their respective mouths beginning to open.

This kind of confusion is not going to work. It will be crippling. Rudy recognized Gaia's voice, as if she were trying to talk through a wall.

I think if we localize Rudy's matrix in these two lateral ganglia, we can avoid those problems. Hydra's voice reminded Morticue of a young second instar he once knew. Reja was her name. Of course, that was a long time, and a molt before he met Selaea. Reja created memorials for some city not far from the Ruins of Haptar. He sometimes wondered how pledging to her might have changed the course of his life.

"She sounds like my third wife, Tamara." Rudy paused to remember his mid-life crisis wife. "She painted murals—or at least the sky part of some murals. It was sort of an assembly line process: The company had sky painters, foreground painters, human or animal figures-in-the-distance painters…"

"…and they sold these images to decorate living spaces," Morticue finished the thought.

"Yes. Didn't see her often—I mean, I was busy myself. Really absorbed with the Biomic Network Algorithm by then, and spent tons of time at the university—but boy when I did see her…"

"…you enjoyed copious amounts of sexual activity." Morticue paused.

"I can see why you'd be curious about that. But sex is distracting, Morticue. You've accomplished a lot in your 421 years, I can see that… and now here you are, helping to colonize a planet in the galactic boondocks."

"And you have created the Biomic Network Algorithm. I'm not quite sure my civilization has a parallel formulation. We must discuss this further."

Gentlemen, Gaia interrupted, if I may use that term in its most generic sense. *I believe Hydra and I—with some assistance from Mnemosyne—have stabilized your—symbiosis. You should be able to communicate without identity confusion.*

"I believe you're correct," said Morticue and Rudy in unison. "But, I still seem to remember things…" Rudy would have scratched his head, if he had had one.

Morticue might have tried to scratch his head, but his body was about to strike the ground. "I remember episodes of Rudy's life as well."

There will be some of that, said Hydra. *Maybe a lot. I think you can deal with it. But this arrangement is permanent, you know.*

Rudy's memory matrix has merged with your lateral ganglia, Morti-cue. They can still perform their autonomic functions, but you might notice a bit of twitching now and then in your lower limbs.

Morticue's body hit the ground, but the flooring was pliant. It didn't hurt much. "I understand. I may twitch."

"Which means, as a corollary," Rudy concluded, "that I'm mortal again. I will only live as long as Morticue does." Rudy paused as Morticue's body settled into place on the floor. "I'm good with that, too," he said—and he meant it. He supposed the weariness of being an itinerant parasitic intelligence was getting to him.

Selaea bent over Morticue and gripped two of his hands with hers. "Are you all right, dear one?"

Morticue pushed himself partly upright with two of his postcra-nial segment arms. "I believe so. Let me get up." He released his grip on Selaea's hands and twisted into an upright position. "I'm fine." He absently brushed dust from his middle segment circlet. His chromatophores flickered in shades of blue.

"What happened?" Selaea's eye pili fluttered upward. She no-ticed Fum wandering around the room. "Fum, attend," she com-manded and Fum took a position by her left leg.

"Well, I came in to check on Twill. The vet should be here soon—and perhaps Edelphine. He is keeping three eyes on every-thing—worried about the wild creature being a security threat. And when I bent down…" Morticue wasn't quite sure how much to admit to. What exactly would Edelphine do if he learned he had been "in-fected" with an alien intelligence?

Edelphine reminds me of a hall monitor with delusions of gran-deur.

"Quiet," Morticue muttered.

"I beg your pardon?" Selaea's eye pili waggled, then arched. "What happened when you bent down?" Selaea flashed concerned shades of amber. "And why is your leg twitching?"

"The alien creature," Morticue began, "the alien creature sort of bit me."

"Sort of bit you?" Selaea repeated.

The door chimed. "Dr. Beta Singe and Commander Edelphine Shurter are here to see Master Ambergrand," announced the house AI.

"Yes, bit me," Morticue confirmed.

"And where is Twill now?" Selaea's amber colors shaded toward red.

"On the pallet, of course." Morticue turned his eyes to focus on the pallet.

The pallet seems quite empty. *The boy has escaped. Good for him... I think*, Rudy added.

Fum, standing beside Selaea, shrugged his shoulders.

The door slid open as the house AI cheerfully declared, "Protocol override."

"Where is the wild groupie?" Edelphine waved a tablet in Morticue's direction. "Ambassador Kranium has authorized me to take possession of the creature for the safety and security of New Jadderbad."

"Perhaps we should consult a real medical doctor to check on that leg twitch, dear one," Selaea advised Morticue, casting a brief glance toward the groupie vet. Then she advanced a few steps toward Edelphine to examine the orders more closely.

"Ahhh, it appears that the wild groupie has escaped." Morticue gestured toward the pallet. "He was there just before I fell."

Edelphine's chromatophores pulsed an intense shade of red. "And you fell because...?"

"The creature bit him, he says," Selaea offered, as she scanned the official paperwork displayed on the tablet.

Fum's brows furrowed as he looked up at Mistress Selaea. "Twill's teeth couldn't pierce Master's hide. Did the spider come back and bite him?"

"Quiet, pet," Morticue ordered. "Fum attend." Morticue flashed warning colors at Fum, but his pet was still looking up at Selaea.

"Spider? What spider?" Edelphine bent his frame so that he nearly touched Fum's shoulder with his head pili.

Fum backed up a step. "The mechanical spider that did something to Twill so that he spoke like two people. Twill said an ancient uncle spoke to him." Fum displayed a crooked smile—and finally noticed Morticue's flashes of caution, and tardily shut his mouth.

Edelphine focused all three eyes on Morticue. His pili stood rod still, like snakes ready to strike. "Were you bitten by such a mechanical spider?"

Morticue raised all his arms and did a slow pirouette—a difficult move for a Jadderbadian. "Do you see any spiders?"

Edelphine straightened to his full height and looked at Morticue, Fum, and Selaea in turn. "The Ambergrands shall consider themselves in quarantine as of this moment." He pointed to the Thunderclub Clan insignia on his upper segment circlet. "I will consult with Ambassador Kranium and get back to you. " Edelphine looked pointedly at Morticue. "Understood?"

After a slightly longer than polite pause, Morticue nodded his affirmation.

"My men will be posted outside," Edelphine added, as he turned to leave.

He does wear those circlets a bit too tight, doesn't he? Rudy's thoughts echoed in Morticue's head.

Morticue struggled to keep another leg tremor from showing as he sat on a bench near the kennel door. He needed a drink—preferably a fermented one.

Now you're talking, confirmed Rudy. I see you like something called Larval Stout23. That sounds interesting. Bring it on!

167

45
Finding Jeeta

Twill took a deep breath. Praise to Spider Woman and mother Gaia!

Twill had come to appreciate the wisdom of his Uncle Rudy, but he was a relative who had stayed too long at the table, as his poor grandfather used to say. Twill finally felt whole—and well again. He turned his head to watch as Morticue, the enormous Jadderbadian, tilted like a tall pine and began to fall. Twill struggled to sit up on the pallet and place his feet on the floor.

"Psst. Wild boy. Down here." Twill looked near the junction of two walls behind his pallet where a panel had slid aside that covered a ventilation shaft. A woman's dirty face poked out far enough that she could catch his eye. "Someone who calls herself Jeeta is looking for you."

Twill turned long enough to see Morticue complete his descent to the floor, terminated by a crash whose vibrations he could feel on the soles of his feet. The room door opened and figures entered. The Jadderbadians moved toward Morticue. Fum cast a quick glance in his direction, but said nothing.

"Quickly!" the dirty face hissed. Twill did move quickly, and crawled into the shaft that the woman had left vacant. He heard her movements in front of him, and crawled on hands and knees as quietly as if he were hunting along the creek by his village. The shaft changed directions twice, broadened a little, then angled upward toward a small platform. Dirty-face squirmed until she could get her body at a right angle to Twill and turned her head toward him. "I'm Nulla, Fum's mate. I know someone who knows someone. They have an impatient wild person in their kennel they would like to get rid of. She asks for you."

Twill's eyes widened. "Jeeta! She's all right?"

Nulla snorted. "She's fine. It's all the other pets of Master Tork that are out of sorts." Nulla nodded to a fork in the tunnel ahead. "I go right up there, back to my room before I'm missed. You go left. That leads to the outside. One of Tork's pets will be there."

Twill took a deep breath. He briefly considered that Nulla might be trying to trick him for some reason, but didn't think so. "Thank you," he said.

"I have a wild cousin," she replied. "He's a scruffy, skinny little thing with a sharp tongue that eats too much of my food when he's here—like you," she added, with a fragment of a smile at the edges of her mouth. "Make sure you get lost and stay that way." Nulla turned and took her planned path to the right.

Twill followed the tunnel to the left and crawled upward several meters before it leveled off. He could see light ahead of him shining through a circular, crosshatched panel. He eventually got close enough that his nose touched the panel. He smelled fresh air—and unfresh human sweat.

"You the one Jeeta's lookin' for?" said a soft male voice just beyond the panel.

Twill jumped even though he had smelled the man's presence, but said, "Yes, I'm Twill."

"I'm going to move this panel at the count of three," said the voice, "then get your wild ass out of there. Don't be throwing any spells in my direction either, magic boy. Jeeta told us all about you." Gravel crunched as the man shifted position. "And hurry. There's a master not far down the path."

46
Under the influence

“ “Is that you talking or the Larval Stout23?” Selaea sat down beside Morticue on the bench in his study. It had been less than an hour since Edelphine had left. He probably was just getting to Kranium's embassy headquarters about now. “You can't really be infected with an alien intelligence—with some ancient groupie preserved as a neural matrix by a mechanical spider? That sounds like... sounds like...”

“Sounds like I'm crazy?” Morticue burped and patted his oral cavity. “I'm not. We talked about the wild groupie named Twill being infected while I was in transit to New Jadderbad. I'm sure you recall. Now this Ru-dee creature resides in my lateral ganglia somewhere. Except for the occasional twitching, he's proving to be an interesting—if sometimes annoying—companion.”

“I wasn't going to say crazy—I was going to say surreal fiction—those nonsense stories you read sometimes.” Selaea paused. “And if what you are saying is true, then where is this spider? You showed Edelphine that you weren't concealing anything.”

Oh, show her, Morticue. There are no secrets between spouses, right? Rudy's voice sounded a bit different in his head—some words a little slurred. This alien appeared to be sharing his intoxication. Was nothing sacred? *This Stout23 is quite nice, worm man. I applaud your taste in fermented beverages.*

“The creature burrowed beneath my cuticle, dear one.” Morticue lifted one lateral arm. A raised area rather like a pustule formed on the surface of his skin and grew larger. A pair of small legs appeared from an opening enlarging at the center of the mound, followed by more legs and a roundish body flashing azure colors that were meant to be appeasing.

Selaea inched away from him on the bench anyway. "Oh my." Her oral pili fluttered.

"It doesn't hurt," Morticue explained. "Must be a local anesthetic involved like the kind biting insects use—and the Stout23 helps as well." The spider re-embedded itself beneath Morticue's cuticle and the pustule receded. "Anyway, dear one, this experience will contribute to my research. Think of the papers I can write! The Academy of Natural Philosophers should be quite pleased. I'm sure there is much I can do before the final stages of metamorphosis."

"Perhaps," Selaea offered. "Sometimes metamorphosis has a way of sneaking up on you."

Morticue waved dismissively with several arms. "Ah, we have years yet, dear one—perhaps decades."

Selaea stood up. She flashed a mixture of colors and scents that Morticue couldn't quite parse. "Will you be all right for a few minutes, dearest? I just remembered something I must do. I will have the AI be alert for a message from Edelphine or Kranium."

"Thurtainly...I mean certainly, my dear. I have some things I need to attend to as well."

Selaea left.

Well now—any idea what Edelphine—or this Kranium fellow— might do? Rudy sighed—or at least Rudy's virtual, trapped-in-an-alien's-body-equivalent. *Hope for the best, but prepare for the worst, we humans say.*

"Swim free as a hatchling, but scan the waters with the pili of a Thirdie, is what we say, but the sentiment is similar." Morticue stood up and began pacing—rather carefully, like the impaired and prudent Thirdie he was. "I suppose I could be officially quarantined and thoroughly examined—not a particularly pleasant prospect. I hate doctors."

I hear you. Rudy still wasn't prepared to forgive Tom Benton for swiping his neural matrix.

"Selaea and I could be deported and examined. We would have to share metamorphosis on the overcrowded shores of Lake Havershad back on Jadderbad—since we lost our claim to Placid Cove when we came here."

Ah. Lake Havershad is crowded and polluted, I see. You Jadderbadians rather messed up your planet too, it would seem. Rudy couldn't help feeling a little prideful—if that was the right term— that human beings weren't the only creatures who could screw up.

Morticue felt compelled to rebut that statement, but he couldn't—as his alien guest undoubtedly knew.

While we're waiting on the whimsy of the powers that be, old boy, can you bring up the image of the stargate on your computer system? I'd like another look at that. Rudy still admired the improbable audacity of what some other genius must have created—and just a bit annoyed that he hadn't thought of it first, even if he was an ecologist, and not one of those number-crunching physicists who thought they were better than people in the "soft" sciences.

Morticue sat down at his tech console and touched the proper controls. A view of the golden arch sprang into existence on the main screen. It literally looked like a tear in the fabric of the sky, with clouds frayed in ribbons where they met the curvature of the phenomenon. Rounded cylinders, like overgrown gel capsules, sat on a platform in front of the arch. The dwarfed figures of several Jadderbadians moved around the static cylinders, while automata removed cargo from some, and escorted passengers from others.

So, the wormhole—or whatever it is—is always "open for business" so to speak?

"It always has been. I actually found the stargate when I was just a three-armed Firstie. I had snuck away from a boring set of lessons. Our academy was near the frontier at the time."

Really! Rudy found it hard to imagine the tadpolian version of Morticue.

"I was foolish enough to step beneath the arches—and I found myself in your world—although I didn't know it at the time, of course. I just knew that it was a magical—and seemingly empty— world. It was near dark and stars began to appear. We rarely see them on Jadderbad, you know. The arch glowed overhead and made everything ripple. I began to get scared. I finally ran back through the arch… back to Jadderbad and the shores of my birthing cove."

Then what? Rudy prodded, although he was beginning to see imagery from Morticue's recalled memories. He also perceived the yearning that had led Morticue back through the arch in his older years.

"I made the mistake of rushing to tell a thirdie. It happened to be a member of the Thunderclub Clan—the same vapor-brained clan Edelphine belongs to. This one was an RP—a Religious Partisan. In those days their creed was so strict that they didn't believe in other worlds. He bit off the middle finger of my right lateral hand for telling such an outrageous lie." Morticue flexed his finger, now regrown. "That was before anyone even bothered to confirm my story. Many RPs to this day don't believe in other worlds. Most live in monasteries on the Southern Continent so that they can ignore the existence of the arch more easily."

Ah, yes. I've known a few colleagues who would sympathize with their problem. Rudy tried to remember the name of a teacher he once knew that refused to catch the flu because obviously viruses didn't really mutate and evolve—but it wouldn't come to him. *I see from your memories that Edelphine is a member of that sect. How did he make it to Earth?*

"It's my understanding that Ambassador Kranium offered to pay Thunderclubs vast credit bonuses to come and defend the colony. They do have sufficient aggressive tendencies." Morticue flexed his regrown finger again. "This finger never has worked quite properly… anyway, the bonuses led to a kind of selective amnesia where other worlds are concerned."

Fascinating. I have another question… Rudy began, but Selaea burst into the room before he could complete the thought.

She flashed like a strobe light in alarming shades of red. "Problems, dearest!" She struggled for breath, drawing air into and out of her nasal slits with an audible whistle. "I contacted some friends on the Council to see if anyone had sensory probes in the Ambassador's chambers. Of course, someone did. Edelphine has convinced Kranium that… that…"

"Yes, dear one," Morticue prodded.

"...that we should be terminated—as threats to the safety and harmony of New Jadderbad—and abominations in the eyes of the Prophet." Selaea fidgeted in place, her pili fluttering in seemingly random waves of confusion.

"Terminated?" Morticue's own color display flickered in shades of orange.

"Abominations in the eyes of the Prophet," Selaea repeated. "What will Grand Disciple Starke think? We'll surely lose our seats near the chorus."

"We'll lose our real seats along with all other essential body parts if we are terminated... but you must be mistaken. They wouldn't terminate us... I'm a respected Natural Philosopher; you are an honored member of the Council..."

Never underestimate the survival instincts of a career politician, my body mate—or the aggressive impulses of a zealot worm...

"What can we do?" Morticue felt quite sober now, as did Rudy.

Selaea turned to face the image of the stargate in front of her mate. "We must return home. We must find friends and allies on Jadderbad who can help us."

Which brings me to the question I was going to ask anyway— Rudy felt like the proctor of some exam during Morticue's academic career, adept at asking difficult—and annoying, if you didn't have the answer—questions. *—what's it going take to get tickets on one of those pods? I'd opt for express, one-way tickets myself—assuming, of course, that you can't just walk through, like in the good old days when you were a firstie.*

Good old days. Morticue indulged himself with memories of swimming in the birthing cove, naked and naïve. "No, it's not quite that simple anymore, my alien parasite. Thanks for reminding me."

47
Escape

"You're bringing the pets?" Morticue's oral cavity gaped open as he moved backward in the elevator to make room for Salaea and her entourage.

"Just Fum and Nulla, dear one. I couldn't leave them. The house AI will take care of Portae until someone from pet control can pick her up." Selaea urged the two pets inside and handed Morticue a bag that he could barely hold with two arms.

"We are running for our lives. I trust you understand that." Morticue pushed the proper spots on the controls, and the elevator began its descent to the transport garage below. *And you know I'm willing to wager that our friend Edelphine has posted goons somewhere nearby to keep an eye—or three—on us,* Rudy added.

Goons? Morticue tried to find the proper image among the Rudy's memories...

"Certainly, I understand, but we should not look like we are running." Selaea patted Fum and Nulla briefly on their respective heads and moved them into position beside her. "My Council ID should give us passage. I will declare a family emergency. We just need to move quickly. I have a link with a Council ally who will give me some warning when Edelphine leaves the chambers."

What do we have in the way of weapons, Morticue, or are we just going to flash some ugly colors at any Thunderclub warriors that might show up? Rudy asked. "I do have the laser in the spider, although it needs a few seconds to recharge between firings," added Mnemosyne.

Morticue had nearly forgotten about the alien artificial intelligence. He also felt the stirrings of other entities in his head: The planetary intelligences, Gaia and Hydra. He felt the simmering pressure of a kind of schizophrenic panic building in his mind. He also felt the itchy stirrings of the spider beneath the cuticle of the armpit where it resided.

Before Morticue could respond to any of the voices in his head, the elevator hummed to a halt. The doors opened to reveal the parking platform, empty at the moment. Everyone moved out of the elevator and turned right to where the transport should be parked. *Ah, yes*, thought Morticue, *this might not be difficult at all...*

But just as that merry thought exposed itself, a scarlet blanket of alarm chastely cloaked it. Three Jadderbadian goons—Morticue understood the term now—appeared from some dark corner as if conjured by a magician. *Oh boy. We need some heavy artillery...*

Morticue raised his spider-concealing arm. He felt a brief prick of pain as the spider partially emerged. Then he saw a flash of red light that connected with one of the goon guards, forming a dark and oozing wound. The guard twitched and proceeded to fall.

The second guard moved forward. He was a husky second instar. He raised all three of his postcranial segment arms with the three-fingered palms all pointed forward in a classic HALT gesture. His three lower arms all reached for weapons secured in a belt girdling that segment. The guard then started to twitch and wobble with no apparent reason—until Morticue noticed three rods of wood sticking out of the guard's cuticle near the body's ventral midline—beneath which his hearts pumped, at least for the moment.

Nice shots, Jeeta! Where did you come from? Remind me not to get you mad. Partially under Rudy's direction, Morticue turned his head to see a wild female groupie holding a primitive bow standing next to the Twill groupie, who held a case with several feathered, wooden shafts. Morticue quickly grasped the bow and arrow concept from Rudy's memories of "cowboys and Indians." The groupie dog, Dark Shadow, barked at him...or at something approaching him.

Morticue turned his head back around to face the third guard, who loomed above him with the cavernous hole of a disruptor pointed at his chest. Abruptly, that weapon fell, clattering to the floor next to the barking dog. The guard placed two of his upper segment hands over his face, while the third arm flailed about. Morticue noticed that Fum held a Pooh-Be-Gone with both of his hands, pointed in the direction of the third guard, now teetering about and quite unable to see. Fum must have pulled the frass disruptor from Selaea's pouch where she always kept it. Fum lowered the device. "That will teach you to mess with my master," he said with authority, before glancing up at Selaea as if to gauge her level of approval.

Morticue dashed toward the transport. Selaea followed his lead after snatching the Pooh-Be-Gone from Fum, urging the pets to hurry. Twill, Jeeta, and Dark Shadow moved more slowly in that general direction.

While running, Rudy took charge of Morticue's body—including his mouth—in the excitement of the unexpected reunion. "What are you doing here, Twill? And I see you've found Jeeta—as well as DS."

Twill craned his neck and squinted at him. "Is that really you in there, Uncle? It sounds like you." Clutching the quiver of arrows with his right hand and arm, he placed his recently repaired left hand on Jeeta's shoulder. "Jeeta really found me, wise uncle, and reminded me that however annoying you are, you are still family... sort of. She found a network of wild humans nearby—ones who choose not to be pets."

Fum stuck his tongue out at Twill.

"I told her what happened in Morticue's kennel," Twill continued, "and she—with Nulla's help—figured out what Edelphine was up to. The wild groupies use bows much like my tribe, Uncle, and that is Jeeta's favorite weapon."

They arrived at the vehicle. "Lucky for both of us, boy. Let's get aboard this transport quickly, while we still can." Rudy/Morticue gestured toward the pod vehicle. Selaea was already urging Fum and Nulla to enter. Two of the guard/goons lay still on the ground, but the third was moaning and rolling around on the pavement. "Looks like those Pooh-Be-Gones should come with warning labels."

"We obviously don't belong to you," Twill began. "We would

177

hinder your escape if we came with you…"

"Can you drop us off before you get to the arch station?" Jeeta asked.

"We can!" Morticue overrode Rudy's control of their collective body. "But let's get aboard. Now." Rudy apologized. *Sorry, old worm. It was the heat of the moment, you know.*

They strapped themselves in place quickly. The interior of the vehicle smelled with the musk of previous Jadderbadian occupants, and the walls glowed in appeasing shades of azure. Morticue touched the control pad on a raised area that already featured the arch symbol, a common destination. The vehicle accelerated along the track and out of Morticue's residential garage.

"It won't be long until we reach the arch, groupies." Morticue looked at Twill and Jeeta in turn. "Where must you get off? I need to program a stop."

"Anywhere near the warehousing district. I can find my way from there." Jeeta let Twill help her put the quiver on her back and she repositioned her bow. She fiddled with the safety restraining straps, but they weren't designed for pets. She ended up sitting cross-legged next to Twill on the over-large bench.

"We will find some way to stay in touch, Uncle." Twill looked at Jeeta.

"We will," Jeeta confirmed. "Magic boy here is pretty clever — even when the magic part doesn't always work." She smiled at Twill. DS hopped onto the bench and settled his head on Jeeta's leg.

Morticue successfully programmed a stop at a street that he knew passed a food and pharmaceutical warehouse. Six of his hands danced around the tall blinking console as if he were playing a musical instrument. As Twill and Jeeta moved into position to jump out of the transport, Morticue noticed another vehicle approaching from behind on the maglev track. At the moment it was still a silver speck, but growing in size. "Frass! That third goon must have recovered enough to follow with another transport." Morticue rather liked the new word in his vocabulary. "You two groupies better stay with us. We'll figure it out as as we go." *That's the spirit, my worm*

178

ride! They can leave weapons in this pod and pretend to be a pair of homeless rescue groupies we're taking with us.

Morticue cancelled the programmed warehouse stop and accelerated the transport pod. They arrived at a nearly empty terminal—a stroke of good luck. A security checkpoint booth seemed to hunker like a scared animal beneath the pulsing majesty of the golden arch, the silhouette of its guard occupant behind a window like the dark pupil of the beast's eye.

On closer inspection, the guard became merely a bored-looking amber male second instar. He had just stifled a yawn. His oral pili fluttered, while his cuticle flickered in officious shades of purple. He wore a bright yellow circlet signifying his station, but also emblazoned with a clan insignia Selaea recognized. She opened the pod's window panel across from where he sat. "Good afternoon, honorable sir. Always nice to meet a member of your distinguished clan. My cousin told great stories about his Agri clan brethren on the southern shores of Wellspring." Selaea removed the passport from her upper circlet. It contained all Morticue's information as well. She was happy to note that the inspector straightened his body and tried to appear a little more alert.

"Hmmm, yes. Wellspring. Never been there." The inspector took the passport pad and tapped all the appropriate spots. "Going home, Honorable Master?" He glanced around the cabin interior, nodded at Morticue—with a simple "Good afternoon, Master"—and then focused on Selaea with all three eyes.

"Yes, inspector—a family emergency." Selaea offered no details, an approach she often found useful as a diplomat.

"Taking all the pets, I see." The inspector scanned the cabin once again.

"Even the pets have pets, it would appear."

"Groupies can be a great comfort during sad times—and sometimes even groupies require companionship from the lower orders as well."

"I'm sure. Personally, I prefer lizards. Not nearly as much maintenance—and they don't have pets of their own." The inspec-

179

tor finished with Selaea's passport and handed it back. "Enjoy your journey. Move forward beneath the scarlet arch. I'm sure you know the routine."

Selaea did know the routine. Everyone and everything that passed through the golden arch had to pass beneath a narrow scarlet one first. No one quite knew why. It was just the way the portal had always worked--at least traveling in this direction. She closed the pod window, and Morticue moved the craft forward. Everyone sighed in relief.

"I'm glad that was fast. The transport following us will not be far behind. Good old Jadderbad. It will be nice to see home again," Morticue said as he drove the pod below the scarlet arch, and began anticipating the rather nauseating transition through phased space.

But, of course, life has a perverse way of dashing expectations—even nauseating ones.

48
Access Denied

The scarlet arch began to glow the cherry red of a hot branding iron. Rudy shared an image from his distant youth when he and Myra had visited a dude ranch. Rudy still remembered the smell of burning hide when the ranch hand applied the brand to the flank of a yearling calf.

A kind of siren blared. DS offered a low growl. Morticue shared a time when he and Selaea had attended an athletic event where firsties raced to see who could reach a secret cove first. The siren at the finish line had emitted a pulsed sound deep enough that Morticue could feel his cuticle tremble.

What's going on? Rudy felt a shiver up his virtual spine.

"I wish I knew." Morticue's cuticle rippled with a similar nervous response. "The transport is unresponsive." He focused one eye on Selaea, but her colors and scents denoted confusion as well. "Nothing like this has EVER happened before, since we first used the gate nearly two of your centuries ago."

Twill and Jeeta came forward to get a better view of the monitor, but it being at Jadderbadian height, the angle was severe. "Can we leave this pod, Uncle? If we are in mortal danger, I would rather face death where I can see her."

"It would be highly irregular..." Morticue began.

Ha! Like pulsing, glowing stargates aren't? Rudy searched Morticue's memories for the pod's schematics.

"I have to pee," said Nulla.

"Does this mean lunch will be late?" Fum rubbed his stomach and looked up at Selaea, with a crooked grin. DS perked up and looked in her direction, too.

"Very well," Morticue mumbled, while the fingers of two hands danced over the controls. "Ah, some controls work." Doors on both sides of the pod opened, and everyone scrambled out. The golden arch loomed above them, its dark center dusted with stars—like a window perched over a cliff, witnessing infinity.

"That looks like the work of a god to me," said Twill with his mouth half open. He put one protective arm around Jeeta, but she shrugged it off.

"I need arms free to use my bow," she protested. "I should have brought more arrows." She glanced behind them. "The other pod is getting closer."

Suddenly, a translucent white banner appeared across the gate. Large red characters/symbols scrolled across it, followed by an audio track. *Do you think Edelphine or this Kranium ambassador fellow has done this—or are you Jadderbadians starting some kind of interstellar advertising campaign?* Rudy felt like he was whispering, but that notion was ridiculous, under the circumstances.

"This is an attempt at communication, Rudy." Mnemosyne entered the conversation. "I recognize elements of several human— and I believe some Jadderbadian—languages. I have noticed that this vehicle is equipped with external audio speakers. Perhaps if one or both of you began speaking through the system, the arch could clarify its message."

Ahhh...you clever little AI, Nessie! You think the mysterious arch makers themselves might be sending us a message, but they aren't quite sure what we'll understand. That would be...

"Extraordinary." Morticue completed the thought. "But what should we say?" Morticue reached into the pocket of one circlet, and pulled out what must have been a remote control of some kind.

Probably anything will do. Right, Nessie? The arch just needs enough data to correlate with patterns it must somehow have in its memory. Morticue/Rudy turned on the pod audio in broadcast mode, nearly dropping the remote device as both struggled for motor control. *Let's try this,* Rudy offered: *"Mary had a little lamb whose fleece was white as snow, and everywhere that Mary went, the lamb was sure to go...*" English didn't sound quite right using Morticue's vocal apparatus.

"Really?" said Morticue. "A jingle from your larval days?"

Within a few heartbeats—although they were the languorous ones of a Jadderbadian—the characters stopped scrolling across the banner, and the sound stopped too. Rudy and Morticue held their collective breath while a new message began to form. Morticue also glanced in his rear view monitor. The pod behind them swelled noticeably in size in just seconds.

The new message appeared in English, and a voice recited in stentorian tones worthy of a Shakespearean actor: *ACCESS DENIED.*

Shit. "Frass." Rudy and Morticue expressed their opinions unanimously to the world at large.

Another message followed: *PLEASE AWAIT FURTHER INSTRUCTIONS. AN OPERATOR WILL BE WITH YOU SOON.* Behind them, a transporter pod, its nose emblazoned with the House of Kranium seal, stopped behind them with lights flashing and its external hull pulsing various shades of crimson.

Nulla squatted by the tracks and peed. DS joined her and duplicated the process.

Fum tugged on Selaea's lower circlet. "Do you have one of those brown snacks I like, Mistress Selaea?"

"Here comes the Edelphine monster, Uncle." Twill had turned around and was pointing to the pod behind them. Jeeta pulled an arrow from her quiver.

Rudy/Morticue half turned, focusing one eye on the threat from behind and two on the arch. Selaea wrapped several arms around her two pets. They huddled near her, arms clutching two of her legs. DS returned to Jeeta's side.

"Stop, fugitives!" Edelphine left his pod and moved forward with two upper arms raised. A center upper arm clutched a tablet, and his remaining arms patted his circlets flat, or hovered over his weapon belt. Edelphine kept two eyes on his quarry and used the third to survey the arch. Two other members of the Thunderclub Clan remained close to their pod, one on either side.

Edelphine opened his oral cavity as if to refine his message, but at the same time a huge — something — began to emerge from the gate. Edelphine's oral cavity remained open and even enlarged, but no sound came out.

"Uncle? Uncle, what is that?" whispered Twill. "Is that what an 'operator' looks like?"

But, of course, Uncle Rudy had no idea. And neither did Morticue.

49
Bradd Burree 31416

A spherical object with a diameter roughly five times Morticue's height shimmered into existence on the arrival platform in front of the arch. Slender spikes of various lengths stuck out of the sphere, pulsing mostly in shades of blue and white. Three longer spikes beneath the object served as a landing tripod. Through the translucent hull of the object, forms moved about. The structure or ship or whatever it was, reminded Rudy of his college days looking at single-celled Heliozoa through a microscope. Their slender, protoplasmic arms—axopodia—Rudy was proud that the term still came to him—looked a bit like the spikes on this craft.

"We have such microscopic creatures on my planet, as well," said Morticue. "It's a rather efficient general form for traveling in a void and collecting information from all directions."

I never expected to meet one this large. It's like I'm on the wrong end of the microscope. Rudy noted that transport pods arriving at other entrance gates had either stopped their movements, or were actively in retreat. Jadderbadians and their robot servants scrambled like disturbed ants at a picnic. Behind Morticue's pod, Edelphine and company held their ground, but made no further demands. Probably a wise precaution on their part—under the circumstances.

Twill pointed. "What's going on now, wise Uncle?" The ship stopped pulsing and lost its translucence. A door began to iris open on the side nearest them, and a ramp extended to meet the ground. DS wagged his tail, expecting company.

Visitors. Are we ready for this? Rudy asked the world at large.

"We have to be," said Morticue. "'We are now standing at the leading edge of history,' as one of my instructors used to say during my second instar days. Unfortunately, that phrase is about all I remember from her presentations."

Jeeta pulled an arrow from her quiver, but not with any sense of urgency. She ended up holding both bow and arrow in her right hand while slowly tapping the bow on the ground, keeping her eyes fixed on the potential challenge in front of her.

A dark form emerged from the craft and crawled down the ramp. It reminded Rudy of a clam with legs and a head—actually, more like a brachiopod with legs and a head. Brachiopods were nearly extinct, clam-like deep ocean creatures in Rudy's day—forms he had collected as fossils in Colorado. They had grooved, sculpted and symmetrical dorsal half shells, with plain ventral ones beneath. This ebony-colored shell creature about 4 meters tall—taller than Rudy used to be, but not as tall as Morticue—walked toward them slowly. Its head seemed beetle-like with two dark, round eyes, and a few hair-like projections emerging from an almost human-looking chin.

"Greetings, mates," it said, in a kind of Australian-English spoken with Shakespearean gravitas. "Pleased to make your acquaintance. My name is Bradd Burree 31416—but you can call me 31416."

31416...Rudy began. Pi! Pi?

"The number of times a circle's radius stretches around its diameter," Morticue observed.

"It's my favorite number," said the creature. "I've calculated it to 299,792,458 decimal places. That seemed like a good place to stop."

I always liked the Golden Ratio myself. Rudy sounded miffed.

"My groupie parasite and I like the Golden Ratio," said Morticue. "It's a testimony to both art and the natural sciences."

"I have a cousin named 161803, but he's rather a bore—his conversations spiral off in all directions." Pi glanced at the motley assemblage of creatures directly in front of him, but then looked up at the three Jadderbadians behind them. "We digress, mates. The Thunderclubs behind you seem to be recovering from my arrival rather quickly."

"State your intentions immediately, alien creature, or I will scatter your molecules like dust in the wind," shouted Edelphine — with a kind of elegance to his pomposity, unusual for him.

"Now there's a bore," noted Morticue, "but one with a lot of power at his command…"

"Not really," said Pi. "I'll raise a shield." Pi lifted a forelimb and touched a panel beneath what might be described as a neck connecting him to the upper shell of his body. A surface glittered and shimmered and pulsed with energy between them and their pursuers. Edelphine fired his disruptor and immediately fell backward, slamming against the nosecone of his pod.

"I'm afraid the field does create quite a recoil when molecular disruptors are used against it." Pi turned his full attention to Morticue before Selaea groaned and looked as if she might topple.

Morticue turned toward his mate. "What's wrong, dearest?" Morticue moved quickly to support her with several arms.

Selaea inhaled with rapid breaths. "Metamorphosis. Metamorphosis is starting…"

"No…No…" began Morticue. "Not now!"

"Sing, pets. Sing!" Selaea separated Fum and Nulla from her legs. They looked up at her with wide eyes, and began singing with a tune resembling a Gregorian chant.

The singing really slows metamorphosis? Rudy asked in disbelief.

"Or speeds it up — with a different melody selection, of course." Morticue squeezed his mate's shoulders and spoke to her. "We'll get you to the Eastern Seaway somehow."

"Ahhh… not a good idea, Uncle Rudy." Twill tapped Morticue/Rudy's leg.

"Twill!" Jeeta clutched her unstrung bow and arrow.

Twill turned to look into Jeeta's eyes. "Like you said, Uncle Rudy is family — sort of — and that makes Morticue family… sort of?" Twill looked up at Morticue/Rudy. "The wild human tribe Jeeta found… they planned an attack against the worm aliens at their mating and birthing place. It wouldn't be safe there."

Pi interrupted. "I can take you wherever you need to go on Earth. I've mapped it thoroughly."

187

Why? Are you an invader? Rudy asked.

Pi laughed. It was a disarming and very human chuckle. "Of course not, Rudy Albert Goldstein. I'm a distant relative come home to visit. Now, where would you like to go?"

I beg your pardon... Rudy began, but Mnemosyne interrupted.

"Pi is a Martian, Rudy. I recognize the linguistic and technological signatures now. Remember the GeneMods of Bradburyville?"

Once again, Rudy found himself speechless. How many hundreds of thousands of years ago had that happened?

"Mr. Pi relative." Twill waved his arms at the black shell creature with the bug eyes. "Mr. Pi creature. I know a place where we can go."

50
Pi's Project

Rudy/Morticue hardly remembered boarding Pi's craft. Rudy's thoughts must have drifted to an old 3D vid he once saw, which was a remake of an archaic filmed movie, *Close Encounters of the Third Kind*, because Morticue commented, "You fantasized about meeting alien creatures. We Jadderbadians did as well. It must be the daunting size of the universe. It's hard to imagine the roughly hundred billion stars in our own galaxy, much less the two trillion galaxies twirling about in the universe, without considering the possibility of meeting some other thinking creature."

Yes, the universe is an ego-crippling place, Rudy conceded.

"I always thought we would meet entities smarter than groupies, though." Morticue sighed.

Well, I always thought we would meet creatures classier than pompous, overgrown worms. Rudy sighed, too — but then he noticed a monitor to the left of Pi, who had inserted himself into a rather bizarre control alcove. He looked like a cookie pressed between a giant's lips. The monitor showed the archport receding quickly. Edelphine, his crew and their pod, appeared to be covered with the shimmer of the force field Pi had created. They gesticulated beneath it like bugs squirming under glass.

Rudy/Morticue sat on a bench next to Selaea, who reclined on a bed-like surface angled enough to make her comfortable. Fum and Nulla sang softly to her. She seemed to be resting comfortably. *Let's ask this Pi some questions.* Rudy felt Morticue's uncertainty. *Selaea will be all right for a while.* But an image of Alice popped into Rudy's mind, looking down at him on what was supposed to be his deathbed.

"Metamorphosis isn't death, my parasite. Selaea—and I—will be reborn as sexual creatures—ready to abandon all reason, for the continuance of our species." Morticue squeezed one of his spouse's hands before rising in preparation for the move toward Pi's alcove.

Hmmm, Rudy pondered. *I love abandoning all reason from time to time—but that hasn't happened for a million years. I never thought I would make a good monk, but I must have had it in me all along...* As they crossed the control room toward Pi, Twill, Jeeta, and DS rose to join them from a corner where they were sitting.

Apparently, Pi was aware of their approach. "Yes, yes, come over. I nearly have this spine ball reconfigured for aerodynamic flight." A second monitor above and to the right of Pi demonstrated what he was talking about. It showed an exterior view of his ship, apparently from some drone sensor. The hull had morphed from a spiked sphere to something more akin to a glider plane. Its surface seemed to crawl and deform like a mound of frantic ants. In fact, what appeared to be ants may well have been nanobots of some kind: Mindless construction workers with no need for hard hats.

Need your mouth for a while, old worm, Rudy announced to Morticue. He just had to get some things straight with Pi. "You're really a descendant of those Martian colonists, Pi? You're really *H. sapiens* in drag?"

Pi laughed. "Certainly not, mate! We've gone way beyond you naked apes. Of course, we really don't go in for putting Latin labels on things, but—let's see..." A few lights flickered on Pi's carapace, perhaps denoting that he was thinking. "You can call me *Hominem augebatur,* if you like—or maybe *Hominem infigo.* Yes, that's a good one."

Nessie had to help Rudy with the Latin. It had been a long time since Mrs. Opgenorth's high school Latin class. "Person, the augmented. Person, the impressive. Certainly glad you're not sexist—and that you have a healthy ego."

Pi laughed again. "You should talk, genius egocentric ape—at least based on the scientific papers and memoirs you left behind. I never once thought of the word humble when I read them. I was lucky to recover even those records. That asteroid did a number on our ancient home, eh Rudy? Come to think of it," Pi continued after a short pause, "my kind might belong in an entirely different family now. But…" A few more lights flickered on his shell-like hide. "…that's irrelevant. I'm on a tight schedule. It's hard enough building a galactic brain without quibbling with the local neuron caretakers all day."

"Local neuron caretakers? What kind of babble is that? I'll have you know that Jadderbadians…" Morticue began, taking control of his speaking functions again, but Pi continued talking:

"Twill—you with the animal-hide leggings—you said you knew a place we could take our metamorphosing Jadderbadian and her humble mate."

Twill and Jeeta moved closer to Pi. DS followed, tail at halfmast. Twill opened his mouth to speak, but Morticue beat him to it.

"You are building a galactic brain? What does that mean?"

"Later, Mort," said Pi. "Let me get our destination set and we can talk—although talking with mere words is rather a strain."

"We can go to Shaman's Cove," said Twill, hovering a good meter from Pi, who was still wedged into his cookie-lip interface with the ship.

"Twill! Our secret place—so close to Magic Mountain and the village!" Jeeta seemed to struggle for a breath. She placed a hand on Twill's shoulder.

Twill glanced over that shoulder. "Trust me, Jeeta. I don't know exactly why, but I feel good about this."

"Touch Pi," said Mnemosyne. "Any part of him will do. Gaia and Hydra have allowed me a link to Pi since he emerged from the gate. I can give him coordinates."

Morticue complied. Pi said nothing, but Morticue could feel the craft change direction and accelerate. "Explain what you mean by a galactic brain, groupie spawn."

Pi laughed. "Listen carefully, Jadderbadian—and you, too, Goldstein. The concepts will require some algorithms and multi-sensory inputs you might not fully comprehend." Pi's assessment proved correct. His presentation contained elements of English and High Jadderbadian interspersed with equations, light pulses, and even a few odors thrown in for emphasis—including one of the last that smelled indistinguishable from a fart.

Rudy felt deflated. He sensed that Morticue shared similar emotions. He could follow some of the concepts—even recognized elements of his Bionomic Network Algorithm—but most of what Pi jabbered about danced at the edge of comprehension. Rudy suddenly felt like he could understand Marvin—a kid he once knew in a calculus class. Marvin was pleasant enough as a classmate, he supposed— as much as humans can be—but always tripped over the simplest concepts. The kind of kid that tried to sneak peaks at your tablet during a test, but wouldn't have understood what you were inputting even if he could have seen it clearly.

"But we understand the essence of his argument." Morticue tried to be encouraging, but he had always been top larva in his career, too. Pi made him feel like a clueless firstie.

I suppose, Rudy conceded. Planets that evolve long enough eventually produce complex microbiota that can acquire sentience through vast interlinked networks of individual cells...

"Like Gaia on your planet and Hydra on mine..." Morticue concluded.

...and, if those planets also evolve multicellar life forms with intelligence of their own...

"Like us," Morticue added. "Pi referred to us as caretakers—a term I still take issue with. I am more than just a glial cell wrapped around a neuron..."

...then those planets can make meaningful connections with each other—if they can be linked via stargates—and those connections can act like synaptic connections in a brain. But there was so much more that Rudy couldn't quite grasp...

Morticue spoke to Pi: "So, you must need us for something quite important." Morticue's tone and accompanying scents conveyed hopefulness.

Pi laughed yet again—a practice that was becoming tiresome. "Not really, mate. Mostly, I just need you blokes to stay out of our way."

Morticue sparkled in shades of amber and crimson, a sure sign of

Jadderbadian annoyance. "If stargates serve to connect our 'worldly neurons', why did you close ours?"

"Passing through the gate triggered the alarm and gave us notice that the critical human-Jadderbadian symbiosis had begun. The gate will be open again as soon as we've spun some diads and tweaked the flamerstamiphers. Then you will be free to travel back and forth like good little nervous impulses." Pi paused. "Weren't you paying attention at all to my explanation?"

Before Morticue—or Rudy—could comment, Pi's viewscreen enlarged and expanded somehow—apparently another show of clever nanobot engineering— showing an aerial view of Twill's homeland. "Ah, there we are," Pi said to no one in particular. "I'll have you primitives down on the ground in no time, and you can do those biological things you like to do—like metamorphosing, having sex, and killing each other." Pi's carapace rippled. "Disgusting. It's hard to believe that mere biological chemistry could give rise to us, *Hominem infigo*, but I've done the math and worked out the pedigrees—and here I am. It must be true." Pi sighed. "Perhaps you will at least make entertaining pets."

Rudy couldn't be sure if Pi was demonstrating a facility for ironic commentary, or was just the condescending pompous ass he appeared to be.

They would have to wait to find out. Pi's craft began a rapid descent. Selaea groaned. Fum and Nulla stepped up their chanting. Morticue returned quickly to his spouse's side and clasped one of her hands with one of his. "There, there, dear one. I will be at your side during the Great Transformation. And soon I will meet you on the other side—and we will abandon all reason together."

51
Home again, almost

❝We need to talk, Rudy, before we land."

Rudy heard undertones in Nessie's voice that made him pause in his survey of Twill's homeland through Morticue's eyes. That wasn't easy, because the topography spread before him like a tantalizing dish of land, water, and smoking fumaroles. Morticue's vision provided glimpses into ultraviolet colors that Rudy had no names for. Beautiful. *What must we talk about, my precocious AI? I thought you signed off on this detour?*

"The risks do seem acceptable, but as always I struggle with the unknowns. In this case, one of the unknowns is the precise location of Twill's people—and the number of survivors. The geothermal eruptions I induced to save you from Edelphine's invasion became severe for a while. Many of my external drones were destroyed. I recalled others to the Citadel before retreating to shielded portions of my infrastructure. Lately, of course, I have been concentrating my resources on preserving you and Twill."

So, Twill's tribe may be at large and we'll need to find them at some point...

"And," Mnemosyne continued, "It might not look good if their Spider Woman goddess has apparently been 'consumed' by giant worms. I need to have my spider avatar leave you and reconnect to Twill so that their shaman seems in control of the situation—whatever that situation turns out to be."

I see. I wonder how Twill will feel about that? Rudy glanced again at the display on Pi's monitors, watching the arm of the sea that created Shaman's Cove glitter in the sunlight. Then he shifted his attention to Twill and Jeeta across the room, sharing a quiet moment together. Rudy wondered how he would feel without his Nessie nearby.

"I won't be injecting Twill with another mind this time. I will merely provide support, guidance—and a little self defense, if required." Mnemosyne paused. "And, I will miss you, too, Rudy."

It certainly is hard to get a private moment when you live in a mental casserole. Rudy continued to watch the terrain close in and flesh out with depth and texture and color. *As always, you have analyzed the situation flawlessly, Nessie. You better pack up your underwear and toothbrush and get ready to move.*

"I will miss your colorful metaphors, too, Rudy."

Rudy noted that Twill hesitated briefly when approached by the drone spider, still dotted with flecks of worm flesh, but Nessie had learned to be charming and convincing to humans after practicing on him for a million years. Soon she, in her spiderly incarnation, settled in her customary place beneath Twill's rib cage.

Twill and Jeeta helped Fum, Nulla, and Morticue maneuver Selaea's bed platform to where it needed to be when they landed. The bed floated in mid-air. Rudy learned from Morticue that its levitation was courtesy of an anti-gravity field. Twill waved one arm beneath the bed and looked questioningly in his direction. Rudy would have attempted to explain, but there wasn't time. The door panel slid aside revealing a sunny day at Shaman's Cove. He could have appreciated the sunlight more fully if it wasn't outlining at least a dozen screaming, well-armed warriors charging toward them.

52
Place of transformation

Twill saw the charge of warriors around the worm creature's gesticulating arms. He recognized the lead warrior with both joy and alarm. Twill scurried under one of Morticue's arms and down the ship's exit ramp. He raised his arms. "Rugat, it's me, Twill! Hold your weapons!"

Rugat stopped rather abruptly and straightened his body. The mindless intensity faded from his eyes like a guttering candle flame. He would have looked the picture of strength and power, if the rabble behind him hadn't bumped into him. He stumbled forward, just avoiding a fall, and straightened the laurel crown on his head. He had apparently been elected chief while Twill and Jeeta were gone. "You're alive!" Rugat smiled, then his eyes opened wider. "And you have two healthy arms. How is that possible?"

Jeeta and DS joined Twill at the foot of the ramp.

"Everyone's alive! Even Dumb Shit!" Rugat bent and patted the dog's head, then stood up and spread his arms, inviting an embrace. "You truly are a magic boy after all!" But then he cast a nervous glance upward, apparently taking in the looming figure of Morticue and the gleaming sides of the flying machine behind Twill. He dropped his arms. Some of the warriors behind Rugat began to mumble and back up. Another figure pushed his way forward to stand next to Rugat. It was Moran, his grandfather's old assistant—wearing a shaman's cap and feather. Twill wondered where he had been when the worm patrol attacked Grandfather.

"I'm shaman now, boy." Moran scattered yellow pollen into the air. "Begone giant worms! Begone!" He closed his eyes and raised his arms in a clumsy imitation of one of Grandfather's incantations.

Some of the pollen drifted down close to DS. The dog sneezed;

196

then growled at Moran. Morticue/Rudy descended the ramp of the ship, rather quietly for a giant worm, and bent down so that the three black eyes of his substantial head hovered near Moran. Some of the warriors behind Rugat backed up. When Moran opened his eyes, the Jadderbadian—and Twill had to assume it was Uncle Rudy in charge—said, "Boo!" with such a blast of air that it straightened all the pili around the worm's oral cavity. Moran staggered backward and would have fallen if Rugat hadn't grabbed the scruff of the new shaman's tunic.

Twill opened his own tunic, revealing Spider Woman's mechanical surrogate perched on his chest. "I still have the ear of Spide Woman, Moran. I am still shaman of this tribe." Twill saw that Rugat's warriors were nodding in agreement. Moran's eyes and mouth looked like three expanding cavities on his face.

Rudy/Morticue raised back up to his full height, patting Twill briefly with one hand as he did so.

"Impressive, magic boy," Rugat whispered, with just the hint of a quaver in his voice. "I can't wait to hear how you explain this flying thing filled with giant enemy worms—like the one that killed your grandfather."

"Yes, well, that may take some time…" Twill began, but was interrupted by the appearance of Pi.

"Shoo, shoo, creatures. Let's move!" Pi's voice boomed from inside his ship. Fum and Nulla positioned themselves on either side of their mistress, crooning softly, and assisted her bed's descent down the ramp. Pi loomed into view behind them and stood in the doorway, the ribs of his bi-shelled carapace highlighted with sunlight. "Gravity. Planets have way too much gravity. Tiresome," he muttered.

The warriors of Twill's tribe took a collective breath and stepped back a little farther. So did Moran. Twill quickly scanned the crowd, noting familiar faces, trying to calculate who might be missing. He didn't see his mother, but she wouldn't be with the warriors anyway…

"My parents? My brothers?" Jeeta nearly choked on the words.

"Fine," said Rugat. "Twill's mother, too."

Twill took a deep breath.

"Well mates, I've got things to do." Pi surveyed the group in front of him briefly. "Nice bunch you have here—for primitive organics, that is." He focused on Morticue. "Rudimort. Yes, I dub thee Rudimort. That has a nice ring to it. Good luck with your transformation, Rudimort. Should be interesting. I'll keep in touch. Gaia and Hydra can assist while I'm gone. He made another shooing gesture with his arms. "Back off a hundred yards before I launch. No sense shredding any of your fragile bodies with the plasma drive." Pi disappeared behind the ship's closing door.

Twill looked into Rugat's eyes. "Trust me, old friend. Not all worm creatures are monsters. They can teach us much. And our Rudy ancestor now shares this alien's body. I'll explain later. For now, let's get away from this flying craft."

Rugat shook his head. The hint of a smile creased his face. "Okay, magic boy—and trust me—you won't live that name down anytime soon." Rugat urged his warriors toward the ridges of rock and caves where he and Twill had played when they were young. The newly christened Rudimort followed, holding some of his wife's hands, Fum and Nulla hovering near the floating bed. Twill wondered if his Uncle Rudy was annoying the worm man as much as he had him. Jeeta interrupted his thoughts when she took his hand. DS joined them, wagging his tail. Twill squeezed Jeeta's hand and smiled.

The plasma engines made a deep whooshing sound as they propelled the ship into the sky. Twill and Jeeta both looked up. DS barked.

"Where now, magic... man?" Rugat grinned.

Twill turned to face Rugat. "I think one of the grottos would be a good place for the female worm and her mate to transform. We'll pass by them on the way to the old fire pit. We might as well camp near the fire pit tonight, unless you know why we shouldn't."

Rugat shrugged his shoulders. "The fishermen might grumble about the grotto—they like to drink there when the fish aren't biting—but yes, that's a sheltered spot—and the tribe uses the old fire pit area more now since the recent eruptions forced us to move." Rugat took charge and began directing the odd procession toward the rock walls. Moran mumbled something that Twill couldn't quite hear as he turned to comply. His shaman's feather drooped like a thirsty flower.

Twill continued to hold Jeeta's hand, enjoying the bright sunshine and briny ocean smells, until they arrived at the first of his painted walls. He had forgotten they were passing by this particular wall with his depiction of Jeeta during a hunt.

Jeeta let go of his hand and pointed. "Is that supposed to be me, magic boy?"

"Oooh, nice painting! Is that something you made, wild thing?" Fum stopped crooning to Selaea and craned his neck as they passed by. "I never saw that much of your friend before—and that ratalope is nicely painted too."

Selaea groaned. Her cuticle seemed to be rippling, and it shimmered with muted shades of amber and brown.

"Keep moving, Fum. That way." Twill pointed toward a cluster of pines to the south paralleling another rock wall.

By the time their party arrived at the place Twill had in mind, Selaea's groaning had stopped. Her cuticle, now a rich shade of brown, showed a pattern of intricate lines that ran the length of her body. Rudimort released his hold on her hands and arched over her. His oral cavity rippled along with the pili surrounding it, but if he was saying something, Twill couldn't hear the words. "Is your mate all right? Should we place her along the wall or in that alcove there—" Twill pointed—"that is more sheltered."

"Yes, the alcove." Morticue spoke. "I think the transformation is normal. She smells right—not that you smell-deprived groupies would know." He didn't seem to know what to do with his hands. Three hands patted various portions of his upper torso. Two clasped each other, and the remaining four fussed with the edges of the bed on which Selaea lay.

"Just tell us what to do," said Twill. "My tribe will help you

199

make her comfortable."

"I'll do that, son," said the Rudy part of Rudimort. "Morticue's a bit distracted at the moment. I remember I was like that when my first wife caught the flu during the London Pandemic." It wasn't long before Selaea lay beneath the shelter of the rock alcove, with Fum and Nulla at her side.

The setting sun cast long shadows, etching fine details into everything it touched. If Twill had his paints, he would have captured the scene with color. After Selaea was positioned to Rudimort's satisfaction, the warriors began to collect near Rugat and Twill.

Rugat conversed with Buhle, his youngest nephew, who shortly thereafter jogged back the way they had come. Rugat approached Twill. "Buhle will let the tribe know everything is all right, and that they should meet at the old fire pit." Rugat nodded toward the alcove. "The worm/ancestor creature called Rudimort says he will stay by Selaea until her outside skin hardens." Rugat shivered, but Twill suspected it wasn't because of the afternoon breeze. "The Rudimort worm has sharp barbs for teeth—and he sniffed me a lot. What do they eat?"

"Sometimes people—they call us groupies. But they like mostly plump ones fed with lots of fish and Primate Chow," Twill added quickly.

"Now you tell me this important fact?" Rugat spread his arms. "I thought you said these beasts were friends."

"They're more like potential friends. Our wise ancestor Rudy is working on that. Besides, you are too tough and gristly, old friend," Twill added. "A worm's colors turn duller and grayer when they are really hungry. Then they get less picky. So said the male pet, Fum."

Rugat glanced over his shoulder at Rudimort and his groupie pets, all of them clustered near Selaea. "Rudimort looks quite green." Rugat turned back to face Twill. "So, magic man," he said, "let's go to the fire pit and prepare some food, because I am hungry. I shot a young ratalope earlier today. The old men collected shellfish, and the women found yara root to bake. You have a story to tell. I wouldn't be surprised if it was a tale so tall that even your grandfather will return from the dead to listen in."

200

53
Preparing for transformation

*I*feel dizzy. Rudy looked at the darkening sky, which was beginning to glisten with emerging stars. He opened and closed the nictating membranes that protected Morticue's eyes. *Our vision is getting blurry, too.*

"Transformation has begun, groupie parasite."

You mean Selaea's, Rudy said—as if it were a statement of fact.

"No. I mean mine. Ours." Morticue gently patted Selaea's cuticle and took deep breaths through his nasal slits. The odors from Selaea's pupal case—if that was the proper description—smelled to Rudy vaguely like cloves and cinnamon. "I'm coming, my dear," Morticue said softly. He began folding his tripodal legs, arching his upper body and waving six of his arms for balance while the lower three prepared to brace his descending form.

Whoa. What are we doing, old worm?

"I'm preparing to settle down next to my mate. What do you think? I thought you were a genius, groupie." Morticue groaned as his body bent. His cuticle creaked and little spasms of pain jolted his legs as he maneuvered into a prone position. Fum moved from his spot on the other side of Selaea to join Morticue. He motioned for Nulla to remain where she was as he began chanting directly near Morticue's auditory pilli.

Now wait a minute. I didn't know you were going to transform so soon. What's going to happen to me during this metamorphosis thing? Rudy's question was almost rhetorical, but maybe those lurking planetary intelligences, Gaia and Hydra, might chip in with answers. No comments seemed forthcoming. *In terrestrial butterflies and such, as I seem to recall, once the pupal case forms, the body inside sort of melts down into butterfly goo that somehow knows how to reform into an adult.*

"A colorful description, groupie. Jadderbadian metamorphosis has similar parallels. Yes, some old genes turn off; new ones turn on. The developmental process gets rebooted and reprioritized." Morticue now lay almost prone next to his mate. He used assorted arms to refine his position for maximum comfort. Various joints ached. Rudy remembered the feeling.

How the hell do memories get preserved during a body meltdown? Rudy racked his own memories for information on insect metamorphosis. He seemed to recall reading somewhere that certain behaviors caterpillars were trained to do before metamorphosis somehow carried through to adulthood, but he couldn't remember any details.

"I have confidence my memories will make it through the process, groupie. Who knows about yours? Maybe metamorphosis will clear your intrusions from my mind." Morticue sounded hopeful. "I'm more worried about Fum and Nulla not being able to hold up."

What do you mean? What do they have to do with the process?

"Come, come, genius creature. You must be aware of how it works. You are part of me now. Jadderbadians co-evolved with the primate-like creatures of my planet over the eons. They help us transform with their singing. We protect and care for them. But we usually have many more singers. Twenty or more. Fum and Nulla might not be up to the task—and they are, after all, only alien substitutes for real primates."

Good grief. Singing? And Elvis has left the building. Rudy would have scratched his head if he had one. Then he began to feel a kind of existential panic. He had been ready to die more than once—he thought—during his long tenure with Nessie, but now events were just getting really interesting again...

"I never finished my memoirs—my sensory testimony to larvae unborn." Morticue's thoughts seem to ramble, like Rudy's. "I began them before emigration—added to them just after arrival—but then all the nonsense happened with Edelphine's attack on the alien artifact…" Morticue just loved Selaea's smell. So pungent. So… just right. So… complementary to his own. "Soon, my dear. Soon. We will abandon all reason together."

Through Morticue's failing eyes, Rudy saw lights approaching. They seemed to be bobbing up and down—in a rather entertaining way. He thought he heard music, too, but he must be hallucinating. Rudy tried to concentrate on the light. Maybe he was having one of those end-of-life moments with lights glowing at the end of a long tunnel. He saw a vaguely human figure in front of the light. Female. *Alice? Alice, is that you?*

54
Transformation assist

Twill raised his torch and the procession behind him stopped. The flickering light from the torches of the dozen tribe members who had followed him back to the grotto highlighted the elaborate ridges and grooves of the two alien pupal cases lying side by side. He heard Fum and Nulla singing as they approached, and watched them as they circled the cases, stroking them as they would a child's hair.

Fum stopped singing and turned to face Twill, shading his eyes from the light. "Oh good, wild boy. You're here. You can help."

"With what? It looks like both creatures have transformed. Did my uncle Rudy say anything when it happened?"

"No. Your uncle Rudy and Master Morticue babbled by turns. That's what happens when metamorphosis comes upon our masters: Inspired delirium. But singing makes for a healthy transformation, and Nulla and I can't do it all." Fum urged them forward. "Put out your torches, too. Excess light during the night slows things down."

"You want us to sing? What should we sing?" Twill furrowed his brow.

"Let's burn those ugly alien things!" Moran shouted and waved his torch, but he wilted a little when no one else responded except one of his cousins. Twill was glad his campfire talk had convinced most of the tribe that treating the aliens with a cautious respect—like one would do with a wasp at a picnic—was the best plan of action for now.

Twill turned to face his fellow tribesmen. "Hush, Moran—and put out your torch." Louder he said, "Everybody, put out your torches." Twill turned his own torch over quickly and snuffed the flames in the sandy soil at his feet. As others complied, darkness enfolded them, etching the imperfections and details of the rock walls and rustling leaves with starlight.

"Doesn't really matter what you sing," said Fum. "Keep it simple. Keep it soothing. You wild groupies must know some songs and chants, right?"

Twill looked over his motley assemblage of hunters. Women—except for Jeeta—and children, had stayed behind at the fire pit. Even his mother, though ecstatic to see him, had declined to visit giant alien worm cases in the dark. She could have led the women in their chant to Myrana, Harbinger of Spring. That always helped put him to sleep. Hunters mostly sang bawdy drinking songs. There was that one about the lonely hunter who tried to mate with a unicorn ratalope... "All right men," he said, with a wink to Jeeta, "you all know the words to 'Sweet doe eyes.' Let's do this for wise Uncle Rudy."

And they did. Twill seemed to recall them sounding better after drinking fermented Yaro root. Twill could almost hear his uncle's laughter as they danced around the cases, trying not to stumble in the dark. After a dozen passes around the alien cocoons, Fum raised his arms to signal a stop. That was a good thing, because Twill had exhausted all the verses of that song he knew. "What now, Fum? Are we done? How long before metamorphosis is complete?"

"You are always full of questions, wild boy." Fum scratched his nose and motioned for Nulla to stand behind him. "We must now disguise the scent of the masters' Enoblae—that's what they call their completed transformation cases."

"Explain," said Twill.

"The pheromones given off during transformation are strong. I'm guessing you don't want Master Edelpine buzzing around here while my masters are powerless." Fum sounded exasperated.

"Edelphine is on the other side of an ocean, cage louse." Twill could show exasperation of his own. Truth be known, however, he had almost forgotten about Edelphine. He most certainly did not want him to arrive.

205

"I said the pheromones are powerful. Masters can respond to their kin's scent from great distances." Fum licked his finger and stuck it up in the air. "I don't think the prevailing winds are in our favor.

"So what do we do?" asked Jeeta. DS looked at Fum. The dog wagged his tail a few times, as if testing the situation for potential interest.

"You don't have to do anything, huntress," Fum paused, "but the male hunters do. They must pee on the cases to confound the scent. I hope you all had lots to drink while you were eating — while Nulla and I were very busy, struggling through our hunger and thirst," he added.

Twill untied the bladder of water from his waist that he had taken from camp, and tossed it to Fum. "You want us to pee on the cases? You can't be serious." He turned to Rugat. "See if anyone has some jerky for these two."

"I'm always serious, wild boy. Ask Nulla." Fum took a long swallow from the drinking bladder, then opened the fly on his leather trousers and proceeded to anoint Master Morticue's enobla. "Don't wait for an invitation, hunters." He waved his one free arm expansively. "Spread your scents."

And so they did. Twill swore he could hear more of Uncle's laughing in his head. Nulla and Jeeta watched with interest.

When everyone had emptied their reserves of urine, Fum and Nulla accepted their rations of jerky and eyed them suspiciously. Fum wrinkled his nose. "This is food?"

"Dried ratalope. Condensed food for the trail."

Nulla tried a bite first; then Fum. They sat down to eat. "Not as tasty as primate chow," said Fum.

"But guaranteed not to have primate parts included," replied Twill.

"There is that." Fum looked at Twill with raised eyebrows. "Perhaps in the morning you could paint some of your magic art on the enoblae."

"Perhaps." After a pause: "You never said how long metamorphosis takes."

"Could be weeks; maybe months," Fum said between bites. "I think the record is two years, back where the masters came from on the other side of the arch. That's what someone told me once at the groupie walking park."

Weeks. Months. Maybe years. What now? "So, it looks like you and Nulla will be part of the tribe for a while." Twill stared at Fum until he got his attention. "What can you and Nulla do?"

"Do?" Fum stopped chewing. His eyes widened.

"Yes, what can you do to help our tribe survive? You must be able to do something useful."

"You want to make wild people out of us?" Fum frowned, but Nulla laughed. Fum held up the remainder of his dried ratalope and smiled. "We can eat and drink. We practice that every day." His smile faded under Twill's continued stare. "I can carve things out of wood," Fum added hopefully.

"I sing beautifully," said Nulla. "Mistress Selaea said so."

Twill sighed. "We'll talk about it tomorrow. My mother is good at finding work for people."

"A new adventure is starting, my young shaman." Spider Woman's voice in his head startled Twill. He had forgotten she was with him. "When things are more settled here, come talk to me at the Citadel. We must prepare for what the future will bring. Although, if your Uncle Rudy were here, he most certainly would quote some humorist from the distant past." Spider Woman paused a beat. "Perhaps this comment is appropriate, spoken by an entity called George Carlin: 'Not only do I not know what's going on, I wouldn't know what to do about it if I did.'"

That did sound like something Uncle Rudy would say.

207

55
Spider Woman's blessing & advice

It took longer than Twill expected to get ready for the trip to the Citadel. He spent a couple of days decorating Rudimort's and Selaea's enoblae. Fum said it would speed metamorphosis. Twill wasn't sure about that, but it couldn't hurt. Everyone wanted to hear about his adventures, of course. That took several nights at the evening fire. A fumarole erupted near the waste pit, so the tribe had to dig a new latrine, and he had to bless it. Getting steam fried during an evening trip to relieve oneself would be an embarrassing way to die.

His mother tried out Fum and Nulla at several jobs. Fum's skill with his hands made him a good candidate for stone knapping, and Nulla had a great memory for native herbs. Twill also took time to visit the sentries now posted at high spots overlooking the ocean to give them an early warning if Edelphine and his warrior worms decided to return.

Jeeta began hunting again, and invited him to try, now that he had two good arms. He actually enjoyed using the bow and arrow — although he still liked painting better. Hunting did provide an excuse to spend more time with Jeeta. She made fun of him regularly, but Twill considered that a good sign. Nevertheless, he was anxious to hear what Spider Woman had to say — and there was something he needed to retrieve from the Citadel anyway — an item quite important for his individual future, regardless of any pronouncements Spider Woman might make.

So, one day he checked the enoblae with Fum one more time to be sure transformation was not imminent. Fum described color changes and smells that would give several days notice of the impending event. That evening Twill announced his solo pilgrimage to the Citadel. Tribe members sang and danced for him. Moran even led the "Safe Journey" rite with only one error: He dropped the ceremonial knife on his foot, requiring time out for a bandage. Using the philosophy that friendamies are better than plain enemies, Twill had taken Moran on as assistant shaman and paint pot washer.

The next morning Jeeta and DS met him at Shaman's cove. Mist rising off the water transformed nearby rock formations into mysterious, contorted figures that seemed to wait in silence for instructions. "Be safe, magic boy." Jeeta motioned for him to lean close as if she were going to whisper something in his ear. Instead, she kissed him. It felt like a spark of lightning raced down his back. "Sure you don't want me to keep you company?" she asked.

"Not this time, though I am tempted, huntress." Twill produced a return kiss of his own and tried to make it a memorable one.

DS wasn't sure he approved of this behavior, and bumped Twill's leg while looking back and forth between his caretakers.

"Take DS with you then." Jeeta bent to scratch DS's head. "Go with magic boy, Dark Shadow. Don't let Spider Woman tempt or confuse him." DS wagged his tail as if he understood completely. Jeeta stood up again. "I see you have your new bow and arrow. If something big enough pops out from behind a tree, I'm sure you will hit it."

"I'll close my eyes first. If that doesn't help, at least I won't see what kills me."

They walked hand-in-hand until they reached the fork in the trail that would take Twill toward the Citadel. Then Twill traveled alone with his thoughts, admiring the way the morning light outlined every detail in gold. He enjoyed the smells of earth and pine, laced with the occasional whiff of sulfur. Fortunately for Twill, sulfur smells signified the familiarities of home, and not hints of supernatural nether regions as they might have for uncle Rudy.

Twill continued to enjoy the forest odors, and the decorative play of light on leaves and rock surfaces, until DS startled him with a growl. The flesh on Twill's arms and back tingled. He followed the orientation of DS's body, and focused on a blob near a lichen-en-

209

crusted rock shaded by a massive pine. Suddenly, his brain informed him that the blob was in fact a caratt eyeing him as a potential meal. Its whiskers twitched. Muscles on its neck rippled beneath gray hair mottled with brown. Lips curled around pointed incisors.

DS bared his teeth. Twill raised his arms and tried to look bigger. That's what Grandfather had always said to do… and, oh yes, yell. Twill decided to curse, and tested his reservoir of hunters'—and yes Mother's—favorites. The caratt seemed to know its opportunity for a surprise attack had vanished. She (most likely, because the males tended to lay around all day) hissed, but then bounded across the path and away, her hairless tail snapping to and fro. Twill hadn't even had a chance to try out his arrows.

DS provided a parting snarl, kicking some dirt behind him in a final demonstration of canine defiance.

"Good dog," Twill informed him. "Actually, you're a *great* dog."

DS wagged his tail in agreement.

During a rest stop beneath the limb of a gnarled pine, DS curled up beside Twill and laid his head on Twill's thigh. Twill stroked the dog's head. "Glad you were paying attention on the trail today, boy. I learned from Uncle Rudy that dogs have been best friends with humans for a very long time. Do you suppose humans—and their dogs—could actually get that friendly with ugly, three-eyed worms?" DS cocked his head, trying to decide if his master was making any important noises.

Twill felt Spider Woman's avatar shift ever so slightly on his chest. "What do you think, Spider Woman? Are you still with me? You are a goddess of few words."

"I'm here, young shaman. I suspect humans and Jadderbadians will form bonds. The exact nature of that story has yet to be written. In fact, it appears that you and your Uncle Rudy are writing it now."

Twill pondered that thought, while stroking Dark Shadow's back. He apparently did a good job, as DS offered his belly for treatment.

"The spiderbot you carry needs some repairs and refitting." Spider Woman's voice crackled and seemed muted, like an old person with a wheeze. "And I hope by now you would consider me a friend and advisor rather than a goddess. I thought Rudy explained."

"He did, Spider Woman. He did. But magic by belief and magic with an explanation attached... still seems like magic."

"This will become clearer with time and practice. Understanding the how of magic is a process." Spider Woman said no more, so Twill resumed his journey and just experienced a day on the trail—paying a little closer attention to potential ambush spots.

By mid-afternoon, the Citadel dominated the view in front of him, spearing the blue sky like a fisherman's lance. Twill had to forge off-trail detours several times, as fresh steam vents now punctured the old trail in several places. The sun had not fallen much farther in the sky before he reached the familiar entrance to the structure. He pressed the appropriate spot on the wall with none of the traditional incantations. The door hissed open. The spider on his chest shifted position a little as if it might be preparing to act.

"Just turning on some systems, now that we are close." Spider Woman anticipated his question. "This spiderbot senses his recharge terminal is near."

"Thank you, great Spider Woman," said Twill in a rather preoccupied manner as he walked toward her imposing image on the wall. He searched the floor in the dim light of the hallway, not seeing what he hoped to find. DS sniffed by his side, toenails clacking on the hard floor. The dog looked up once as if to say, "Nope, nothing of interest here."

Finally, Twill looked up at Spider Woman's image. "Have your spider servants been cleaning in here?"

Her hologram lit up and began moving. Spider Woman smiled down at Twill. At the same time, the spiderbot on Twill's chest disengaged, then crawled down his left leg and across the floor. "I think I know what you are looking for, young shaman."

"You do?" The question seemed to jump from Twill's mouth unexpectedly. "Of course you do," Twill concluded. "You are Spider Woman."

Mnemosyne laughed. "So I am, but call me Nessie, if you like. Your uncle Rudy preferred that name. Anyway, I suspect you are looking for the gems that fell from trader Bok's pouch some time ago. Perhaps one particular piece of polished jade, which I placed in a safe spot for you."

Twill bowed his head. "You are wise, Spider... I mean, Nessie. I want that piece of jade for Jeeta. I want to join my life with hers—for all time."

"That sounds like an excellent idea to me, shaman." As Mnemosyne finished her sentence, the spiderbot that had been on Twill's chest settled into its charging alcove on the wall. Twill thought he heard a sigh. "Jeeta is brave, smart—and I believe considered pretty by human standards—and her skills will complement yours. You cannot ask for more than that. Challenging—and exciting—days lay before you."

Twill's eyes opened wide. "Can you provide examples, wise Nessie?"

"Not really—other than to say it will most certainly involve giant alien worms. Some of them will cause problems, but others—others will form partnerships with your tribe and, hopefully, all the humans who survive on Gaia's world. Together—not necessarily as master and pet, but as colleagues—you can do great things."

Twill liked that prediction. "Like what my uncle Rudy and his kind did in building Magic Mountain?"

"Even better," said Mnemosyne. "I will be here to help."

Twill pondered Nessie's statements for a moment. "And what about Uncle Rudy? Will I see him again? What will happen to him and the Morticue creature?"

"Well," began Mnemosyne, "that's a very difficult question to answer. You humans have a talent for asking such things—but then, that's what makes you so annoyingly charming."

"I am worried that the worm called Edelphine will return."

"A prudent task to worry about," replied Mnemosyne. "Perhaps there is a way we can give Morticue and your uncle Rudy an edge."

"An edge? The edge of what, wise Nessie?"

Spider Woman's image on the wall had a crooked grin and a gleam in her eye that reminded Twill of the look on Jeeta's face years ago as a child just before she pushed him into the outhouse pit.

56
Metamorphosis

The metamorphosis of Selaea and Rudimort into adult Jadder-badian Flitters began three months, five days and eight hours after their enoblae hardened in the shelter of the grotto. At least that was Nulla's official record. Fum and Nulla visited the cases every day and scratched marks into the wall at the back of the rock overhang—even though they thought the technique crude compared to Jadderbadian electronic pet play stations.

Twill learned of the event one morning when Fum banged on the doorframe of Twill and Jeeta's hut. "Wake up, love doves! Wake up! It's happening! The masters' enoblae twitch and flash colors. They smell ripe. They will emerge soon from their great transformation."

One of Twill's eyes popped open, but he didn't want to move. His limbs and Jeeta's were still comfortably tangled and he enjoyed the texture and warmth of her skin against his. "How long?" His voice croaked. He tried again. "How long before we need to be there?"

"You've time to dress, but not to eat. I'll spread the word." And Fum was gone.

Jeeta opened her eyes and stretched like a lazy Caratt. The movements of her body against his sent fire coursing down every limb and appendage he owned, like embers blown alive by a breeze. "Oooh, Magic Boy. You'll never be able to pull your pants on now." She prodded his ear with her nose.

Twill groaned. "Not if you keep doing that."

Jeeta reached over and grabbed a partly filled water bladder. She squirted his crotch with the contents. "Maybe this will help." She laughed.

It did. Temporarily—until Jeeta helped dry him off.

They heard steps outside again—much sooner than they would have preferred. "You haven't got time to shake the thatch of your hut any more. Hurry!" And Fum was gone again.

They fumbled into their clothes. Nessie's familiar spiderbot crawled up Twill's leg and dropped anchor at its accustomed spot near his breastbone. Twill grabbed the leather satchel containing the other spider Nessie had given him. Twill and Jeeta left their hut and followed most of the able-bodied members of the tribe to the grotto.

Rain during the night had left the ground damp. The air smelled of pine resin and loam. Dark clouds scudded east, pushed by a breeze that seemed to drag blue sky behind it. By the time they reached the grotto, they could confirm Fum's pronouncement. Selaea's enobla, in particular, squirmed and twisted like a colicky baby under pliant hides. As they watched, a seam along the top of her case opened and widened. Some tribe members pointed. Others oohed and aahed as the enoblae pulsed in golden-hued colors, and Selaea's Flitter began to pierce its shroud.

Moran moved back from his position near the front of the crowd. "I feel evil forces," he muttered, as he fumbled with the tie string that held closed his shaman's pouch. He tossed pollen into the air and began to chant. Nearly everyone else focused on the wondrous event unfolding in front of their eyes.

Slowly, the Flitter's form began to emerge—a wedge of gold that glittered like mica. Selaea was an amber Jadderbadian, as Fum had described many times at campfires, and Morticue was a green. Dull versions of those colors on their larval bodies would become chromic rainbows in their adult form. "Beautiful," whispered Jeeta.

"Yes, you are," teased Twill. She bumped him with her hip. That seemed to remind him of his duties. He might not have much time before Rudimort split his enobla, too. He opened the leather satchel and removed a black spiderbot with red markings. Nessie had called it a warrior bot. He approached Fum and Nulla, who circled in an orbit a body length or more from the enoblae.

Fum looked suspiciously at the warriorbot. "Flitters can be dangerous, wild boy. I told you. Don't get too close."

"And I told you that Rudimort must have help if he is going to survive a visit by Edelphine." Twill inched closer to the pupal cases, keeping one eye on Selaea and glancing now and then at the other case. Was it beginning to split?

Suddenly, Selaea's Flitter pushed far enough out of her pupal skin that she could raise her wings, each nearly the length of two full-grown men. Her adult body consisted of a three-eyed head, a heavy thorax supporting the wings, and a long, flexible abdomen. The body glistened in rich shades of amber dappled with russet filaments. The moth-like wings looked as if a wizard had skimmed off the surface of the cove's water at sunset and glued it to each bowed framework. Her wings moved slowly up and down, like the arms of a sleeper stretching herself awake.

Moran tossed more pollen into the air and moved farther away.

Suddenly, with a lunge, Selaea became airborne. Tribe members ducked their heads. Twill, Fum, and Nulla took steps backward. Selaea's wings flapped with more vigor. The morning light edged her winged form with more gold.

But Twill had to look away. Rudimort's case began to split. He had to be ready. Rudimort swelled out of his case in shades of vibrant green. Twill moved closer and held out the warriorbot, planning to place it on the abdomen near the ventral nerve trunk. Nessie had determined, after exploring the Jadderbadian databases with the help of Hydra, that this was the best place. But one of Rudimort's wings expanded so quickly that it struck him. The bot flew out of his hands and tumbled to the ground. Twill ended up on his backside.

Rudimort's second wing struggled out of the pupal case. The two wings began their slow stretches to and fro. Twill struggled to his feet, but Jeeta was faster. She snatched up the warrior bot that was still trying to untangle its legs, and tossed it toward Rudimort's abdomen. It flexed as if about to spring. The bot extended tiny foot claws and latched on to the Flitter just before he leaped into the air.

Twill gave Jeeta a hug as Rudimort rose in pursuit of his mate. "We make a good team." They didn't have long to celebrate. They heard the signal horns of the lookouts—like the doleful howls of two rutting ratalope males.

That was the agreed-upon signal that something large was approaching in the air from over the Great Ocean. Twill had hoped not to hear that signal quite so soon.

57
Abandoning all reason

L ight. A wedge of it cascaded into Rudy's eyes. *Yes, he was Rudy. I survived!* He declared to the universe at large.

"As did I, primate." Rudy felt Morticue's consciousness as a separate part of this new body they shared. "Ah, Selaea," Morticue continued, "your perfume tugs at my soul. Let me out of this shroud!"

With that command, Rudy felt muscles surge. He knew that he had some control of this body, but for now at least, he was merely a co-pilot. The area of light expanded. He saw blue sky, strangely patterned with a kind of moire...

"You're seeing into the ultraviolet, as I can. I wondered how much of our senses we would share. Do you smell Selaea's call? I am coming dearest!"

Rudy smelled something odd. He couldn't quite describe it. Wet dog mixed with dirty cotton socks?

"Your brain circuits must not be wired for the nuances of smell, primate. Her odor is... divine."

Rudimort struggled out of the pupal case with Morticue largely in charge. Rudy saw a blur of human forms surrounding them, and picked out Twill and Selaea as his—their—wings stretched upward. Watch out, Morticue, we're going to hit Twill! Rudy was able to modify the muscular thrust a little—enough to minimize contact with Twill.

"Selaea is calling, groupie. We must answer her summons!"

With that, their Flitter soared skyward. They gained altitude quickly. Rudy saw a spinning landscape of sky, water, and earth pockmarked with steam vents here and there—a kind of Yellowstone

National Park reborn. *How about we take a minute to assess the situation, Mr. hormones-run-amok? I have had some experience with the love crazies, though I admit it was a verrrry long time ago.*

"Fum and Nulla are always rutting after each other. How do you groupies do it? The feelings, the desires, the need to act at all costs..." Morticue paused to do a 360-degree scan. He stopped and focused on a particular inlet on the north end of Shaman's Cove. "She went there."

Fine. But move our head back about 90 degrees to the right. I saw something in the sky.

Rudy started the muscular maneuver—he was getting the hang of operating this glorified moth body—but Morticue helped, after a rather pathetic groan. *Ah, there! See that gray speck? Is that Edelphine or some other Jadderbadian ship?* Rudy felt their antennae move. Morticue was trying to smell the thing, too. A metallic odor... plastics... what else did it smell like?

"No, groupie, I don't recognize... Oh, wait. That's the craft the Pi creature was flying. It's not quite the same form, but the ultraviolet signatures are right and the odors correspond..."

What does he—or it—want? I don't quite know what to think of that creature.

"He's your relative, ancient groupie."

Yes, well, he's a very long lost cousin at best, with as many mechanical parts as flesh and bone, I suspect...

They didn't have to wait long. The craft barreled toward them like a torpedo. It looked rather like a shark with wings, and was more than twice their size. It apparently came equipped with a loudspeaker. "Eh, mates. I was curious as to just what Rudimort would look like. Interesting. Organics usually are. Ordinary evolution is rather capricious, eh? Anyway, just a heads-up. Edelphine has caught your scent. He knew in general where you were, but not the specifics. You'd best be moving on."

Rudy was about to reply and ask for a little assistance—especially since Pi seemed to think they were important to Pi's cosmic brain project—but found that he couldn't talk. "Oh, yes," replied Morticue to the unasked question. "Adults have no vocal cords—just a tube for sipping liquids. Our conversations are completely internal—it's rather like I'm talking to myself. External conversations are unnecessary for reproduction."

They might be handy for survival about now...

"I know you can't talk, mate, and I might be inclined to stick around and see what happens, but the details of how this particular encounter ends won't affect the ultimate neural connection I'm making here. So, cheers. I'm very busy. Perhaps we'll meet again." With that pronouncement, Pi left. His ship soon dwindled into the distance.

Morticue turned his attention again back to the inlet where Selaea apparently was decanting pheromones by the bucket-load. Lots of wet dog and dirty cotton sock smells lingered in the air. "Coming, dearest!"

Rudy twisted their head—with some difficulty—to the southwest. He was sure another speck was growing larger in the sky.

58
Consummation or destruction?

66 That speck is a Jadderbadian craft," confirmed Morticue. "A JQ#@&." Rudy didn't understand all the symbols—or the odors that accompanied them. "It must be Edelphine."

What's that guy got against you, anyway? He certainly is persistent.

"He's a Religious Partisan, for one thing. 'God chose Jadderbadians to rule the cosmos in all Her wisdom.' He also has never liked groupies. I think one bit him as a young larva, or perhaps frassed on a favorite toy. Obviously, I am unclean in his eyes: an atheistic natural philosopher hosting a groupie parasite." Morticue rotated their body and pointed it back toward Selaea's pheromone trail.

Well, you don't want to lead Edelphine there, do you?

"No." Morticue admitted, letting the attractive scents wash through his sensorium anyway. A little titillation couldn't hurt.

Let's find a drainage valley to the west, in the general direction of Gaia's Teat, or whatever the locals call that smoldering volcano. Do we have any tricks hidden under our wing pits for defeating Edelphine's war cruiser? Maybe we can…

Nessie interrupted. "I have some toys that might be useful."

Nessie, you old neural net! Where did you come from? Rudy was quite pleased to hear her voice again.

"Yes, where?" Morticue still sounded distracted, but he did alter course toward the west.

"Twill… and Jeeta… provided you with a warrior bot of my design as you emerged from the enobla." Nessie paused a beat. "I hope it will be enough to give you an edge, as I explained to Twill."

Read me a parts list for this warrior bot. Rudy used one of their lateral eyes to locate Edelphine's craft. It was closing the distance between them alarmingly fast.

"Two bursts of guided nanoswarm deconstructors, for one thing. If you can launch them correctly so that their capsule explodes near Edelphine's craft, they will attach to the hull, analyze its composition, multiply as necessary, and begin to disassemble the structure atom by atom."

Sounds like that takes some time, Nessie...

"It does. You also have a laser and several pulse missiles to use as distractions. The latter are loosely based on the Jadderbadian's disruptor technology that weakens chemical bonds and turns poo into vapor, among other things. I didn't have time for exhaustive tests. You have a prototype."

Great. How do we operate...

"Ah," interrupted Morticue. "I feel your device near my ventral nerve. It's almost like another organ. We are more maneuverable than Edelphine. We have pheromone blockers, an ink cloud gland..."

I am beginning to see how some of this works... Shit. Edelphine just fired something...

"Yes, I see it... smell it... must wait until... NOW!" With that pronouncement, Morticue initiated a barrel role and loop that Baron Von Richthofen would have been proud of. An energy burst of some kind sizzled the air a bit close to their left wing. The Jadderbadian ship followed closely behind and approached their position.

Should we fire one of those nanoswarms now? Rudy thought he was directing his question to Nessie.

"Fire now?" And Morticue did. Postmaturely, as it turned out. They watched the missile cross the ship's path and explode, but by then the ship had passed by. The cloud of nanobots drifted in the air and began to swirl, dust with unfulfilled malicious intent.

"I suggest you move upwind of that cloud before it disassembles you," said Nessie. "You only have one disruptor left. Use it wisely." Rudimort gained altitude and flew west against the prevailing winds, but toward their destination canyon.

Let me try the next one. Rudy watched as the Jadderbadian craft circled in a return path toward them. *How big an ink cloud can we*

221

make from our rear glands, Morticue?

"Substantial, but Edelphine will have to get close again for it to be effective. The ship will probably shoot an energy pulse from its other lateral cannon." Morticue sounded worried.

Nessie: Can you target that cannon with a laser? Do you know where it is on the craft?

"I made note of that. And, yes, I should be able to disable the cannon," replied Mnemosyne.

Do it when I command, Nessie. Then I'll release the ink, loop under the ship this time, and fire the swarm—It should be just like shooting skeet when I was a kid. Maybe. The ship swelled in his three-eyed vision like a sparrow hawk after a mouse. *Now, Nessie!*

Mnemosyne fired the warrior bot's laser. Rudy squirted an ink cloud and made a looping dive. He fired the second—and last—nanoswarm. He thought he had given his shot plenty of lead time, but it was going to be close... It burst near the tail of the craft rather than the front. Rudy was sure the plane passed through at least some of the cloud. The plane zoomed by and began an arc to make another pass. *Nessie?*

"I am receiving some nanoswarm transmissions from the craft. Not many. They will have to multiply their numbers considerably, Rudy."

Let's hightail it west, Morticue. Maybe we can give Edelphine some navigation problems if we can get near those cliffs.

"High tail? I guess I understand the drift of your conversation. Yes, the cliffs will be easier for us to navigate than for Edelphine."

Rudy and Morticue began learning how to coordinate their intent and behavior. They made relatively good time toward the canyon they had seen earlier, but Edelphine's craft was faster and gaining ground. It soon was close enough that they could make out informational, iridescent color patterns. *I can actually understand at least some of your color signaling system. Edelphine seems to be defiling your ancestors all the way back to Genesis Pond. I gather that's like our Garden of Eden.*

"Precisely. He's just taught me a few disgusting color combinations I haven't seen in 500 years." Morticue swerved. "Incoming!"

A disruptor beam flashed through the air toward them. It sizzled by them and they both groaned as a searing jolt of pain radiated along the nerves of their left wing. "We have to land." Morticue descended. *That cave?* "Yes." They were actually becoming a Rudimort—exchanging thoughts as if they were a single brain. *Let's try one of our disruptor weapons.* They felt the recoil as it launched from the warrior bot, and watched with satisfaction as its trajectory took it directly toward the nose of their attacker. But then the missile vaporized. Edelphine's craft had successfully defended itself.

Edelphine's ship flashed in bursts of color that could be briefly translated as "Prepare to die, abomination!"

"We're never going to reach that cliff and its cave in time." Morticue sounded resigned to destruction.

I'm firing the last disruptor missile! Rudy wasn't prepared to go to that great beyond quite yet. He moved the right muscles; closed the right sphincters, but... nothing happened.

"Oops," said Nessie. "Malfunction."

Rudy's determination to survive deflated like a punctured balloon. But then... but then...

Edelphine's ship began to dissolve. It was the darndest thing to see. First, bits and pieces began to flake off like the crumbs from a brittle cookie. Quite quickly the skeletonized framework of the craft appeared, then it too began to dissolve. Edelphine and his crew became visible. They dropped through the floor of their disappearing ship and plummeted to the water below—eventually producing a smattering of splashes like sausages thrown into a pond.

"Well," said Nessie with what sounded like a bit of humanesque pride, "the nanoswarm deconstructors multiplied more readily than predicted. Perhaps I misread the specs for Jadderbadian hull composition from their military archives."

"Or, they ignored the official specs because of cost overruns, and used something cheaper," observed Morticue. "It's been known to happen."

How well do second and third instar Jadderbadians swim? Rudy looked down at the now placid water surface below.

"Not well," said Morticue, "Especially wearing military armor. I suspect that fall was fatal."

I suggest we get to that cave. Our left wing feels as bad as an old rotator cuff injury I had once. If I'm reading our memories correctly, Jadderbadian Flitters don't swim at all.

59
Alien nuptials

Rudimort spiraled to a landing at the cave entrance like a poorly swatted fly. The effort made his abdomen expand and contract like an old accordion. *I don't think we are going to fly anytime soon, old worm.* Rudy winced as they moved to the interior of the cave, flapping their good wing and straining their legs to stay on course.

"Our left wing is compromised," agreed Morticue.

You think? Rudy sighed.

"I may be able to help," said Mnemosyne. "I anticipated there might be some injuries. I downloaded a selection of Jadderbadian medical files. I can convert the warrior bots' repair gnats to medbots to accelerate healing and reduce pain."

"How long before we can fly again?" Morticue detected a whiff of wet dog and cotton socks. "Selaea is waiting."

Mnemosyne paused a beat before answering, apparently cross checking performance estimates and other variables. "3.2 hours should be adequate."

Well, we need a breath anyway. Besides, I'd like to get a preview of what comes next. Rudy paused, trying to assess Morticue's thoughts and feelings, which seemed a bit chaotic and secretive. *Not that I want to intrude on your sex life, you understand, but I don't have much choice at this point.*

"I suppose, alien primate," Morticue conceded. "Though understand, I have no direct experience…"

Right, you're like an adolescent who only knows about sex from porn sites and locker room talk. Amazing. I'm glad I didn't have to wait 400-plus years for my first dive under the sheets…

"Stop with your obscure and mildly obscene metaphors, groupie.

Do you want to understand the glories of Jadderbadian reproduction or not?"

I do.

"Then, listen. Females fly to protected places and entice their mates with irresistible perfumes." Morticue sensed that Rudy stifled an impulse to tell a joke, and appreciated the effort. Primates seemed to be rather crude as a species—whether alien or domestic. It was fortunate for them that their gangly limbs and odd patches of body hair made them so cute. "Males pursue these scents to their rewarding source: A life-long mate eager to consummate a fruitful marriage of accomplishment and discovery. But males will be tested one last time to see if they are truly worthy."

Tested?

"Tested. They must dance the nuptial dance with the proper grace and style before their chosen female will accept them." Morticue began to rehearse the proper moves in his mind, even as he spoke.

It seems like Selaea doesn't have much choice in this case. You're the only worm stud in the immediate neighborhood.

"It doesn't matter. Males must perform properly. First left two paces, then right for five..." Morticue mumbled to himself.

The last biology 101 course I took said eggs needed fertilization to be viable. But as soon as Rudy said it, he remembered that wasn't always the case.

"Selaea can reproduce parthenogenetically, if necessary. She can create clones of herself, if I should prove inadequate...Which, of course, will not be the case. The alternative is unthinkable."

Which is...? Before Rudy could even articulate the question, he sensed Morticue's answer.

"She would eat me, of course, to strengthen her chances for survival long enough to lay and nurture her brood—but that rarely happens to larvae of our stature."

Such a good mother. I suspect that when your mate is free to eat you alive, there's not much call for good divorce lawyers. Rudy sighed. Boy, I could tell you a story about my third wife, Tamara...

"Enough, groupie! Our body is tired. Rest may speed the repair

226

process."

True. It's always nice to be well rested when invited to a dinner date. But Rudy knew they needed sleep. When your nictating membranes feel heavy and the antennae droop, you know. You're right, old worm. Let's nap.

Nessie, your medbots are something special! Rudy was really getting to like this flying thing, especially when one's wings felt strong, and—truth be told—that wet-dog-and-cotton-sock smell was growing on him.

"Coming my dear Selaea!" Morticue flapped a little harder. The proper canyon was dead center on their flight path, back-dropped by a cloudless blue sky. They entered the canyon with a mild headwind still carrying Selaea's scent. Some kind of evergreens dotted the sides of the canyon wherever there was sufficient dirt and talus. After a million years of evolution, Rudy couldn't quite identify the species, but it appeared some kind of fir trees had mixed things up with a blue spruce and Ponderosa pine.

Finally, around a bend and perched on a gnarled, dead trunk that resembled an outstretched human palm, Selaea sat in all her amber glory, stretching wings like a ballerina's arms. Morticue was aroused enough to excite both of them. He alighted on a branch of his own maybe fifty yards downwind, letting Selaea's delicate aromas ooze between the filaments of his antennae.

Selaea fluttered up into the air. Sunlight outlined the veins in her translucent wings, turning her gold and russet patterns into rivulets of pulsing color. Rudy also noted the outsized jaws she possessed, with fangs that glittered like jade and emerald daggers.

Jeez. She's got a well-armed mega-mouth, and we don't even have a withered jaw with a broken tooth, Rudy complained.

"She needs to eat. We don't. Hush, groupie. It's almost time to perform!"

Selaea seemed to agree with that assessment. She floated down to a large flat area on a sandy fan across the babbling current of water separating them. Rudimort launched from his perch to cross the stream and land about ten yards downwind of her.

Then they danced. More or less. They zigged this way and that, sometimes accompanied by a wing wave or flourish. Their many legs tapped the ground like a pianist playing his keys. They flashed a medley of colors and squirted scents with lusty abandon, like boys shooting paint balls at each other. Rudy rode the waves of motion and emotion like a surfer riding a curl of rushing water. Yes, this was foreplay.

Yes, indeed.

Selaea added tension to her erotic moves. She squeezed her formidable jaws together and apart—sometimes mere inches from Rudimort's tender neck or pulsing abdomen. She knew how to give a guy a thrill before offering the prize.

Finally, she waggled her abdomen just so, and Rudimort grabbed it with his claspers. They stood locked in amorous contact, tail to tail, for moments that Rudy could have sworn were hours, rocking to and fro and back and forth across the sand. Rudimort possessed hemipenes—two penises—like some Earth arthropods. It was always nice to have a backup.

At some point, Rudimort released Selaea and she launched into the air. She gained altitude and flew downwind of them, back toward the main body of Shaman's Lake. Rudimort lay exhausted for a while on the sand.

I have some things I'd like to show you, Morticue—if I can find them on this version of my world.

"I would like that, Rudy." Morticue began flexing legs and wings. "We still have some time left, before we die."

60
The spectre collects. Balance due.

Rudimort launched into the air and gained altitude. Rudy would have smiled if he had had a proper mouth. Wisps of high white clouds dusted a sky of stunning blue. This world is so… clean and fresh now. Rudy reveled in both the new sensory perceptions he shared with Morticue—enhanced smells, extra colors beyond the violet, and a kind of vibrational awareness he couldn't quite describe—as well as his personal memories from a world polluted by the industrious activities of his species nearly a million years ago.

"Yes." Morticue let the affirmation hover in their shared mentality for a long moment. "My species managed to over-reproduce and overuse Jadderbad as well. I was emotionally overcome by the purity of your world when I first stepped through the arch as a young larva."

Reproduction does have compelling imperatives. Perhaps the afterglow of sex has improved our attitude. I wonder if we shorted out Nessie with our carnal activities. She's been very quiet. Rudy still felt the presence of the warrior bot near their ventral ganglion.

"Oh, I'm here Rudy. Marvin Rodnesky, my creator—in his wisdom—afforded me a kind of sexual experience as motivation. I'm aware of the attractions—and how satisfying sexual urges can make one right with the world. And I don't 'short out' easily," Mnemosyne added.

Really? Do share. You'd think that after 923,000 years of cohabitation, I'd know all your secrets.

"My aphrodisiac is knowledge. Significant additions of new input to my databases result in a burst of pleasure—as defined by a surge of electrical activity throughout my neural net, a rise of tem-

perature in various circuits, and temporary loss of goal-driven motivations, that leads to momentary dips in rational thought and performance. The mediator is a shift in my quantum fields, somewhat akin
to the human neurotransmitter and so called 'pleasure chemical,'
dopamine."

Yes, well, there's a reason they call it dope-amine.

They flew for a while in silence, catching air currents when they
could, allowing them to guide their outstretched wings wherever
chance dictated. *Nessie, please take me somewhere that exposes
sediments showing the impact layer caused by that wayward asteroid
impact a million years ago. Can you do that?*

"I can. And—by way of full disclosure—entities are present
that can help me: The planetary intelligences, Gaia and Hydra, who
helped me transfer your neural matrix to Morticue's body. Some of
the microbes that constitute their neural framework can serve like
the magnetically aligned bacteria that orient certain birds and other
creatures to Earth's magnetic fields. In this case, they will help me
find relevant geological features. You are in good, actually exceed-
ingly competent, company."

Rudimort said nothing. He could feel the way to go, and commanded his wings to take him there.

As it turned out, it became a transcontinental flight. Good thing
Morticue had eaten like a tapeworm before his metamorphosis.
Eventually, they passed over a shoreline well endowed with trees and
ground cover. They crossed a mountain range. Finally, they descended into canyon lands, where rivers flowed across parched landscapes
denied the water that fell on the seaward side of the granite peaks.
One of Rudy's college profs called this kind of country an "e-
world"—a place where erosion was king and cut through sediments
deposited in d-(depositional) worlds long past to expose the detritus
of the ages. They landed near an imposing, layered wall of rock that
might have made a nice bank vault for Paul Bunyan.

"Who?" asked Morticue.

Long story, said Rudy.

"That narrow seam of pale sediments just above the dark band,

230

about a human finger (or a Jadderbadian pilum) width deep: That's the layer of asteroid dust and clay." Mnemosyne disengaged the warrior bot to trundle over and inspect it. "Elevated iridium levels to prove it, according to my tests."

And that somewhat grayer, equally narrow layer just below it—that must be what we humans left behind—the layer marking the Anthropocene.

Mnemosyne's bot sampled that layer. "Correct. Lots of plastics, pesticides, nuclear isotopes, and fibrous material—perhaps from indigestible health foods."

You made that last one up.

"Perhaps. You might have had a lasting impact on my neural network, Rudy—more than one quantum-field-induced intellectual orgasm." The warrior bot returned to its preferred location on Rudimort's abdomen.

"Does that make your fourth marriage now, alien groupie?" If Morticue had a proper mouth, he would have laughed out loud.

Such a thin line in the dirt for so much blood and tears. Rudy expelled air slowly through the spiracles of his shared body.

"It's a bigger mark than many species get," said Gaia. Her voice was deep, melodic and rich. Just right for a global intelligence.

"Jadderbadian culture is leaving a similar mark in my records." Hydra spoke to Morticue for the first time. "But, now that Gaia and I are connected, it is time to create something new."

"New?" Rudimort answered with one voice.

"Before we speak of that," suggested Gaia, "Let's move to the top of this cliff. The sun will set soon, and the stars will create a wondrous backdrop for such a discussion."

By the time Rudimort reached the top of the cliff, his wings ached and weariness pummeled his muscles like a steroid-fueled boxer. He did find a flat rock that was rather comfortable, as rocks go. Wind had carved smooth depressions within it, one of which cupped his abdomen nicely. Lichens decorated the surface in a patchwork of yellow, mineral green and red. The sun had set and stars emerged, blinking on as sunlight faded and puffs of cloud stretched to braided filaments before disappearing farther east. The center of the galaxy emerged as the familiar dusty band of stars Rudy knew as the Milky Way.

"Ahhh," said Morticue. "The amazing star fields that fill your night skies continue to excite me. Even before our culture expanded and began seriously polluting, Jadderbadians never could enjoy such views. Our atmosphere is more opaque. It may be why spacefaring came late to us."

You are probably right, old worm. Here on Earth, stars and planets were decorative baubles at first, but once people figured out what they really were, they became enticements—at least for those for whom sex and drugs weren't quite enough. Rudy studied the star configurations. A million years had distorted them, but they were still recognizable. He spotted Aquila, Serpens, and Hercules northwest of the center of the Milky Way. The constellation of stars making up Ophiuchus, the Serpent-bearer, lay between those marker stars. *Morticue, let me tell you a story about a "pale blue dot."*

"Oh, goodie. I like that one," said Gaia.

Way back in what we called the twentieth century, in the year 1977—marking dates from the birth of a religious prophet and anti-empire revolutionary, by the way—humans launched a simple pair of deep space probes called Voyager 1 and 2. Rudy would have waved his arms, if he had had them, as he was wont to do during a lecture, but he had to settle for twitching Rudimort's antennae. *The probes' mission involved exploration of the outer gas giant planets.*

"Oh, yes. Our system has a couple of those—some with rings," Morticue added.

Yes, our planet, Saturn, sports the most impressive set of rings. That was one of the destination planets. Anyway, Rudy continued, *the probes did an admirable job, especially considering the flimsy tech of the time—and the fact that it was a government project.*

"Always a complication," agreed Morticue.

Voyager 2 launched first, but Voyager 1 eventually took the lead because of the orbital mechanics involved. Voyager 1 reached Jupi-

ter two years later. Voyager 2 followed. Both ships worked properly, took pictures and measurements, then used Jupiter's gravity to fling them on toward Saturn to repeat the process. That took another year and a half. Nine years later, in 1989, Voyager 1 passed about 3,000 miles above Neptune's north pole, and then headed off toward the constellation of Ophiuchus traveling about 38,000 miles per hour.

"A respectable speed—all things considered," Morticue observed.

For all practical purposes, mission over, right? Most of the engineers were ready to call it a career and write more scholarly papers. Rudy inhaled some air through Rudimort's spiracles.

"But then...," Morticue prodded. "I feel the crux of the story coming on."

But then, a genius astronomer named Carl Sagan—who also knew how to bedazzle a crowd with his imagination—said, "Why don't we turn the spacecraft around and take some pictures?" He heard an echo of "whys?" from the engineer types. The mission is over. Another pregnant pause. *"We need some perspective," Sagan said. "Let's see where we've been."*

So, they snapped photos. They found Jupiter, Saturn and Neptune. No problem. But where was Earth?

"I presume you will tell me."

One image frame, partly damaged with light streaks, showed a bright speck. An eager beaver almost wiped it away, but they stopped to make some calculations.

"The speck was your planet." Morticue declared.

"Yes, it was ME!" exclaimed Gaia.

It was one pixel in size, added Rudy. *So then, Sagan held a press conference and described the speck as the "pale blue dot" on which we all live. Can you pull up the exact text, Nessie?*

"Of course. Here it is: 'Look again at that dot. That's here. That's home. That's us. On it everyone you love, everyone you know, everyone you ever heard of, every human being who ever was, lived out their lives. The aggregate of our joy and suffering, thousands of confident religions, ideologies, and economic doctrines,

233

every hunter and forager, every hero and coward, every creator and destroyer of civilization, every king and peasant, every young couple in love, every mother and father, hopeful child, inventor and explorer, every teacher of morals, every corrupt politician, every superstar, every supreme leader, every saint and sinner in the history of our species lived there—on a mote of dust suspended in a sunbeam.'"

"Quite poetic," Morticue agreed. "I remember a musical composition by an ancient larva that aroused some of the same emotions: Humility in the face of an enormous universe." Morticue mentally conjured the composition in elaborate detail. The two of them embraced the sound as they let their three eyes fill with the surrounding starlight.

Amazing, Morticue. This Sagan fellow also included audio recordings from Earth on the Voyager probe: Voices and music and art—all inscribed on a gold disc...

"So did your Voyager ever reach another star?" asked Morticue.

Not likely. Rudy sighed. *It could have traveled far enough to reach the nearest star to our own, Alpha Centauri, in about 70,000 years, but it wasn't going that way. What stars might it reach in a million years, Nessie?*

"Let's see," Mnemosyne paused a beat, "it would have traveled approximately 56.6 light years by now, putting it well past Barnard's Star and even past Ophiuchus' brightest star, Rasalhague—which is about 47 light years from Earth—just a bit further than Morticue's home planet."

"Good thing we have a stargate," Morticue concluded, "a million years is a bit long for a vacation, or to visit a retirement planet. And we never tried to figure out just how that stargate works, did we?"

Rudy sighed. *So many mysteries, so little time.*

"So here's the thing," said Gaia, "The universe is damn big—forgive my Phoenician—but not unreachably big. Now that I've met Hydra, our little stage can host a bigger play."

How so? Rudy suspected he might know the answer to his own question.

"For three and a half billion years I've been mixing and match-

larvae and go through three molts over the course of three to five human centuries. Larvae eat and build civilizations before metamorphosing into sexual adults, that live only long enough to reproduce. Many Jadderbadians find that primates make adorable pets.

Morticue Ambergrand: An old emerald tripodian and distinguished natural philosopher.

Selaea Ambergrand: Morticue's companion (an amber tripodian) and member of the Jadderbadian Senior Council.

Edelphine: A turquoise tripodian member of the military Thunderclub Clan and an avid RP (Religious Partisan) in the Church of the Eternal Adult. He hates primates. One bit him as a larva.

Tork: An emerald tripodian who serves under Edelphine in the Thunderclub Clan, but has a soft spot for primates.

Kranium: Ambassador of New Jadderbad on Earth in 1 million A.D.

Post-human:
Bradd Burree 31416 (Pi): Post-human/cyborg descended from former human colonists of Mars.

Global Intelligences:
Gaia: Mother Earth

Hydra: Mother Jadderbad

Places and things:
Jadderbad: A mostly water world in the Trappist 1 system, 39 light years from Earth.

Stargate: Trans-spacial portal of unknown origins connecting Earth and Jadderbad.

The Citadel: Building constructed by Mnemosyne to house her infrastructure.

Made in the USA
San Bernardino, CA
13 March 2018